Divine Legacy Series, Book 3:

Hearts United

C.J. Peterson

Texas Sisters Press, LLC

This book is dedicated to my loving husband, Trevor, who is my heart. I am grateful God united our hearts together! I love you!

It is also dedicated to my dear family who love and support me. You all mean more to me than you will ever know. Thank you!

This is especially dedicated to my parents, Gene and Sue, who are celebrating 65 years of wedding bliss this month. May God grant you many more happy years together!

A portion of the proceeds of this series will go to Airborne Angel Cadets of Texas – a non-profit group of hardworking volunteers who send care packages to our soldiers overseas. You can find them at: http://www.airborneangelcadets.com

This book is also dedicated to the men and women of our military. You are not forgotten. You are in my prayers until the last one of you comes home!

To learn more about C.J. Peterson, you can find her online at: http://cjpetersonwrites.com/
'While the stories are fiction, the journey is real!'

C.J. Peterson

<u>Summary</u>

With the loss of a prominent A.N.G.E.L. fresh in their minds, the team focuses on trying to get to Angel without losing anyone else. Angel is doing her best to fight Cassius, Calliope, and Korax in complete isolation, with only God's strength to pull her through. Already tortured, how much more can she endure?

In the meantime, Jerrod's battles with the ghosts of his past become overwhelming. Will he be able to see past them to find his future?

As the A.N.G.E.L.s converge for yet another memorial service, Jesse struggles with feelings of anger and resentment. Knowing Angel's choice triggered this loss, he fights within to reconcile his feelings.

With emotions at an all-time high, ricocheting all over the place, the team is more divided than ever. Will they be able to focus on God enough to center themselves and carry on their legacy? Will they continue to be divided or will they become ***Hearts United.*** (Book 3 of the ***Divine Legacy Series***.)

Proverbs 4:20-23 *"My son, pay attention to what I say; turn your ear to my words. Do not let them out of your sight, keep them within your heart; for they are life to those who find them and health to one's whole body. Above all else, guard your heart, for everything you do flows from it."*

Table of Contents

Prologue
God Is The Strength Of My Heart

"Oh, dear Lord!" Casey said into the phone, color drained from her face, as she talked in the living room at the Haven in Nevada. "Are Charlie and the others okay?"

"Yes. We're sending Charlie your direction, along with Katia and Liliya," Nico explained. "All three need the Spirit to touch their hearts. I don't think it's sunk in for Charlie yet. Liliya's been held captive. And, Katia just about killed Sergei on sight. You got your work cut out for you. I'm thinking of checking with Kit to see if she wouldn't mind coming to help you guys."

"That would be great!" Casey said. "If she can't, it's nothing we can't handle. If she can, that would be a huge help. How is Mark? How are Jon and Jesse? I can't imagine what they must be feeling for having to leave Angel. I'm sick just thinking about it. I pray every spare moment for her safety."

"I'm sure. As her mum, I would expect no less. She is a brave warrior for Christ, though," Nico reminded her. "She yelled at me, and wouldn't let me release her until the others were released. I'm really sorry we weren't able to get back to her. We left another as well. The other two we rescued said he is a pastor."

"Wow. What are they doing?" Casey asked, shaking her head as flashbacks of what Jackie had done to her shot through her mind. "I pray she doesn't have to face what I did at their hands."

"She's strong, Casey. You and Mark did a phenomenal job raising her for the Lord. Without that foundation, I doubt she would have survived this long."

*   *   *

"Knock, knock," Casey said, poking her head into Rachel's room as she lightly knocked. "Got a minute?"

"Got nothing but," Rachel said, holding her ribs. "I'm obviously not gonna sleep with this pain."

"I'll give you more pain killers in a bit," Casey said, looking at her watch. "You still have an hour."

"Great." Rachel sighed. Then she got a good look at Casey. "What happened?" she asked, heart racing as she struggled to sit up.

"How do you know something happened?"

"The look on your face. You may be able to hide it from others, but you can't from me. Are Josh and my dad okay? Is the team okay? What about Angel and Liliya?"

"I just got off the phone with Nico."

"Not Mark?" Rachel asked, confused.

"Mark was with the others still in the Tanami Desert," Casey explained.

"Where did my dad call you from? Why didn't he talk to me when he called?"

"Well, he called from Alice Springs, because they brought part of the team back, along with two they rescued."

"Wait. What? Why? What happened? They wouldn't come out and leave the others there if everything went okay. Why did Dad leave the others and go to Alice without them? What's going on?"

"Calm down," Casey said, sitting on the side of the bed. When Casey took her hand, Rachel looked from her hand to Casey nervously. Casey knew she would have to tread carefully. "Lord help me," she whispered, looking to Heaven.

"What is it? Please talk to me, Casey," Rachel said, holding her breath.

Psalm 34:18 came to Casey's mind, so she quoted it, "'*The Lord is close to the broken hearted and saves those who are crushed in spirit.*'"

"No." Rachel shook her head in understanding. "Who was it?"

"I'm afraid Danny Hawk…" As soon as Casey said his name, Rachel felt like a knife slashed through her gut. Grabbing her stomach, she felt as if she would throw up at the loss of one of her mentors. Casey continued, "…is no longer with us. Charlie's bringing him home, along with Katia and Liliya. They'll be here tomorrow afternoon. I'm so sorry, Rachel."

"He-he was one of the ones who trained us," Rachel said in shock. No tears, no thoughts or feelings. Complete shock. "Does Mum know?"

"Your dad was calling her next. He wanted to give me a head's up before the other three got on the plane, and he knew it would be a long conversation with Kit."

"How did it happen?" she asked, looking back up to Casey.

"Nico said they were trying to get the six out they found in the caves. Angel and Liliya were with them. They were able to rescue everyone but Angel and one other man."

"*They still have Angel*?" Rachel asked, wide-eyed, heart racing as she tried to process. "How did this happen?"

"Angel insisted they free the others before her. And you know Angel." Casey sighed, shaking her head. "Once she gets something in her mind, that's it."

"Right." Rachel nodded, still trying to focus as her world spun around her.

"Well, when they were almost done freeing those they first went to, and went to get Angel and the other guy, a demon caught them. Danny insisted that they get the others out, that he would hold them back. The demon got him. Jon ran back for him so they wouldn't have the satisfaction of having his body, and carried him out. A group headed back to Alice Springs, but left part of the team behind to keep an eye on the situation. If the other side moved Angel, they wanted to know about it. In the meantime, a portion of them got those rescued to safety. Charlie took Danny to the morgue, for Danny to be cremated and brought back here. Then they got plane tickets for Katia, Liliya, and Charlie to come here. The remaining should be heading back to the others in the desert soon. Hopefully the others will already have a plan formed so they can get the last two out quickly."

"Was anyone else hurt?"

"Not that I know of."

Rachel dropped her head in her hands. "I don't know how to process this."

"Just give it time and a lot of prayer. When Katia and Liliya get here, I will need to do some heart work with them. You and Charlie can work together through this. It's a lot to deal with, but you guys can help carry each other through the tough days."

*   *   *

After they got everyone situated in Alice Springs, and stocked up on supplies. They picked up what Jacob had asked for before Nico, Jerrod, and Jon headed the eighteen hours back to the others, who were tucked away safely with the other Jeep, deep in the Tanami Desert.

*   *   *

"While we're waiting, we need to work on a plan," Derek said to Jacob and Josh, as he and Mark walked up to them. The moon was high deep in the Tanami Desert, and there were numerous stars in the sky above. "We're now four short with Charlie and Katia going to the Haven, Danny's passing, and Amarina back with her people."

"No, I am not," Amarina said, climbing onto a rock next to Josh and Jacob.

Jacob jumped. "Where'd you come from?"

"I came from home," the young Aboriginal girl said, adjusting in her seat to a more comfortable position. "I checked with the elders. They said I can help again."

"Amarina, we can't ask you to help. It's way too dangerous," Mark said, shaking his head. "We've already lost Danny, and possibly Angel. We don't want to lose you too. You're too valuable."

"I talked to the elders. They say it is my path. They knew you were coming, and would need me," Amarina insisted.

"I know they have their ways, but did you tell them we lost one of the A.N.G.E.L.s?" Josh asked. "Do they understand what they're sending you in to?"

"Yes," she said firmly. "It is my choice. I saw them. I felt them. I *know* what they are. I have known for a long time. They are evil. I will *not* leave innocent people in there. I want to help get them out…even if it may cost me my life. If I was in there, I would want others to rescue me. I am going to help."

"We could use as much help as we can get," Mark said, kicking the idea around in his head. "*If* we let you stay to help, you are not to go any closer than you did before. I *do not* want you going in. I don't want to lose you. We could use your help with backup, though."

"Agreed!" She grinned. "I am going to help. Let's make a plan! We need to get Jesse and Jon's sister outta there."

* * *

Nico drove around Jerrod's and Jon's Jeeps and spun around to the side. Both Jeeps slammed on their brakes, and swerved to avoid hitting Nico's Jeep. "What in blazes are you doing?" Jerrod snapped, getting out of his Jeep, closely followed by Jon from his.

"We need to take a break. We've been awake and driving for more than twenty-four hours. Those energy drinks won't keep us alert enough to get in and out safely. We're not doing Angel any favors by going in exhausted," Nico said.

"All right. Pull off to the side of the road," Jerrod grumbled. "A little warning next time would be appreciated. Having said that, we *should* take a break. You're right. We'll do something stupid if we're exhausted. The others are okay where they are."

After they pulled over, Jon made a fire, while Nico and Jerrod got MREs and water. After they were settled and eating, Jon asked, "Jerrod, want to share some of that?"

"I hate your gift," Jerrod griped.

"What's going on, mate?" Nico asked.

"Nothing." He shook his head, feeling sick to his stomach.

"Spill it," Jon snapped. "The anger, anxiety, fear, and hopelessness are overwhelming. You need to get rid of it, or it'll swallow you whole."

"I'll deal with it when we get back to the Haven," Jerrod said.

"You need to deal with it now so you can focus. If it's strong enough to send Jon into a fit, then it's pretty big," Nico pointed out.

"It's just…" He shook his head. "I thought I had wrestled those demons and won. Seeing Danny die in Charlie's arms brought back so many…" He shook his head again.

"Any in particular?" Nico pressed. "I've had a few of those types of demons to battle myself."

"It was one of those middle-of-the-night wake-ups for a casualty evacuation. When we got there, it was a hot zone, when it wasn't supposed to be. We couldn't leave them there, though. The Marines did their best to fight them off while the choppers laid cover fire and we landed. They loaded up the two injured. I was in one chopper with this young kid." Jerrod shook his head. "They kept getting younger and younger every year. Kids. They were just kids outta high school. They were still a glint in their momma's eyes, and now here they were, lying in front of me fighting for their lives, miles away from their families. Their lives were in my hands." He looked at his hands, seeing the faint bloodstains. "He fought with everything in him. He said he felt like he was on fire…which he practically was. He was near an IED when it exploded. He had severe burns over eighty percent of his body, including his face. His entire left arm was missing, and he had shrapnel in his thigh. It cut the femoral artery. He didn't have a chance."

"Wow," Jon said, feeling everything Jerrod did as he told the story. Feeling like he was going to throw up from the emotions Jerrod was emitting, he asked, "How did you manage?"

Staring off, as if the scene were right in front of him, Jerrod went on, "At first he was somewhat cognizant enough to know I was the one helping him. After a few minutes, he was begging for his mom." He wiped the tears that had escaped. "It broke my heart. I knew I should shut my heart off in the field, but I couldn't." As tears welled in Jerrod's eyes, he refused to let any more fall. "That kid fought for as long as he could. He finally said, '*Mom, I need to go. Jesus is standing there waiting for me. I'll save you a seat next to me at the great banquet when Jesus comes back.'* With that, he was gone. There was nothing I could do."

"I'm not going to comfort you with some malarkey," Nico said. "There's no way to comfort someone after they watch people die right in front of them. Watching Danny die in Charlie's arms today, I didn't know what to wish for. He was a great man, and a terrific friend. I didn't want to watch him suffer, but I also didn't want him to leave. I know we'll see each other again in the ever after, but it doesn't make it hurt any less."

"It doesn't," Jerrod agreed.

"While we generally only have to process the actual life that has passed, those of us who served in various parts of EMS, military, or civil service, fully understand what it's like to watch someone die right in front of you," Nico said.

"Exactly. You really don't know *what* to wish for," Jerrod said. "Serving in the capacity we served, you only wish to not see them in pain. Most of the time, you don't know what they were like before. You don't know their families. Being in the military, you *may* know their spouse or kids, but not always. Yet, there they are, right in front of you, with their lives in your hands. You do your best, but in this case, your best isn't good enough."

"We've had this conversation before, mate," Nico reminded him. "You're not God. He is the only One who truly has their lives in His hands. You can do your best, and your best is *always* good enough, but you're not the One who determines who actually lives or dies."

Jerrod pointed to his head. "I understand that here." Then he pointed to his heart and said, "It's here I have a hard time processing that. My heart wants to save them all. It's not for my glory. It's more so I don't have to contact the CO who has to write the memorial letters to their families. I know what it's like to see that black SUV drive down the road. You see them coming, praying they're not coming to your house, but you know. When I lost my dad, I saw them coming. He was deployed. We knew as soon as we saw the vehicle park in front of the house. Mom grabbed my shoulders and told me to stand strong, but…" Taking a deep breath, he did his best to process. "It's not something you get over."

"You never get over a loss," Nico said. "You only learn to live with the hole left in your heart by that person. Danny was a great mate. It *is* a struggle between the head and the heart. It's one you'll have to battle more than most in what you did."

"Definitely," Jerrod agreed.

" *'Therefore, they are before the throne of God and serve Him day and night in His Temple; and He who sits on the throne will shelter them with His presence. Never again will they hunger; never again will they thirst. The sun will not beat down on them, nor any scorching heat. For the Lamb at the center of the throne will be their Shepherd; He will lead them to the springs of living water. And God will wipe away every tear from their eye,'* " Jon said, quoting Revelation 7:15-17.

"That's one of my true sources of comfort," Jerrod said. "My only fear is that the nightmares will ramp back up, just when I was starting to get them under control."

*   *   *

"You are a pretty, young thing," Calliope said, tossing a portion of her long brown hair over her shoulder as she stood in front of Angel. Leaning down, her yellow eyes looked deep into Angel's green eyes. "If we were in a different time and place, I am sure we could be a good team."

"We could *never* be on the same team," Angel shot. "You have an evil within you that anyone with an inkling of humanity can see from a mile away."

"Oh," she countered, "I have led many a man into battle or their ruin. Men are putty in my hands…much like Korax and Cassius."

"The A.N.G.E.L.s see you for what you *truly* are."

"Nice try, young one," Calliope said, condescendence evident in her tone. "You see, it is in a man's nature to fall to beauty."

"Our guys see below the surface."

"We will see, young one. We will see," Calliope said.

*   *   *

"Look," Calliope said, inches from Allen's face, deep in the caves of the Tanami Desert. She lightly ran her fingers down his arms as she continued to coerce Allen to follow Cassius, "the Spirit is nothing. Jesus was just a man. As for God? Well, I promise He won't do anything. All you have to do is renounce them all."

Seeing the pain Angel was in from the torture she'd just endured, he didn't think he would survive, so he relented, "Jesus is not my Lord or Savior."

"And finish with…I choose to follow Cassius for the rest of my life. Come on, Allen, you are almost done," Calliope encouraged. "Once you finish, I get to be with you forever!"

"He is not my Lord and Savior, and I-I choose to follow…" He stopped for a moment. Seeing the tears in Angel's eyes as she shook her head, he knew he had already broken the Spirit's heart, so he finished with, "And I choose to follow Cassius for the rest of my life."

"Wonderful!" Calliope said, delighted. "So, you would like to join us then?"

"I…" He sighed, distraught.

"You get to be with me. I want you to come wholeheartedly."

"I…" He looked to Angel, who dropped her head. Knowing he had already done it, he sighed before he said, "Yes. I want to be with you forever."

Humming near his ear again for a moment to calm him, Calliope then looked him right in the eyes as she said, "You are mine. Right?"

When he shook his head to clear it, Calliope started her song again. As the song took over his will, her perfume enveloped his senses. After a few moments, she mesmerized Allen.

"Now, are you mine?" she asked again.

He slowly nodded. Lost in her eyes, he whispered, "Yes. I am yours."

Angel narrowed her eyes at Calliope. *What had she done to him?*

"Yes, my dear," Calliope said with a pleased smile.

The other demons danced in joy, while the demon that had held Angel, let go and immediately freed Allen. "Do you want to eat?" the demon hissed.

"Yes, please," Allen said as his wrists were released. While he rubbed his wrists, he looked toward Angel.

" *'The fear of man bringeth a snare: but whoso putteth his trust in the Lord shall be safe,'"* Angel said, quoting Proverbs 29:25.

*   *   *

Once Korax was out of hearing distance, the demon with Angel attempted to feed her. It said, "You *will* bend, or he *will* kill you."

Spitting out the food all over the demon, she snapped, "That will *never* happen."

"Fine then! Starve!" Face red in anger, the demon punched her midsection.

She groaned, gasping to get a breath of air. Sweat dripped into the cuts covering her arms and legs, the salt burning as if the demon doused her with alcohol.

"Sssee how you like being in complete isssolation," it growled, and left her alone.

As soon as the demon was out of earshot, the angel who had been speaking with Angel the entire time approached her. He stood there, translucent, in appearance so he could disappear at a moment's notice if the demons returned.

In her pain, she had a difficult time lifting her head. The angel tilted Angel's chin so she would look at him. Then the angel whispered Joshua 1:9 to her, *"'Have I not commanded you? Be strong and courageous. Do not be afraid; do not be discouraged, for the Lord your God will be with you wherever you go.'"*

As the angel rested his hand on Angel's cheek, Angel nodded in understanding. She looked toward Heaven. "Lord, I needed You today, and You sent someone for me. I am grateful for all that You are and all that You do for me, Your servant," she said, and groaned, twisting in pain. "Lord, I cry out to You, and I feel You near me. I will hold tight to all I know of You. I know I am never alone, despite what it may look like. Although I can't see You, I am reassured that You are here. I am trusting You with all of my heart, body, mind, and soul." Squirming in pain, she took a moment before she continued, "I know my pride got me into this mess. I'm sorry for that. I will follow You and Your instructions in whatever happens here. My soul is Yours. Please protect it, and hold me close to You. While he fought, Allen fell today. Lord, please give me Your strength! You are my source of strength. You are the strength of my heart. G-give me the endurance to…" She stopped to catch her breath from the piercing agony she was in. "Give me the endurance to make it through this, or please bring me home to You. Please do not let me fall. I do not want to let You down. You *are* my Lord and Savior. Without You, I am nothing. I commit my soul and this situation to You. Your will, not mine."

Psalm 118:6 *"The Lord is with me; I will not be afraid. What can mere mortals do to me?"*

Chapter 1
Above All Else, Guard Your Heart

"I hate it when they make us do this at night," Alexander Bennett said to his passenger, Paul Green, as their Humvee bounded down the dirt road. The convoy travelled deep in Iraq in a line of five Humvees. "I mean, I understand *why*, but it doesn't make me feel any better."

"I don't really think there *is* a good time for this," Green said, watching for any sign of movement near them. Their vehicle was the second in a line of five. "However, Captain said we had to move. When we're given orders, we go. It's a little easier for us to operate in the cover of darkness," he said, tapping the night-vision goggles on his helmet. "During the day, you might as well paint a target on us."

"Are you scared, Bennett?" Charles teased. He was in the back with Hernandez and Adams, who chuckled in response.

"Not necessarily. While I realize there's strength in numbers, a friend of mine got blown to bits two weeks ago on a night mission. Driving around at night, convoy or not, *really* has me on edge."

"Don't let Cap hear you say that," Charles warned.

"I won't."

"He'll make you do extra night duty if he thinks you're scared," Hernandez said, reminding him of the lecture they received prior to their takeoff from Camp Pendleton almost nine months ago.

"Yeah, he's sadistic like that," Adams pointed out.

"Do you think he's there this time?" Charles asked.

Green shrugged. "Intel says he is."

"Is the intel good?"

"Let's hope so, or this will be a colossal waste of time," Adams said. "Hey, Green? How's your girl?"

"I heard from Jenny the other day," Green said, with a boyish grin.

"Oh yeah?" Bennett glanced over at him, surprised. "Why didn't you tell me? How's she doing?"

"Great! She's finally over the morning sickness. She sent me a pic," he said, taking his helmet off. Pulling the photo from his helmet, he held it up for Bennett to see before passing it to the back of the vehicle for the others. In the green hue of the vehicle lights, they saw a very pregnant Jenny Green.

"She's a beaut!" Hernandez commented, handing it to Adams.

"Definitely a looker!" Adams said, handing it back to Green. "Does she have a sister?"

"No." Green chuckled, accepting the photo back. Then, turning to Bennett, he said, "She *did* say she has a friend she wants to introduce *you* to when we get back next month."

"Really?" Bennett asked, heart skipping a beat in excitement.

"Yep. She's got great taste in helping hook people up," Green said, returning the photo to his helmet. As he replaced the helmet back on his head, he explained, "She's helped at least –"

BOOM!

In a flash of blinding light, an explosion rocked the ground under their vehicle. With the crushing metal, yelling and screaming of the guys, and the roar of the blast, it was difficult to distinguish any sound. The ringing in Bennett's ears overpowered any other noise.

…What seemed like minutes, was only a few precious seconds. To him, it could have been an eternity as memories from Bennett's life flashed through his mind. There was his first ten-speed bike he got for his tenth birthday present. It was a top of the line red one with thin white stripes. Then, there was his first date with Erica when he was fifteen. She was also his first girlfriend. Erica was only about 5'3", but the sweetest girl he knew.

Bennett felt his body leave the seat, throwing him all over his position in the cab. The Humvee flipped, landing on the roof. As his arm was trapped in the collapsed roof, he felt the metal carve into his wrist before blood from his wrist created a warm river down his arm.

…The next memory was of the first touchdown he scored in a varsity game as receiver at seventeen. It was the first of many in his football career. Then, there was his high school prom with Erica as his date. Unfortunately, it was also their last date, because that night she found out he joined the Marines and broke up with him. She insisted that she wasn't cut out to be a military spouse. This memory was closely followed by his high school graduation. His parents beamed as they took plenty of photographs to document the occasion.

The vehicle went for the second roll. The Humvee landed on the driver's side, pinning his legs. He felt metal slice his body in multiple areas as the front of the truck collapsed around him.

...His graduation from boot camp was another proud moment for him, as well as one of the worst things he ever went through up to that point. The brutality strengthened him, but also took a toll on him. He would wake up before the sun came up, and wasn't allowed to go to bed until well after sunset. The drill sergeants would work them night an day, until they were satisfied that the recruits were ready. Then came his graduation from technical school, which was the same day he was assigned to a unit. Being officially assigned to the unit was an exciting day in his life. Within that unit, he found fellowship, learned valuable lessons, and learned to work as a team. On that unit, he found his family. The next memory was standing in line with his unit, loading into the C130 for Iraq. While everyone's nerves were completely on edge, they knew what they had to do and why. This was what they signed up for. As he took his seat among his fellow military members, he looked around with pride. He thought sure at that moment, if they tested his blood, it would be red, white, and blue. He knew he was where he was supposed to be. He was a patriot. The last memory he saw, was a conversation with Doc, Green, Hernandez, Adams, and Charles, where they were laughing while playing poker a few nights ago.

Another flip crushed the sides of the vehicle into him. His body jolted as the vehicle rotated again, landing on Bennett's side of the truck. It rocked back and forth before coming to rest fifty yards from its original position.

As much as he tried to focus on any one memory, the intense pain jetting from his legs and arm, along with his lack of oxygen, and the constant ringing in his ears, prevented him from zeroing in on only one. When the concussion wave passed through Bennett, it felt like a vacuum sucked out all the air around him. He had a difficult time catching any breath of air. Any air he did inhale was laced with the taste of dirt, gunpowder, and blood.

Bennett's arm hung in the air, wrapped in a piece of metal from the roof. Unable to release it, he did his best to see around the sheet of roof that separated him from his best friend, Sergeant Paul Green.

When the truck stopped moving, the chaos that suddenly erupted sent shockwaves through Bennett as he did his best to process what was going on around him. "Green!" he shouted for his friend. Barely hearing his own voice, he shouted several more times. It sounded like an echo to him, but he continued to shout for his friend. The sound of gunfire flew around them at an alarming pace. Bennett was desperate to hear an answer from Green…really from anyone at that point. "Hernandez! Adams! Charles! Green! Anybody!"

"I'm here," Adam's groaned. "My leg is trapped. Hernandez is unconscious. I already checked on Charles. He's gone."

"C-can you see Green?"

"No."

Tugging the portion of the roof that separated him from the others side of the cab with his free hand, he could barely move it to see the starry night sky through the thick, black smoke. Shouting again in a voice that was barely audible to his own ears, he was desperate to find any of them, but especially his best friend. "Green!"

After a moment, unable to move from his captured position, he moaned and groaned in pain, joining the faint chorus of Adams and Hernandez in the back. When the reality of what his body experienced hit him, he rested his head back, doing his best to get the pain under control. Hearing the shouts and yells of the fellow members of his unit from the other Humvees was a relief. They not only scrambled to get to their men, but also returned fire to the enemy who surrounded them. He couldn't fully comprehend, nor could he hear what they were saying over the ringing. The blasted ringing was getting to him.

"Bennett, man, don't move," Pierce, his Captain, said, sticking his head through where the windshield used to be.

"Green?" Bennett asked. He sounded weak to himself.

"Barlow's with him."

"Charles is gone. Adams and Hernandez are hurt."

"I need you to focus on my voice, Bennett," Pierce said, scaring himself at how calm he was despite the pandemonium that besieged the convoy. Ducking a few bullets that strayed in their direction before ricocheting off the vehicle, he kept low as he yelled to Bennett, "They've called for help. They're on the way. Just focus on me. There's a lot of blood on you, so I want to make sure you stay with me."

"What happened?"

"IED. They created a choke point. We're returning fire, but we're waiting on air support before we go after them. We don't know who all is out there."

"The other vehicles?"

"Some are still searching the wreckage, while others are keeping the enemy at bay."

Hearing gunfire in the distance, mixed with the shouts of other men, Bennett begged, "Don't leave me, Cap."

"Wouldn't dream of it. Adams, are you and Hernandez okay back there?"

"Think my leg's broke, but other than that, I'm just shaken up…and cold," Adam's voice responded from the darkness. "Hernandez is barely conscious. I don't want to move him."

"Don't. Where's Charles?"

"He was right behind Green," was his only response. From where Adams was, he could clearly see the empty space where the passenger seat used to be.

Pierce shook his head at the devastation around him, at a loss for words. Seeing movement to his left, he noticed the man wore the gear of their enemy. He whipped out his gun and fired off three rounds. When the body dropped to the ground motionless, Pierce looked to the sky, and yelled, "Can we catch a break here?"

"I can't feel my legs," Bennett moaned, bringing Pierce back to him.

"One of mine's on fire," Pierce said, glancing at his own leg, which had tourniquet strapped just above where a piece of shrapnel impaled his thigh.

"I-I can't breathe, and I-I think I'm going to be sick."

"No. Please don't do that. We've got enough going on." Taking another good look around, Pierce placed his gun on his lap before resting his hands on either side of Bennett's face, forcing him to look at him. "You need to focus on me, and work on slowing your breaths." Glancing up at Bennett's arm, he shook his head. The amount of blood soaking Bennett's clothing deeply concerned him. He feared what Bennett's arm would look like once the compression was released. He wasn't sure that Bennett would make it out of this one alive.

"Green's wife is pregnant. Is he okay? He needs to get back to Jenny. Sh-she's due any day. He needs to get back to her before their baby is born."

"Focus on me, Bennett. I need you to worry about yourself. You're –" Pierce swore again as more gunfire neared their position. Aiming into the darkness, he emptied his weapon. After a moment, the gunfire abruptly ceased. Reloading his gun, he watched in the distance at someone maneuvering through the vehicles, to see Jerrod coming toward them. Pierce turned back to Bennett, "Doc's coming. Just focus on me. Okay?"

"I'm trying, Cap. I can't feel…Ahhhhhh!" He shrieked when his arm dropped from its metal encasement, doused in blood. As it landed on his chest, he clearly saw that his hand was missing from just below his wrist…and Bennett completely lost it!

"Just breathe, Bennett!" Pierce yelled over Bennett's shrieks and shouts. "Focus on me, Marine!"

Wide-eyed and frantic, Bennett shouted, "Cap! My arm! Where's my hand? Where's Doc? Why isn't he here yet? What do I do? Help me! Find my hand and put it back! What do I do? Do something! Help me!"

"Bennett! Focus on my voice!" Pierce shouted.

"It's okay. I'm here, Cap," Jerrod said, running up to the truck, sliding in front of Pierce. "How bad?"

"Make him comfortable," was all Captain Pierce said. "As for the back, Charles is already gone. Adams has a broken leg. And Hernandez is semi-conscious, but –"

"Adams! Does Hernandez have a pulse?" Jerrod called to Adams, cutting Pierce off while applying a tourniquet to Bennett's arm in an attempt to slow the bleeding. By the amount of blood loss already, he wasn't sure how much more time Bennett had, but he would fight for him.

"Just a minute," Adams said. After feeling the pulse in Hernandez's neck, he confirmed, "Yes. It's weak, though. He's going in and out of consciousness."

"Which is he right now?"

"Unconscious."

"Okay. Don't move him."

"I won't. Hey, Doc?"

"Yeah?"

"I'm stuck back here. I'm not getting out without help. The seat has crushed my leg. Pretty sure it's broken."

"I'm sure. Just do me a favor and…Bennett?" Jerrod asked, glancing down to Bennett, who closed his eyes. "Bennett? Bennett, can you hear me?" he asked, looking into Bennett's eyes with a penlight.

Shaking his head to wake back up, Bennett glanced down at his arm and started panicking again. "M-my arm! Doc, it's gone!" he shouted, wild-eyed. "Where'd my hand go? You need to find it and put it back! Help me! Ahh! It feels like it's on fire!"

"I need you to calm down," Jerrod said, doing his best to get further into the vehicle to find out the condition of Bennett's legs. By the looks of the vehicle, unless there was a pocket open for Bennett's legs, he feared the worst. He also needed to assess as to how much it would take to get him released.

"My-my legs! My hand! Help me, doc! I'm going to die! I don't want to die! You need to help me!"

"*You need* to calm down, Marine!" Jerrod ordered. Hearing helicopters in the distance, he said, "The cavalry's coming. I need you to stay with me, okay?"

"I don't know what to do! My hand! Look at my hand, Doc!" he said again, holding it up in the air. "It feels like it's on fire! Please put it back on! Help me, Doc! I don't want to die!"

"Calm down," Jerrod gently said.

"My legs! There's pain, but I can't move them."

Trying not to get hit by the hysterical Bennett, Jerrod wiggled back out of the Humvee. "Relax," Jerrod coaxed, giving him a shot of Morphine for the pain, and Valium to calm him.

"I-I…"

"You can do this. Think of home. Think of Buck, your puppy back home. He's waiting for you," Jerrod said, shaking his head as he kept count of the beats of Bennett's pulse for five seconds. He counted for five, and then multiplied it by twelve to get the approximate pulse rate. Due to multiple patients, he didn't have time to count the full ten seconds for a more accurate heart rate.

"He-he's with my sister and her family."

"Good. That's a good place for him. There ya go," Jerrod encouraged, feeling Bennett's pulse slow. He didn't want it to go too slow, but as fast as it was when he reached him, he was sure Bennett would bleed out before he could be extricated from the vehicle. "Buck's waiting for you. Think about playing with him in your backyard. You need to focus on something good. Where was Buck's favorite place to go? Where did he like you to take him? Somewhere you both relaxed," Jerrod said as he bandaged Bennett's arm.

"He loves the beach, like I do."

"Think of the beach," Jerrod said, putting his hand to check the pulse on Bennett's neck to keep track while he searched the skies for reinforcements. Seeing the helicopters nearing their position, he turned back to Bennett and said, "Think of the waves. Imagine sitting there on the beach in the bright sunshine. I'm sure you threw the ball for Buck to chase?"

"Yes."

"Close your eyes and pretend to toss the ball for Buck on the beach. Can you do that?"

"Yes."

"Good. Stay there for me while we work on getting you out of here," Jerrod said, feeling Bennett's heart rate beginning to calm.

Bennett nodded as he closed his eyes. "Oh. Okay."

Jerrod kept his fingers resting on the pulse of Bennett's neck. "We need to get him out of here," Jerrod said in a low voice to Pierce. "Choppers are here. He needs to be the first one out if he is to have a remote chance of getting through this. I also need to get to the others in the back as soon as possible."

"I'll go grab a couple other guys."

"With what? You can't walk on that." Jerrod pointed out. "I don't even know how you got all the way over here in the shape you're in," he said, before he swore under his breath. "Seriously, I'm surprised *you* haven't bled out. Where's your common sense?"

"Watch it, Lucas!" Pierce snapped. Then he shouted out, into the darkness, "Murphy! Garcia! Grab a couple guys and get over here! We have to get these guys out!"

In an instant, there were six guys at their side. Together, they extricated Bennett carefully from the truck while the gunfire slowed around them. A couple men chased after the stragglers so the others would be safe. Meanwhile, after they got Bennett out, they headed inside the vehicle to get to the others.

Two helicopters landed, while two others hovered in the air, keeping an eye overhead. They fired where they would see flashes from gunfire, and knew they weren't friendlies.

"Over here!" Jerrod shouted as the two Corpsmen got out of the helicopters.

"What do we have?" asked one of the Corpsman, running up to what was left of the mangled Humvee.

"His left leg is crushed, and the right arm is missing about the mid-radius and ulna," Jerrod said quietly to the Corpsman, as he finished bandaging Bennett's arm. "He hasn't lost consciousness, but he's not all there either. He's lost *a lot* of blood. He also keeps asking about his partner, Green. Green is DOA. There's another DOA in the back, Charles, along with at least one unconscious, and one with a broken leg. They're working on getting the others out."

Stunned for a moment, the Corpsman only nodded in response. "You take him. I'll take care of the others," the Corpsman told Jerrod. He then went over to where they pulled the others from the vehicle to start on them, while Jerrod stayed with Bennett.

After they loaded him onto a stretcher, Jerrod ran with them to the helicopter. He made mental notes on all he would tell the Corpsman in regards to Bennett's condition once they landed. As he started an IV on Bennett, he looked up to see a couple guys load a covered body on a stretcher next to Bennett in a body bag.

"Who is that?" Bennett asked.

"Green," one of the men said, not thinking.

"Green! Paul!" Bennett panicked. Trying to grab at the bag, Bennett yelled, "That's Paul Green! What happened to him? Why is he in there? They only do that if they're dead. You have to help him, Doc. He can't be dead. He needs to see his baby. Jenny's due any day. Please help him, Doc!"

"Great!" Jerrod groaned, giving up as he injected another dose of morphine into Bennett. He wouldn't be able to do anything in the state Bennett was in until he was calm. If the pain and the status of his hand and legs weren't enough to freak him out, the fact that his best friend laid dead right next to him was the final straw that through him over the edge. "Calm down, Bennett. I need you to calm down *now!*"

While he waited for the morphine to kick in, amongst Bennett's shouts of pain, agony, and panic about Green, Jerrod feverishly worked on getting the blood flow from Bennett's arm back under control before moving back to care for his legs.

After a moment, as another Corpsman neared the helicopter with Adams, Bennett's body suddenly went limp and the screaming abruptly stopped. Jerrod jerked his head up toward Bennett, to see his eyes wide open with a faraway look to them. Other than that, there was no muscle movement. "No-no-no-no-no-no-no-Noooo!" Jerrod shouted, scampering toward the head of the stretcher. "No! You come back here!" he yelled, feeling the side of Bennett's neck for a pulse with his glove-covered, blood-soaked hand. "Bennett! You can*not* die on me! I've worked too hard!" He shouted.

"Noooo!" Jerrod yelled, sitting straight up in the back seat of his Jeep. Sweat poured off his face as he tried to catch his breath, almost hyperventilating. The trio of Nico, Jerrod, and Jon were deep in the Outback of Australia, on a dirt road several hours outside of Alice Springs in the middle of the night. They were en route back to the others in the Tanami Desert with the Jeeps.

Nico snapped to attention in his Jeep, as it was his turn to keep watch. Running over to Jerrod's Jeep, grabbing his face so he would look at him, Nico said, "It's all right, mate. You're safe. You're not there anymore."

"But, he –"

"I have a pretty good idea what happened t' him, but I need you to snap out of it before you wake –"

"I'm up," Jon said, coming over to the Jeep, cutting Nico off. "Don't worry about me," he said, sitting in the driver's seat. "Worry about him. You don't *want* to know how he's feeling," he said. Sometimes Jon's gift of feeling what others felt was a curse, and sometimes it was a blessing. In this instance, it was a curse. If Jerrod didn't calm down, there would be no way for Jon to get any sleep, and Jon only got to sleep an hour ago, after being up for over twenty-four hours.

"No, I don't, and nor do I want to," Nico acknowledged before he turned back to Jerrod. "Jerrod, mate, come on. Who am I?"

"I…I…" Jerrod shook his head.

"*Where are you?*" Nico pressed.

Looking around for a moment in a daze, he shook his head again.

"Jerrod Lucas!" Nico shouted. "*Look* at me, mate! Who am I?"

"I don't…" He shook his head again.

"Let me take a crack at it," Jon offered.

Nico shook his head. "I dunno."

"Which one of us literally knows how he's feeling?" Jon asked, raising an eyebrow.

"Too true," Nico agreed, switching places with Jon.

Taking his hand, Jon knelt on the floor of the backseat of the Jeep. Positioning himself in front of Jerrod, Jon calmly said, "Jerrod, I'm Jon English. You're in the Outback of Australia, not in Iraq. Can you see me?"

Jerrod just looked at him blankly.

"Let me try this another way," Jon said, getting a little closer. "Jerrod, you did your best," he encouraged, praying for the words to come from the Spirit. "You helped those you could before returning to base. You then went into the bathroom and washed the blood from your hands, safe, out of the nightmare you just experienced."

"How do you –?"

"Shh!" Jon cut Nico off. Turning back to Jerrod, he continued, "After you washed your hands, you collapsed on your cot, and drifted off to sleep. That was years ago. Now you're in the Outback of Australia with Jon English and Nico Sullivan. Do you know who we are?"

Looking at Jon and Nico, Jerrod slowly shook his head, before he nodded after a moment. Still in a bit of a daze, he looked around at their surroundings. Turning back to them, he let out a slow breath of air and asked, "What happened?"

"You had a night terror," Jon said, moving back to the driver's seat, giving Jerrod some space. "Do you know where you are?"

"Sort of. No. Not really. Give me a few," he mumbled, looking around the landscape, hoping to get his bearings.

"Want some water?" Nico offered.

"Yeah."

After getting him a bottle of water, Nico leaned on the Jeep up next to Jerrod's head, crossing his arms. Over his shoulder, he told Jon, "Go back to sleep. I got this."

"Thanks," Jon muttered, shuffling sleepily back to his Jeep, grateful they got Jerrod's emotions landed for the moment.

"All right, mate," Nico said, turning back to Jerrod. "Is it always that bad?"

"Sometimes it's worse."

"Who was Bennett?" Nico asked. When Jerrod looked at him wide-eyed, Nico asked, "Did he live?"

Slowly shaking his head no, not taking his eyes of Nico, Jerrod admitted, "His name was Alexander Bennett. His injuries and blood loss were too much. I couldn't save him. He lost part of his arm in the blast, and his legs were crushed. How did you know his name?"

"You shouted it in your sleep. Look, mate, you're not God. You can't work miracles. You're only human."

"His best friend, Paul Green, died in the blast. Green's wife was pregnant at the time – due any day. I found out later she had a boy, and named him Paul Alexander Green, after the two of them. Bennett was in a body bag right next to Green. He didn't know it was Green, until one of the guys said his name, and then Bennett completely lost it. There was no bringing him back from that one."

"I'll bet," Nico said, trying to process how he would feel.

"You have no idea. We were on a mission to take out one of the leaders at the time. We had intel of his position, and had to move right away. It couldn't wait until daylight. We knew it was a risk, but letting him get away again, was a risk we weren't willing to gamble. I was in the Humvee behind them. A couple more seconds and I would have been in Green's position. There were five of ours killed on that day," Jerrod said, holding his stomach, as he curled up in the seat.

"When the smoke cleared, it was a mangled mess. Captain Pierce had a lacerated leg, but he crawled off to their vehicle, while a bunch of us did our best to take cover from the weapons fire that immediately ensued, and returned fire. We had to take out those firing on us before we could even *think* of getting to the wounded."

"Wow."

"When it slowed enough, the others sent me to Bennett's Humvee. By the time I got there, Bennett was already losing it. He already knew he lost part of his arm," Jerrod said using his hand to show where Bennett's arm was taken off, "and his legs were crushed from here down. I have no idea how the guys got him out of there, but they did it quickly enough for me to give Bennett a chance. When the choppers landed, I went with Bennett. He was the worst one there. Green and Charles were already dead. Adams' leg was crushed. He just thought it was broken, but he ended up losing part of it. We lost Hernandez and another one in the firefight. It was a cluster –"

"I got it," Nico said, cutting him off.

"I played poker with all of them just the night before. I *knew* them. *All* of them. As a Doc, you don't just come in at the last minute. You are part of their unit…for better or worse."

"I'm sorry you had to go through that."

"If it was only the one instance, I would probably be able to process it, but it wasn't. We were pretty much on edge twenty-four hours a day for seven days a week for months on end. What I don't get is when we live like that, and then return, or get out of the military, civilians just expect us to *get over it*," he said, shaking his head. "There's no getting over watching good men die. There's no getting over living with the threat of being blown up or shot at any time. They even hid bombs in stuffed animals or toys that the kids carried. Can you *believe* they sent kids in to their deaths just to blow us up? And we were trying to *help* them!" Taking a deep sigh, Jerrod looked up at the vast amount of stars that filled the sky. He was amazed at how many more were visible away from the lights of the city. He took a deep, cleansing breath in hopes of clearing his mind. "That's amazing," he said, hoping to get lost in the stars.

Deciding that sidetracking Jerrod's train of thought would be the best approach at helping him, Nico said, "That's what happens when you're out of the city. You can see all of God's creation in its splendor. When we're on the station, nighttime is actually my favorite time of the day. It's cool, and there are a billion stars up there. When you're in the city, you can't see them as well, but they're always up there."

"I feel like my mind's all over the place," Jerrod said.

"That's understandable. Look, you got five hours of sleep. You can try for another hour, or you and I can talk some more?" Nico offered. "We take off in a couple hours. I may give Jon a bit more time to sleep since his sleep was interrupted."

"Yeah, I'll have to apologize to him when he wakes."

"No, you don't," Jon called from his Jeep. "Just relax so I can get back to sleep."

Nico and Jerrod laughed, as they admired God's majesty above, lost in conversation, while Jon drifted back to sleep.

*   *   *

"Mum!" Rachel grinned. Tears instantly stung her eyes when Kit walked into the house, dragging her suitcase behind her.

Upon seeing her daughter on the couch, Kit dropped her suitcase and coat at the door, and ran over to her. Gently sitting on the couch next to Rachel, Kit wrapped her arms around Rachel's neck and hugged her tightly.

"Mum…can't…breathe!" Rachel finally said.

"I'm sorry," Kit said, pulling back, wiping the tears out of her eyes before she wiped the few tears on Rachel's cheek away as well. "I just missed you so much. To hear you had been hurt made my heart drop into my stomach. Knowing Angel's still in danger, and that Josh is still out there in possible danger as well, terrifies me. I was so relieved when your Dad told me you were here. And then hearing your voice…" Kit's voice trailed as Rachel cried a little harder. "It's okay, Rach. Really. I'm here. I *did* bring someone with me, though. She wouldn't let me leave without her," Kit said, gesturing toward the door.

When Rachel saw Leah, she couldn't hold the tears back anymore, and they turned into sobs as Leah ran over to her. Getting on her knees next to the couch, Leah grabbed her twin sister without shame or embarrassment, and they both burst out in tears of joy at being reunited.

"There are two of them?" Kai asked with his thick Irish accent, eyes wide and mouth gaping. He and Cori were standing in the doorway of the basement, with Charm (Cori's seeing eye dog) leaning on Cori's leg.

"Shut your mouth," Cori whispered.

"How'd you know my jaw was dropped?" Kai asked, glancing at her sideways, as he stood there with his arms crossed. "You're blind."

"Probably because I *know* you. You don't have to have sight to know that you've seen a gorgeous girl…let alone two a' them. I assume by your reaction that they're identical?"

"Yes. Seriously! How are there two a' them?"

Katia walked over to Kai, and using two of her fingers, she pushed up his chin, shutting his mouth. "Not nice to stare," she pointed out, her Russian accent still thick within her English.

"Way to go, Katia," Cori said with a grin.

"Seriously! How did all the good genes end up in one family?" Kai asked. "The girls are gorgeous, and there are two of them. Delaney thinks Josh is hot, and I *know* there are two of him too. I've seen them. Seeing Nico, and now Kit? It makes perfect sense. Even with as old as she is, she's still pretty."

"Hush!" Cori reprimanded him.

Giggling, Katia moved to the opposite side of the doorway from Kai and Cori, leaning against the wall. "You are funny, Kai."

"Glad you think so, but I'm serious!" Kai defended himself.

"Beauty is only on the outside," Katia reminded him.

"And, from what I've seen of Rachel, she's just as pretty on the inside," Kai pointed out.

Suddenly, the group heard a scream from upstairs. "Liliya!" Katia breathed out, before bolting up the stairs to her sister.

"I'm afraid it's been this way every few hours since she got here," Casey explained when Kit gave her a questioning look. "I want to talk with her, but I really need her to get some decent sleep first. Unfortunately, she's not getting any."

"Mind if I speak with her? It's been almost a year since they've seen each other, so I'll let these two get reacquainted," she said, gesturing toward Rachel and Leah, who finally let each other go enough to make sure they were really looking at each other. When Casey nodded, Kit stood and asked, "Would you please boil some water for a tea for her. Pete makes a tea that helps one sleep, and he sent me with a few baggies. She won't be able to fight it."

"Sounds good," Casey agreed. "Her room is upstairs. At the top of the stairs, go left. It's the second room on the right," Casey explained. "In the meantime, I'll boil the water and get breakfast for these two, so we can get homeschool started," she said, ushering Allie and Callie to the kitchen.

Allie and Callie were on another couch with Charlie, listening to a story Charlie was telling when Casey went to pick up Kit and Leah. Charlie followed Casey and the girls into the kitchen to lend a hand.

"Too many twins," Kai said, shaking his head as he finally turned to go back down the stairs. He followed Cori and Charm, leaving Leah and Rachel alone in the living room to catch up privately.

*   *   *

"Knock, knock," Kit said, sticking her head in the doorway, to see tears slowly crawling down Katia's cheeks as she held Liliya. Liliya was crying and rocking in place, her face pale.

"Does she speak English?" Kit asked, knowing they were from Russia.

"Yes. We both do." Katia nodded, her heart breaking for her sister. Wiping the few tears that escaped, Katia curiously watched every move Kit made.

"If we get anymore tears in this house, we're going to need a mop," Kit said with a smile as she walked into the room. Taking the chair next to the bed, she gave Liliya some space to breathe. "Your name is Liliya?"

Liliya sniffed, wiping her cheeks. "Yes."

Shaking her hand, Kit said, "Hi. I'm Kit. I'm Rachel's mom."

"You do not sound like her. Little different," Katia pointed out, with her head cocked to the side, studying her.

"That's because I was born and raised in America. I didn't live in Australia until I was in my twenties. While I *do* have somewhat of an Australian accent, it's more of a southern American accent. You tend to pick up certain parts of speech when you move to a different place."

"Yes. This happens," Katia agreed.

Moving her chair closer to the bed, Kit retook her seat. Leaning forward, with her elbows on her knees and her hands together, she said, "Liliya, I understand you've had quite an experience." Liliya only nodded in response. Reaching up, Kit went to move part of Liliya's blond hair out of her face.

Initially, Liliya pulled away, but then she allowed Kit to touch her. "There ya go, sweetheart." Kit smiled warmly. "May I sit on the bed with you?"

Liliya nodded. She and Katia moved to make room for Kit, as Kit moved onto the side of the bed.

"Casey tells me that you've had some trouble sleeping?" Kit asked.

"Yes. Very scared," Liliya admitted, as she sat there looking like a terrified animal, cowering on the bed.

"You know you're safe, right? The man who took you is probably locked away in some freezer in Siberia," Kit explained, praying Sergei was getting his due justice in prison for what he did not only to Liliya, Angel, and Elena, but also to the other girls…or would be as soon as he got deported back to Russia. "Or he will be as soon as the Russian authorities get their hands on him."

While Katia smiled at that, Liliya didn't. Taking a moment to form the thought in her head, Liliya then explained, "It is not Sergei who frightens me. It is the evil in the cave. It is fear for Angel. She is in danger."

"Aww, honey," Kit said, resting her hand on Liliya's arm. "God has you in the safest place possible on this earth. The Haven is surrounded by His angels. Trust me, they won't let anything get to you here. That's probably the only reason Rachel's been able to get some sort of rest here. Trust me," Kit said, tossing her long auburn hair over her shoulder, "you are perfectly safe here."

"Can they find me at school?"

"The Devil and his minions are everywhere on this planet," Kit admitted, much to Liliya's horror, "but – and this is a big *but* – but God is bigger than anything here on earth. He didn't just *create* this planet and its inhabitants. He only had to open His beautiful mouth and *speak* them into existence. Trust me, you are on the right side of this."

"Then, why is Angel still there?"

"Knowing what Nico told me, and knowing Angel the way I do, I'm pretty sure it's because she knows where she's going when she dies. She wanted to give the rest of you a chance to live your life. You and Katia have had one doozy of a life so far," Kit said with a gentle smile. "You are now in a safe place. Casey and Mark will look after you as one of their own. You may not have been born to them, but you are now theirs. You will have many doors here in the States open to you. As to what you want to do with your life, it's completely up to you. Katia has looked after you as much as she could, and has done an amazing job at it, I must say," she said, smiling at Katia, who nodded in appreciation. "But, now she has her own path she must follow. She's given you the gift of being here at the Haven while she moves forward. In the meantime, she's fixin' to go out to fight for, and with, the others. God has an amazing plan for both of you. Did you know that when I was in college, I was kidnapped as well?"

"You were?" Liliya asked, as both she and Katia looked at Kit wide-eyed.

"Oh yes," Kit assured them. "There was a sadly misguided man who thought I was meant for him. God had a different plan, though. While I was being held captive, the one verse that allowed me to keep my sanity was Jeremiah 29:11. It says, '*For I know the plans I have for you,' declares the Lord, 'plans to prosper and not to harm you, plans to give you a hope and a future.'* God had an incredible plan for me. He sent Mark to help me out of another mess too. He, along with my husband, Nico, whom you've already met, finally got me out of all of that. Now we have lived in God's grace and mercy on Serenity Wells Station for years. He gave us the gift of twin boys, Joshua and Caleb, and twin girls, Leah and Rachel, as well. He also gave us the blessing of, when a young neighbor girl of ours got pregnant out of wedlock, having the opportunity to save the baby's life. The parents wanted the girl to have an abortion because she was too young." When she said that, both girls gasped. "I know, but God had a better plan for that little baby. She was born into that family and raised by the young girl's parents. And now, that beautiful little baby has grown into the young woman my Caleb married. He and Willow run the station now. And, the little girl who got pregnant is married with three children of her own. She's also a doctor."

"Really?" Liliya asked, stunned.

"Yes. See, despite all the bad, God had a plan, and He knew who needed to be there for it to come to fruition. We may never know the why, but we know the Who…God. We know that no matter what has happened, that God is still there, looking out for those of us who are His. He'll never leave you now that you are one of His."

"But…still scared," Liliya admitted, as Katia still had her arm protectively around her sister.

"You will be. That's natural and understandable," Kit explained. "You're mind and body will continue to battle what all has happened for a long time. Thankfully, though, you are in a safe place, surrounded by safe people. There is only love and protection here," she said, choosing her words carefully. "I won't lie to you, though. In 1 Peter 5:8, we are reminded to, *'Be sober, be vigilant, because your adversary the devil walketh about as a roaring lion, seeking whom he may devour.'* I'm not telling you that to scare you. I'm telling you so you stay on your toes. We don't fight against flesh and blood. You've seen firsthand what we're fighting. I *know* you know what's out there. However, in this moment in time, you need to relax, and rest in the fact that you are safe. In order for you to work through what you've been through, you *have* to get some rest. Now, I've brought a tea from our station doctor for you to drink so you can get some sleep. Will you drink it?"

"Yes, ma'am," Liliya agreed.

"Wonderful," Kit said, getting off the bed. "I'll go get it. I'll be back as soon as it's finished. When was the last time you ate?"

"She ate a little dinner last night," Katia explained.

"Right-oh," Kit said in a sigh. "I'll bring ya up some breakkie too."

"Breakkie?" Katia cocked her head to the side again. "What is this breakkie?"

"No worries." Kit smiled gently. "That just means breakfast. I'll be back in a tic," she said and left.

When she was out of earshot, Katia looked to her sister, and they spoke in Russian. "We are out of there, little one," Katia encouraged Liliya.

"I know that. I do not know if it is okay to rest, though. Every time I do, I see those creatures," Liliya said with a shudder.

"You have to rest. You are safe. I trust these people."

"You do?" Liliya asked, wide-eyed. "You do not trust anyone!"

"I know. God has shown me amazing things in my dreams. I know these A.N.G.E.L.s are good people. I know God is bigger than any of this, or you wouldn't be here. I also know without sleep," she said, lifting Liliya's chin so she would look at her, "you will not get any better."

Looking down for a moment, Liliya organized her thoughts now that her head was a little clearer than when she woke. When she looked back up to Katia, she explained, "You are my sestra. You are the only person on this planet that I love."

"As are you *my* sestra, but you know you are not the *only* person I love."

"There is another?" she asked, stunned.

"Three. They are God, Jesus, and the Spirit. One day, little one, you too will know these as I do. Right now you are young in the Lord. Allow Kit to help you. Let her show you who Jesus is, and the sacrifice He made for you. Let her give you insight into Who the Father is. Let her tell you of the Spirit and His guidance. You will grow, much like the wonder twins downstairs," Katia said, smiling at Allie and Callie's nickname. "If you trust me, and you trust Jesus with your life, then you must trust Kit to help you."

"I will," Liliya agreed.

"The dreams will continue," Katia said, resting her hand on the side of Liliya's face, gently lifting it so she would look at her with her big blue eyes, "but they will become less and less with time. With each one you conquer, you will be slowly released from this nightmare. For now, though, know you are free from living the nightmare you were in."

"I know. Thank you for coming for me."

"Of course! I will come every time. Just like God, I would move heaven and earth to find you. As Kit said, the angels of the Lord are protecting us here. You will need to eat, and drink the tea so you can sleep. You have not slept for days."

"Yes. The last time was when I was taken from that horrible house and drugged," Liliya admitted.

"You are too young to have such problems. It was my hope to keep you from them."

"The world is cruel."

"Not here. Here you have a fresh start."

"Thanks to *you*."

"No, thanks to God, little one. Thanks to God."

*   *   *

"Seriously, that last one was a soup sandwich!" Jerrod said as they talked about a new plan with the others when the group finally got together deep in the Tanami Desert. It was about midday, and a hot one at that. The closer summer came, the hotter and dryer it got.

Laughing, Joe asked, "Okay, what's a soup sandwich?"

"It's something that's a mess...a disaster," Mark explained with a smile on his face. "I haven't heard that in a *long* time."

"Oh, I'm full of them!" Jerrod grinned.

"I'm sure you're full of *something*," Jon added with a smirk. When Jerrod smacked his arm, he was laughing too hard to respond, so Mark continued.

"Okay," Mark said, still smiling, "here are the previous points marked on the map." With the map on the ground in the middle of the group, he explained, "We can't go in with the same plan we had last time. It's too predictable."

"Not to mention virtually impossible to get to now because it's blown to smithereens," Jacob reminded them.

"This is true," Mark said, stroking his chin in thought.

"We go this way," Amarina said, pointing to the other side of the caves. "There is an exit there too."

"Wait! What?" Nico looked at her stunned. "There's another way out?"

"Yes," she said, not sure why they were all looking at her in shock. "What is wrong?"

Groaning, Derek dropped his head on his hand as he explained, "Because we thought there was only one entrance. We haven't been watching the other side." Looking up at her, he added, "They could have taken her out the other side, and we won't know because we weren't watching there."

"Oh," she said, kicking herself on the inside for not mentioning it before then. "I did not think of that. I am sorry."

"You didn't know," Josh said, hoping to ease her conscience. "Now that we know, we're going to have to have two plans of attack.

"We were going in thinking they were in there," Nico continued, "but they may be gone. If they aren't, then they may very well be waiting for us to show up again, and will attack us outside the caves on the way in, or could very well seal us in there before we get out."

"I see the problem," Amarina said in understanding. "I am sorry."

"Seriously, you have been invaluable," Mark pointed out. "There is no way you should have thought to tell us that. It just means we need to change our strategy going in. We're going to have to have a few in, and the rest outside cautiously moving in, looking for traps all the way in. Jacob, you are mission critical. You are to stay outside. I need your eyes on the ground. You know what to look for, because you set them all the time."

"True," Jacob agreed.

"At the same time, I need you to stay near, so when we come out you can set them off at a moment's notice."

"Consider it done. I'll need some help mixing stuff and setting them up. You got everything on the list, right?"

"Yes," Nico chuckled. "Not sure why you need part of this stuff, though."

"Well, for the toilet paper I just need the rolls. Then I'll use the rolls, the sugar, and the potassium nitrate to make smoke bombs. Those are going in with you this time," he said sternly.

"They'll fill the cavern, giving you a chance to get out without losing anyone."

"The bucket? The PVC pipe? The ammonia?" Jon questioned.

"Dude! You'll find out. You asked me to make something that will explode. Trust me. It *will* blow."

"While I don't doubt that, moth balls and diesel gasoline?" Nico raised an eyebrow.

Jacob sighed, crossing his arms. "Do you trust me?"

"Yes."

"Then, trust me. You want it to blow? It'll blow. You want to blow the entire cave system? I can do that for you too," Jacob pointed out. "You want to fill the entire thing with smoke? I can do that. You want to blow a tree stump, or sufficiently blow a vehicle sending them both a fair distance? I got that covered too when you need it. Don't doubt me, though."

"Never," Jesse said, ruffling his hair. "You're too smart."

Shoving his hand away, he grumbled, "I hate it when you do that."

"No you don't," Jesse said knowingly. "You only like complaining about it," he said ruffling his hair again. Ducking, he missed it when Jacob took a swing at him. Jesse grabbed him, taking him to the ground as they play wrestled.

"Can we calm the testosterone down a bit, and focus on getting Angel and the other man out?" Delaney asked, trying to be the voice of reason, putting a halt to the wrestling.

"I need at least until tomorrow," Jacob said, as they got off the ground, brushing the dirt off. "One of the explosives has to settle before I can pull out what I need."

"Done," Mark agreed. "Now," he said, directing everyone back to the map, "Amarina, the other entrance is *where exactly*?"

Pointing on the map, she said, "Here."

Marking the spot on the map with an 'x,' Mark asked, "Are there any trees or hills on that side?"

"Oh yeah!"

Looking up at her, surprised again, Mark just sighed as he shook his head.

Amarina blushed. "Oh. I did it again. Didn't I?"

"It's okay," Derek assured her. "This is new for you."

"Yes. I usually just go on walk-about…not looking to pull someone outta danger."

"It's just a matter of adjusting your line of thinking," Mark explained. "Okay, if I give you a couple pieces of paper, could you draw what the other side of that hillside looks like?"

"I can draw what it looks like before Jacob gets his presents ready. I can have it for you in the morning," Amarina offered.

"Can you get it to us sooner than that?" Mark asked. "I can't do anything until I know what it looks like."

"In a couple hours?" Amarina proposed.

"That'll work," he said, looking toward Derek, who went to the Jeep to get pencil and paper.

"I'll make it quick," Amarina said, accepting the paper and pencils.

"Take your time, but hurry up," Mark added. "We have to come up with a plan. In the meantime, the rest of us can keep watch, and help Jacob as much as possible."

*   *   *

Groaning from the pain, Angel woke to her living nightmare. "Ohhh, why can't this just be a really bad dream?" she said aloud.

"You are awake," the angel said, as he got off the ground. Still translucent, he kept a vigilant eye and ear to everything around him.

"You're still here? I didn't imagine you?"

"No. I am still with you. I am not a figment of your imagination. God sent me here to stay with you so you know you are not alone. While I am here doing my best to keep you focused on God, you need to do your part and guard your heart against what the other side is trying to do," he said. Standing around six foot, with blond hair, and royal blue eyes, he was dressed in a chiton, with a belt around his waist that carried his sword. His wings hung loosely on his back, while he kept his hand on his sword at all times, on alert.

"How do I do that?" Angel asked, exhausted.

"You follow the words of Proverbs 4:23. It says to, *'Above all else, guard your heart, for everything you do flows from it.'* You committed your spirit and heart to the Lord before you passed out. Do you remember that?"

"I *vaguely* remember that," Angel admitted. "Did Allen really give up?"

"Unfortunately, yes." The angel nodded. "As for guarding *your* heart, you do as you did last time, staying focused on the Lord and His words, and you will do well."

"Will I make it out alive?"

"That is not known to me. I am ordered to stay by your side. I will die before I leave you."

"Thank you," Angel said, appreciatively. "Do you…do you think they'll be back anytime soon?"

"I know you are hungry, because you have not eaten in two days, but remember to whom you belong. You are a daughter of the Lord God. They will use food and drink to tempt you."

"Man does not live by bread alone," Angel said, remembering when Jesus was tempted in the wilderness.

"Exactly!" the angel said with a smile. "You can do this, Angel!" Suddenly turning to his left, he looked toward the entrance to the cavern for only a moment before he disappeared right before her eyes.

"Ohhhh, you are awake!" a demon hissed, walking into the cavern, wringing his hands in delight. "Deliciousss! Time for another round!"

Chapter 2
Be Strong And Take Heart

"Cori, if I copied this for you to listen to on your computer so you could do your thing to it that you do, would you take a listen?" Kai asked, taking off his headset. They were down in what had become affectionately known as the cyber cave. The cyber cave was located in the basement of the Haven, and contained all the equipment Cori and Kai needed to do their thing. They were only on one side, though, knowing eventually the other team's IT people would use the other side.

"Sure. What is it?" Cori asked.

"I just picked up some chatter, but I can't separate things enough to distinguish what I'm hearing."

"Where did you get it?"

"Tsk!" Kai clicked his tongue. "Is that really a question?"

"*How* did you get it?"

"I thought we didn't ask that question around here either. Now be a good lass, and take a listen, yeah?" he said, putting the thumb drive securely in her hand.

"Fair enough." Taking it from him, she inserted it into her computer, and then picked up her headset and put it on. After only a moment of tapping on her computer and listening, she whipped them back off. "Go get Casey, Kit, Rach, and Charlie."

*   *   *

"What's going on?" Casey asked, coming downstairs with Kit, Katia, Kai, Rachel, and Charlie, while Liliya stayed upstairs with the twins.

"We have a problem," Cori explained.

Kit raised an eyebrow. "Could you be a little more specific?"

"Kai gave me something to listen to. Have a listen for yourselves," she said, unplugging her headset from the computer before she played the recording.

At first, there was a sound of very loud white noise, along with a lot of indistinct voices.

"Too loud!" Kai shouted over the noise with his ears covered. Everyone else immediately covered their ears as well.

"Sorry," Cori said, adjusting the sound before she started playing with the program to cut out the white noise.

As it cleared, everyone took their hands off their ears to hear Korax say, "We have Allen. We need to get Angel as well. If we get her on our side, then we will have the A.N.G.E.L.s right where we want them."

"We cannot risk moving," Calliope pointed out. "They will see us. We are well hidden here."

"We have to. Our other choice is to sit here and be taken out by those blasted A.N.G.E.L.s!" another female argued.

"We need the time to work on her," Calliope pointed out. "They do not call me the muse of heroic poetry for no reason. *I* can get her to rethink her position as an A.N.G.E.L., or at least get her ready for you to come in and change her mind."

"I do not want her to change her mind *or* get her to rethink her position. I *want* her to turn on them completely, and join *our* side. Anything less than that is unacceptable," Cassius growled.

Tapping the computer to turn the recording off, Cori turned in the direction of the others and said, "That's all I got. Well, technically, that's all *Kai* got."

"How did you get this?" Casey asked, taking the portable drive out from the computer tower.

"In the cyber cave, we are under a *don't ask, don't tell* policy," Kai said with a smirk. Crossing his arms, he leaned on Cori's desk.

"Okay," Charlie said, taking a deep breath. "How do we get ahold of them?"

"We can't." Kit shook her head. "It's too far out. There's no cell out there."

"*We* can't, but *they* can," Rachel said knowingly, looking toward Cori and Kai. "Can't you?"

"Well..." Cori said hesitantly.

"We *have* to tell the others. Angel may not even be there," Katia pressed.

"Or worse yet, they may be walking into a trap," Casey pointed out.

"Give me a minute," Cori said, turning to her computer. Tapping feverishly, the group watched as one screen after another flashed on the monitor. After several minutes of everyone holding their breath, Cori used her computer to dial a phone number.

"Hello?" Delaney said, answering her phone.

"Delaney, this is the Haven," Cori explained.

"Okay, and *how* are you doing this?"

Cori chuckled. "Don't ask a question you don't want to know the answer to, love."

Hearing her giggle before she spoke, Delaney said, "Gotcha. What's going on?"

"I'm going to play something for ya, but you need to put it on speaker with the others around."

"Will do. Just a sec," she said.

As she gathered the others around her, Cori booted up the recording. After they listened to it, Mark said, "Thanks for the head's up."

"Mark, you are caught between a rock and a hard place. There's no telling if Angel's there or not," Casey said, stress evident in her voice.

"I understand, sweetheart. Angel's strong."

"But even strong people reach their max," Casey reminded him.

"Thankfully God doesn't have a max for *Him* to reach," Mark pointed out. "And, she's not alone."

"I know. How are we going to find her if they've moved her?"

"We'll let God lead. Until then, we'll go forward with the plan that she's right where we left her."

"I'm worried for her," Casey confessed.

"So am I."

"Keep an ear out," Nico said. "If you hear anything else, let us know."

"You know our ears are to the ground on this one now that we're set up properly," Kai assured him.

"Thanks," Derek said. "We're working on things over here. We should be ready in the early morning."

"Just know we're here praying for you," Kit said.

"We're counting on it, love," Nico responded over the computer phone line.

"Be careful," Rachel added before the team in Australia hung up.

*   *   *

Out in the Tanami Desert as they hung up, Nico turned to Mark, and said, "Look, I know it sounds bad, but your daughter is strong."

"I know," he said, deep in thought. "I also know Allen was a pastor, and he obviously fell."

"Pastors are men too," Jon reminded them. "Yes, they are to be held to a higher standard, but maybe the temptation was too great."

"Then we need to pray that it's not too great for Angel," Jacob said, turning back to work on his explosives. Joe and Val were helping him.

"Amarina? Do you have that drawing yet?" Mark asked, visibly on edge.

"Yes. Here," she said, gathering the papers off the hood of the Jeep. As she handed them to him, she mentioned, "If she is anything like her father, she is strong."

"Thank you. Come on guys," he said to Nico, Jon, Josh, Derek, Jesse, Amarina, and Jerrod.

As the group went off to themselves, Mark spread the papers out on the ground near the fire so the others could see. Delaney and Sasha were keeping watch while the others took care of their various assignments.

"This is where the other entrance is." Amarina pointed it out on her drawings.

"This is where Jacob blew the ground," Jerrod explained, pointing out several areas. "I saw him plant the IEDs."

"That leaves this portion of the hill open," Derek said, motioning to a portion with his hand. "It's heavily treed up here, and a rock hill down there, so we have to be careful on how we go about this."

"Yes, or we could find ourselves in the middle of another…what did you call it?" Amarina asked Jerrod.

"A soup sandwich," Jerrod offered.

"Yes. That. Now," Amarina directed everyone back to the map, "here and here are good points of lookout."

"We can't follow the same pattern we did last time," Jerrod disagreed. "That will set us up for failure. We hit them hard last time. I *highly* doubt they'll not be expecting something like that again."

"Okay. My vote is that only three go in," Derek suggested. "That'll leave three at the Jeeps, three inside, and leaves seven outside."

"Who are the three going in?" Mark asked.

"I'm going in this time," Derek said firmly. "I was at the Jeep last time."

"Wouldn't want to miss out on the fun this time?" Jerrod remarked, as a grin spread across his face. "I would have never pegged you for an adrenaline junkie."

"I don't get to do the fun stuff all that often anymore." Derek shrugged. "Besides, this could be my last shot. I *am* getting older."

"You're not *that* old, old man," Jesse nudged him.

"Glad you think so, because you're going in with me," he said to Jesse.

"Me? Why?" Jesse asked, wide-eyed.

"Because it's *your* sister."

"Then I'm going in too," Jon volunteered.

"Me too," Mark said.

"I'm not a math whiz by any stretch of the imagination," Jerrod said, "but I'm pretty sure that's four, and not three."

"Fine," Jon said. "I'll hang back outside."

"I think that's a good idea," Derek agreed. "We need to be quiet. Jesse needs to be on the inside, so we don't get caught by surprise like you guys did last time. With Jesse's gift, he can tell whoever goes in how close the other side is to us."

"The other's need to be spread out in these two regions," Amarina explained. "This will give them a clear view of the opening, but still hidden in case there are surprises."

"Do you honestly think we'll get surprised?" Jesse asked.

"Why not?" Jerrod shrugged. "There's more chance of them breaking any type of former rules of engagement, than there is the off chance that they'll follow them. They've already shone that by taking Aden Knight out in broad daylight in London, and when they attacked and killed Stepan in a park in Russia – both of them out in the open. There are no rules, here, folks. To think anything else would be naïve. You are delusional if you even *remotely* think they are still playing by the rules they played by before Black Rock. That was a turning point in this battle."

"And one, it seems, that has completely changed how they operate," Mark agreed.

"Whatever, or *however* they played before, you can throw out the window," Jerrod went on. "We're dealing with an anything goes situation."

"Then, we need to play by the same rules," Jesse said.

"With the exception that God is our gauge," Derek added. "We may be able to change *some* of the rules, but there are still some hard and fasts."

"Agreed," Mark said. "Okay, let's rethink this. We need Jacob and Jerrod outside, but close."

"We need at least three at the Jeeps. There are four Jeeps they have to keep safe. We need to make sure there are enough people to cover all four," Jerrod pointed out.

"After Black Rock, that needs to be a priority," Jon agreed. "That's our only means of escape out here."

"Okay, that's five," Mark said.

"I *am* a bit quieter than you," Derek pointed out to Mark.

"Right, so you're inside," Mark agreed.

"We should really make sure Jesse's inside as well," Derek reasserted. "You guys got caught last time. We need his gift inside."

"That leaves one more opening," Mark said, writing the names down to keep track of where they were assigning people. "We need someone we know who won't freeze."

"Honestly, I think Josh needs to go this time," Jesse said. "He's the other team lead."

"While that's a good point, we have to look at the gifts we have," Nico said, stroking his chin in thought. "Doesn't Sasha have Jesse's gift, *and* the gift of premonitions?"

"Yes, but we'll need him outside so we don't get surrounded," Jerrod pointed out. "I'm going to suggest one a little less conventional."

"Really?" Mark asked. "Who?"

Turning to Jesse and Derek, Jerrod asked, "Would you be opposed to taking Val in?"

"*Who*?" Jesse asked, stunned.

"Did you say *Val*?" Derek asked, shocked.

"What? Who?" Josh asked, surprised.

"What? Did I hear my name?" Val asked from where he worked with Jacob and Joe.

"Working on something. Just keep working with Jacob," Jerrod dismissed him.

When Val turned back to the explosives, Mark looked at Jerrod and asked, "Have you lost your mind? He's the biggest pacifist on both teams! While there's nothing wrong with that, I have a *huge* problem with potentially sending him in somewhere that he'll be *forced* to kill. Pretty sure that goes against everything in him."

"Hear me out," Jerrod said, trying to calm everyone. "What is Val's gift?"

"Spiritual sight," Jon answered.

"Derek is extremely quiet. Jesse's big, so he makes a bit of noise. Val's quiet as a church mouse, *and* has spiritual sight. If they've moved her from her original position, Val would be the first one to know."

"You should *really* take someone who's already been in there," Josh disagreed.

"Katia's not here. She has the most knowledge of what that place looks like," Jon pointed out.

"Right, but after Jacob's bombs, that place could look entirely different," Jerrod added. "Again, this is where Val's spiritual sight will come in handy. He's just as trained as everyone else…with the exception of Delaney and Sasha, who we're not sure of how strong they really are."

"Do you think he'll do it?" Jesse asked.

"I *think* he's part of this team," Josh said confidently, realizing Derek was right. "He'll go where he's needed."

"Okay then. Are we agreed that Derek, Jesse, and Val go in?" Mark asked. When everyone nodded, he went on, "We're also agreed that Jerrod, Amarina, and Jacob need to be outside, but near the caves?" Everyone nodded again. "Okay then, who's staying with the Jeeps?"

"I think if we're not going in, you may need the muscle nearby, so Josh and I should be outside," Jon said.

"Joe was by the Jeeps last time with Delaney. They should be closer this time," Derek suggested.

"That leaves Sasha, Mark and Nico," Jerrod pointed out. "Are those the ones we really want left at the Jeeps? Mark and Nico bring in a lot of experience."

"I don't think that's a good idea." Derek shook his head. "If something happens, we need someone who can think on the fly nearby."

"Not to mention the muscle of Mark, Sasha, *and* Nico," Amarina pointed out. "Besides, we said Sasha should be outside so he would know when other side is near, yeah?"

"Good point. Okay," Mark said, taking a deep breath before slowly blowing it out. "The Jeeps will be about a half-hour walk out. Whomever we leave, we need to make sure they can handle themselves." After gathering everyone over, Mark explained the dilemma. When he finished, he asked, "Any suggestions?"

"Are you really sure I should go in?" Val asked hesitantly.

"For the reasons that Jerrod pointed out...yes," Mark said firmly.

"I'll stay at the Jeeps again," Delaney volunteered. "I know I was there last time, but I think others that are more skilled should be closer in this instance."

"Thank you," Mark said appreciatively.

"I could stay at the Jeeps too," Amarina offered.

Mark shook his head. "We need you so we don't get lost."

"Right-oh."

"You need me outside, right?" Joe asked.

"Definitely!" Jerrod said.

"Maybe," Mark countered.

"With Jesse going in, if he's not outside, we could get caught by surprise," Jerrod objected.

"While I agree with that, he may be needed at the Jeeps so those at the Jeeps don't get caught off-guard. Sasha may be a better idea to have outside with Josh," Mark pointed out.

"Fair enough. I'll be at the Jeeps. Look, since we know where we are, Delaney and I are fixin' to go on lookout," Joe volunteered.

"Go ahead," Mark agreed. "I'll fill you two in after we finalize the plan."

"Sounds good," Joe said, and then he and Delaney took off for the boulder they used for lookout.

"I'll stay with the Jeeps," Nico offered.

"Thank you," Mark said. "That'll put you, Delaney, and Joe at the Jeeps. I think you three are more than capable to head off any attack on them."

"Okay. Can I go back to the explosives? I need a couple guys with me," Jacob said, standing. "I know what I need to do."

"Take Sasha," Mark said. "The rest of us need to work on this."

"Let's go," Jacob said to Sasha, and they left.

When they were gone, the remaining group poured over the map, as well as the plan for the morning. They decided to go early in the morning, around dawn. That was the only way to remotely catch the other side off guard. Then they prayed for the next few hours over the mission, and for safety for everyone, especially Angel.

Chapter 3
Love The Lord Your God With All Your Heart

"You know to keep an eye in every direction, right?" Mark asked Delaney and Joe, knowing Nico already knew to do so.

"Yes, sir," they said in unison.

"And, once again, Jacob's got us covered, yeah," Delaney said, nodding toward the makeshift bombs in the back of the Jeep they were standing near.

"Good," he said. Chuckling nervously as he rubbed the back of his neck, he admitted, "Have to say that I'm a little anxious on this one. I'm not completely sure what we're walking into."

"I understand. Know we're with you all in spirit, and will continuously be in prayer…as is the Haven," Nico added.

"I appreciate that."

"Not to cast another shadow, but I have a bad feeling," Delaney mentioned. "It's the same feeling I had when you went in last time."

"We'll leave it to God to guide and direct us," Mark said confidently.

"Just gently reminding you that one of her gifts is discernment," Joe pointed out.

"I understand," Mark said, taking deep breath as he continued to rub the back of his neck. He wouldn't admit to the others, but he was just as nervous as they were. He had a sick feeling in his stomach from the time Cori played the recording for them, even up until that moment. For sake of leadership, though, he had to stay focused on the mission, and brushed off his concern regarding his daughter.

"Please don't make me have to make that call to Casey again, mate?" Nico added. "That was hard enough to talk t' Casey last time. She and the girls are waiting for *everyone* to come home this time. And, I *know* Casey wants to hear *your* voice on the other end of that phone after this, and not mine."

"I know," Mark said. Taking one more look around, he sighed as he said, "Time to go."

Leaving the trio at the Jeeps, the others hiked through the tall grass, going parallel to the path they took last time, but followed a path that went lower on the hillside. They figured with their other path marked by the destruction from Jacob, that the other side probably laid traps on it so they wouldn't be able to use it again.

Hiking in two groups, they spread out along the way. They dropped off Amarina at the second lookout with a radio, and instructions to turn it on in fifteen minutes. Jacob followed the rest of the team in so he could set up his explosives as they maneuvered through the bush.

Then they dropped off Jerrod about halfway between Amarina and the others. He settled into an alcove out of sight. His position was close enough that if something happened he could be there in a matter of minutes, yet far enough that if something happened he wouldn't get hurt. Resting his medical bag at his side, he tucked in, safely out of sight.

Once the others reached the allocated position, they stopped. "We only have two radios," Mark explained. "I'm going to keep one with me and Jon. Josh, I want you and Sasha to have the other," he said, handing it to him. "I have the lower lookout with Jon. And Josh, you're in charge of the radio for you and Sasha. We'll give you some time to set up before sending Jesse, Derek, and Val in. Are you all ready?"

"Ready as we're going to be." Josh nodded. "We're bathed in prayer, and Angel's waited long enough."

"Agreed. Let's go get her," Mark said, and they disbursed into three groups.

Josh and Sasha headed to the high terrain to make sure they could pick off anyone coming out, while Mark and Jon were to watch the lower. Once Josh and Sasha were in place, Jon moved to where he had a clear shot of the entrance behind a boulder, and Mark had a good view of the lower terrain, positioned behind a tree lying flat on the ground. Both Mark and Jon were positioned at the top of a hill, slightly lower than the cave entrance, in order to duck if someone exited the cave. Derek, Jesse, and Val were near Mark until Jacob was ready.

Once the guys were in place, they watched as Jacob snuck up to the doorway and placed explosives on either side of the entrance. To his left, just past where he buried his explosive, he brushed a little dirt, and cocked his head to the side. Looking toward Josh, he narrowed his eyes. He took a moment before he made his way over to Josh. "Something's fishy."

"What do you mean by fishy?" Josh asked Jacob.

"The dirt around the entrance has been moved recently…and not by me."

"Did you see anything buried?"

"No, but –"

"Then it's probably just from them going in and out. We would expect there to be dirt disturbed if this is the only way in or out."

"Are you sure? It doesn't look right. I could dig a little to make sure. There may be explosives underneath."

"Don't worry about it. You're just being paranoid. We need to get to Angel. Go finish up and get back to Amarina," Josh ordered.

"Yes, sir," Jacob said, and went back to the entrance.

Mark clicked the radio, and Josh looked at him. When he did, Josh just shook his head that nothing was wrong.

Once Jacob got his explosives set up, he slowly made his way back to Amarina. From his position, he would wait until he saw them come out before he set his explosives off.

"Now or never," Mark said to Derek. "You got this, my friend." Mark gave Derek a brief hug. "Take care of my boy, and bring my girl home."

"I'll take care of them and Val with my life."

"Let's not go there. Just get Angel, and get out."

"I will. We're *not* leaving her behind this time."

"Thanks, man," Mark said appreciatively. As he retook his position, Derek, Jesse, and Val took off for the entrance.

Hearing them doing radio checks as they left, Val asked, "We're going to be okay, right?"

"God's got this covered," Derek said confidently.

"Good, because if He didn't, I'm not sure I would be here."

"Knowing you, I *know* you wouldn't be here," Jesse chuckled nervously. "You don't tend to look for a fight."

"No. Not really."

"Jesse?" Derek asked, as they neared the cave entrance.

"Of course there are some here," he said. "That's a no brainer."

"How close?"

"We have a bit," he said confidently.

"Val?"

"Nothing new," Val said, silently praying as they maneuvered their way toward the entrance. "She's in a cavern of some kind, but we already knew that."

"They're breaching the entrance," Mark said into his radio from his position.

*   *   *

"What do you want now?" Angel grumbled, as a demon came in to where she was being held. The demon had drugged her when he finished torturing her earlier.

"I *want* you to agree to come to our ssside," the demon hissed, slowly walking around Angel. "Haven't you had enough pain?"

"Guess not," Angel said with a shrug, "because I'm not giving up on God, and there's nothing you can do to me to make me change my mind."

"Allen sssaid the sssame thing."

"I'm *not* Allen."

"Oh no. You are one of the archangel's preciousss A.N.G.E.L.sss."

"Love the Lord your God with all your heart and with all your soul and with all your mind and with all your strength," the angel with Angel whispered Mark 12:30 to her.

Nodding, Angel said, "Take your best shot. You haven't got a prayer."

"Ohhhh, you are a brave one. Aren't you?" the demon hissed. Then, getting into her face he added, "We'll sssee how brave you are when *I* am finished with you."

"Cast all your cares on the Lord and He will sustain you; He will never let the righteous be shaken," the angel whispered Psalm 55:22.

"Do what you want. I will *never* bend."

"Never sssay never, my friend," the demon hissed, and then cackled with an evil laugh.

*   *   *

"It's time to start praying," Casey said, looking at the clock that said it was one o'clock in the afternoon where they were near Reno, Nevada. "They should be heading in."

Kneeling in the middle of the living room to pray, the entire group, except Cori, Kai, and Rachel focused their efforts on those in Australia. The group prayed for continued safety for Angel, along with God's hands of protection around the remaining A.N.G.E.L.s. They prayed that this time the rescue would be successful. They prayed most of all for *all* of the A.N.G.E.L.s to return from this mission safely. With the loss of Danny Hawk so fresh, they didn't want to have to add anyone else's name to the boulder.

While they were praying, the trio in the cyber cave worked on being able to see what was going on in Australia. When they finished, Kai popped his head out of the basement door, and announced, "I have the satellite view downstairs."

"How'd you do *that*?" Kit asked, her green eyes wide.

"That's a question we never ask around here," Kai pointed out, as they made their way back downstairs to Rachel and Cori.

"Why not?"

"Plausible deniability," Casey explained. "They do what they do. Frankly, being able to see and talk to them this time is a blessing. I don't care *how* they do it."

"Okay, this is Joe, Delaney, and Dad," Rachel explained, pointing them out to the others. "They are with the four Jeeps."

"Right. And that must be Amarina," Kit pointed to the lone person standing on the hillside, as another slowly neared her, stopping periodically. "And that must be Jacob." What they saw had a green hew to it. The people were lighter blobs, indistinguishable except for their position. "This must be Jerrod," Kit said, pointing to another small blob off by itself, right before it disappeared. "He must be near a cave."

"Right. That means these two are Josh and Sasha," Charlie pointed out the two on the upper portion. Pointing to the two lower down the hillside, he added, "And these two are Mark and Jon."

"The other three have already gone in," Rachel said, nibbling on her nails as she watched. "While this is nerve wracking, at least we get to see what's going on this time."

Suddenly there was a flash of light near the cave, followed by multiple other bright flashes.

"What was *that*?" Casey asked, wide-eyed as her heart raced.

"*That* was an explosion," Kai explained, jumping on his computer to see if they could get a better view from another satellite. He was unsure if it would be possible due to the time of day. "Looks like it took out the hillside," he reported.

"Mark! Jon!" Casey gasped.

They watched in horror as one bomb went off after the other. It looked like one bomb triggered Jacob's two bombs at the entrance, which in turn set off the others.

"Oh, dear Lord, help them!" Kit whispered.

"Jesse," Rachel whispered, dropping to her knees, feeling like she would throw up. "God," she said, unable to look away from the screen, "Please help them all. Please send the archangel, and Your angels of protection to surround them. Please say it isn't too late."

*   *   *

One explosion after another occurred around them. What was calm only moments before, suddenly burst into a chaotic rain of debris and explosions that echoed in their ears. The trio inside the caves felt the blast blow through their bodies as dirt and stone rained down on them.

"What was that?" Derek shouted, ducking, as he turned toward the entrance. When the mouth of the cave collapsed, the trio looked at each other, horrified. The roof of the cave slowly disintegrated right before their eyes. "Run!" Derek yelled, and the trio took off in a full sprint down the tunnel.

When they turned left, another explosion went off above their heads, and the roof caved in, landing on top of them, pounding their bodies with rock, debris, and dirt.

*   *   *

The original explosion created a chain reaction, setting off all of Jacob's explosions in succession. Mark and Jon watched, wide-eyed, as the explosion created a landslide around them. When the small boulders, rocks, and rivers of dirt headed toward them, they ran, only to be caught up in the landslide when the ground gave way under them. The river of dirt swept them off their feet, sending them sliding down out of control.

Bounced around by the rocks and boulders, the cuts and scrapes were the least of their worries, as they each heard a loud crack of bones breaking.

*   *   *

Ducking the flying debris as they hid behind a giant boulder and tree, the wind was knocked out of Josh and Sasha, and they hit the ground. Feeling the air sucked out around them, as the air from the blast washed over them, they couldn't see or feel anything for several moments. The ringing in their ears overrode anything they could remotely focus on as they inhaled mouthfuls of dirt. Disoriented, they struggled to find their way to each other.

*   *   *

Amarina and Jacob watched in terror at the devastation that appeared from seemingly out of nowhere. "I didn't do this!" Jacob said, horrified, as the bombs went off, one after the other. "That wasn't me! I swear!"

Placing her hand on his shoulder, Amarina said, "While I know this isn't you, we have a problem."

"We need to get to everyone," Jacob said, heart racing, "...fast!"

*   *   *

"This isn't right!" Joe said, alarmed at the amount of debris that suddenly filled the sky. "They weren't in there long enough!"

"I agree," Nico said, recovering from the shock. Grabbing the explosives Jacob left them, he went to head toward Amarina and Jacob.

"Nico! We can't leave!" Joe grabbed his arm.

"That could be what they want," Delaney added.

"We can't leave them. We don't know what shape they're in," Nico argued.

"I get that," Joe said. "However, if we leave here and they get control of the Jeeps, we're stuck here. We learned the importance of an exit vehicle in Black Rock. If we let them get ahold of the Jeeps, we'll have to walk out. If any of them are seriously injured, we *need* these Jeeps to get them out."

"Walking to the nearest town is *not* an option," Nico agreed. Sighing, he set his pack down. "Not sure what t' do here. I was never trained to stand by and wait when people were in danger. I was taught to act on instinct."

"I know, but we need your talents here," Delaney explained. "We're not trained for any of this yet."

Getting on his radio, he called Amarina and Jacob, "Eagle one, this is the nest."

"Go ahead," Jacob said in response.

"What's goin' on?"

"Looks like they set off one or two presents, which set off a chain reaction of mine," Jacob explained. "This *wasn't* me."

"I know."

"What do we do now?" Jacob asked.

"Can you two come here, so we can get together and figure out how to get to the others?"

"Be there as soon as possible," Amarina said over the radio.

"We'll be a bit. Remember, we're twenty minutes out," Jacob explained. "But we're running."

*   *   *

"What do we do now?" Casey asked, pale. "No one's moving, except Amarina and Jacob, who were away from the blasts."

"Why are Amarina and Jacob going back to the Jeeps?" Rachel asked.

Kit looked at the screen, wide-eyed. "Why aren't they all running to help the others?"

"Give me a minute," Cori said, and feverishly tapped on her computer. In a few minutes, she said, "Nest, this is the Haven. Do you read?"

"Go ahead," Nico's voice came over Cori's computer.

"Nico, what happened?" Kit asked, adrenaline pulsating through her entire body.

"They blew Jacob's presents. We can't leave yet. We can't leave the Jeeps unattended or we could be stranded."

"Want me to call the station and see if we can get y'all some help?"

"Go ahead. See if Pete can get ahold of Amarina's clan to get help here a little quicker. Afraid we're not sure what the status is on the others. Eagle one's team is coming to meet us. We'll come up with a plan when they get here."

"We will," Rachel said. Then she asked, "Have you been able to reach the others yet?"

"Haven't tried. Just a sec…" Nico said, and then he continued, "Nest to Eagle 2 or 3. Come in." After white noise, he tried again, "Nest to Eagle 2 or 3. Come in."

"Does not sound like they are responding," Katia said, with a nervous edge to her voice, as she played with a portion of her hair. "Try again."

"Nest to Eagle 2 or 3. Please come in."

"Nest, this is Eagle 1, they are not responding. The radios *are* working," Jacob said into his radio.

"Can you two double-time it?" Nico asked. "I think we need to get there sooner rather than later, and I want your partner here with the nest team."

"*We're going*!" Joe objected.

"I need ya here with Amarina and Delaney," Nico explained. "You three need to watch these. You convinced me how important they are, and I agree."

"We'll be there in another ten," Amarina responded.

"Anyone know Jerrod's status?" Leah asked.

Realizing that they had someone near, Nico asked, "Eagle 1, were you able to see Jerrod?"

"Negative," Jacob said into the radio. "Now, quit talking to us. We run faster when we're not talking."

"Copy. Thank you," Nico said. "Haven, did you copy?"

"Yes," Cori said into the microphone at her desk. "Haven will contact Serenity," she said, and Kai nodded toward Kit to go call. "We'll keep this line open."

"That would be appreciated," Nico said with scenarios running through his mind on what to do once they reach the teams while he waited.

Running up the stairs, Kit's heart was racing. When Willow answered the phone at the station, Kit explained what happened and that they needed help.

"We'll get in touch with Alice Springs," Willow explained. "We'll get rescue sent up there immediately."

"I don't know if we want to involve the authorities. That may take a bit more explaining than we have time for," Kit pointed out. "Just have Pete get word to the clan, and send some of the bigger ranch hands. There's a lot of debris from what we could see."

"Are ya sure?" Willow asked, doubtful. "I think the rescue teams would be more effective help."

"We would have to explain *way* too much. Remember the stories of all that happened when the kids were younger?"

"Yes, ma'am."

"That's what is going on. We need to handle this ourselves."

"Yes, ma'am. I'll tell Caleb."

"Thank you," she said and hung up. Dropping to the couch, she rested her head on the back of the couch. "Lord, I don't know what to do here, but I know You have a plan already in place, and I trust you."

*   *   *

"I just want to sleep, and you're getting on my last nerve," Angel snapped at the demon. With the exception of when they drugged her to move her, every time Angel tried to rest her eyes over the last twenty-four hours, the demon would start back up again with questions. The demon seemed to avoid hurting her anymore. For that, she was grateful. She was struggling with collecting any type of clear thought after not having any food or water for those twenty-four hours as well.

"By now, your preciousss A.N.G.E.L.sss are buried under a pile of rubble," the demon hissed, as it wrung its hands in delight once again.

"What do you mean?" Angel asked, confused.

"We drugged you, and moved you after you passssssed out. You are no longer in the Tanami Desert."

"Where am I?" Angel asked, heart racing. "Why didn't you tell me?" she asked the angel, who was still invisible.

"Why would we tell you anything?" the demon asked.

"I am sorry. I was too worried about your condition, and did not want to worry you further," the angel whispered. *"You are not in good shape, Angel."*

"How am I supposed to fight until they get here, when they don't even know where I am?" Angel demanded.

"I do not want you to fight," the demon pointed out. "I want you to give up and join usss."

"You fight with a strength that is not your own, no matter your location," the angel whispered.

"Fine," Angel snapped. "What do you want from me?"

"Oh, it isss not what *I* want from you. You will be in the handsss of Calliope," the demon hissed.

At the sound of her name, Calliope appeared in the mouth of the cavern. "Hello, Angel. We meet once again."

"Where am I?" Angel demanded.

"That is of no concern. What *is* my concern, is your mental state. You have not been yourself lately." Resting her hand on the side of Angel's sore face, Calliope explained, "You seem distraught. Lonely maybe?"

"Nope."

"Well, if not now, you *will* be. You don't seriously think the A.N.G.E.L.s will forgive you for the loss of one of their founding fathers, so to speak, do you?"

"What are you talking about?" Angel questioned, anger in her eyes. Glancing at where the demon once stood, she was shocked to see Danny Hawk standing there instead. "What's going on?"

"Because of *your pride*, I lost my life." The creature had taken the shape of Danny Hawk, including his mannerisms and voice. Angel shook her head to clear it before she looked back into the face of Danny, who continued to speak, "How many more A.N.G.E.L.s will lose their life because of your actions?"

"I don't know what you're talking about!"

"You chose to go after Liliya all by yourself, to prove to the others that you were worthy to lead. Because of that, you got captured. Once captured, it was the responsibility of *all* the A.N.G.E.L.s – young and old – to come rescue you. You do not seriously think we would leave you in the hands of the demons and Cassius, do you?"

"Well, no."

"So, instead of working with your team, you chose to go after Liliya all by yourself. That is the sin of pride."

"Oh," Angel said, mulling over the demon's words.

"Do you *seriously* think Josh will *ever* be able to love you after you cost one of his mentors his life?"

"I…no," Angel said, dropping her head in shame.

"How can anyone love you if they have to keep cleaning up your messes?" the demon demanded. "You know you are almost too much to handle, right?"

"I-I don't know."

"How are you supposed to lead a team, when you can't even get out of your own way?"

"I-I didn't do it on purpose!" Angel defended herself.

"Really?" he asked, crossing his arms. "You are *really* going to tell me that you did not go after Stepan without the others on purpose?"

"I…" She shook her head, beside herself. The more the demon spoke to her fears, the worse Angel felt.

"You *know* Rachel is a better leader than you, right? That is why Val said he was going to change teams," the demon said knowingly.

"He did," Angel admitted, "But –"

"But nothing! The archangel even replaced you already. Did he not?"

"He did," she said, as her heart sunk.

"Why did God choose you when all you do is keep failing Him? What use are you to Him *or* the Kingdom?"

"Please stop?" Angel begged. The more he talked, the more her heart broke. The more her heart broke, the more the tears stung her eyes.

"Who will want to be on your team now?" the demon pressed. "You have royally messed up. You know that, right?"

"I did."

"Your looks, which were your *only* redeeming quality, are even in question right now. Look at all those scars up and down your body. How do you expect Josh, or anyone else for that matter, to love someone with scars all over their body?"

"I…" Angel went to object, but she hung her head instead. Unable to stop them, the tears flowed freely down her cheeks.

"Josh said you were at least pretty on the outside, but you are not even that anymore. You are now as ugly on the outside as you are on the inside," the demon pointed out.

Angel just shook her head.

"Blessed is she who believed that the Lord would fulfill His promises to her," she heard the Spirit whisper through her mind Luke 1:45.

"No," Angel moaned, shaking her head.

"Your beauty should not come from outward adornment, such as elaborate hairstyles, or the wearing of gold jewelry or fine clothes. Rather, it should be that of your inner self, the unfading beauty of a gentle and quiet spirit, which is of great worth in God's sight," Angel heard the Spirit whisper 1 Peter 3:3-4.

"Stay focused on the Word," the angel whispered to Angel. *"You are beautiful on the inside, and the outside."*

"It does not matter what you *think* you look like on the inside," the demon continued, speaking to her fears again, contradicting the Spirit's attempts. "Josh already told you what he thought of your inside. You *are ugly* on the inside," the demon pressed. "How do you *ever* expect to be worthy in the sight of God with your hideous appearance inside *and* outside?"

"I do not think he can hear me," the angel whispered.

"Oh, yes, I can!" the demon said, and immediately shifted back to its creature self before slashing through the middle of the angel.

Taken by surprise, the angel appeared and fell back to the wall of the cave. In that instant, the demon jumped on the angel, killing him with its bare hands, ripping out its insides, tossing them to the side.

Shock replaced the despair, as Angel watched the horrific scene unfold before her.

"Look," Calliope jumped in. "See? You have done it again. This time it cost God one of His precious angels. You think the archangel is already angry with you for the loss of Danny Hawk? Wait until you deal with your God for getting one of His angels taken out as well. He was sent to protect you, but obviously you are such a screw up, that an angel cannot even protect you."

Angel just shook her head in response, as she watched the angel who had been with her the entire time, die right before her eyes.

"Remember what Josh said?" Calliope continued. "He said the packaging is good, but the inside is not. You have created *such* a mess! And now, your fellow team members are getting blown to smithereens…all because of *you!*"

"What do you mean by that?"

"You know those nifty little presents Jacob likes to plant?"

"Yes," Angel said, heart racing.

"Well, we figured out a way to set them off…while your friends were still there."

"*What?*" Angel asked, stunned, as she turned pale.

"They went in to rescue you. Want to see?" she asked. With a wave of her hand, a cloud appeared, and then transformed into a screen. Watching the group separate, she was beside herself and horrified at the same time, to see Derek, Jesse, and Val enter the cave, and moments later, the cave entrance blow out.

"Oh, we are not done," Calliope said, full of glee. "Watch."

As soon as the cave entrance blew, she watched as each of those set off two more of Jacob's bombs. The landslide swept Mark and Jon off their feet. Watching Mark and Jon ride the river of debris, she saw the rocks beat them up on the way down. Settling at the bottom of the hill, to her horror, they weren't moving.

Then the next scene she saw was Josh behind a boulder, and Sasha behind a tree. When the bombs went off, both stood, looking toward the entrance, just in time to have two more bombs go off near them, blowing them off their feet, throwing them back, over ten yards. As the debris showered over them, both curled up in a ball. When the debris settled, she saw them lying there, not moving.

The next scene was inside the cave. Seeing the front entrance blow, she watched as Val, Jesse, and Derek ran for their lives, only to have the cave collapse on them when another bomb went off. Seeing no one move, Angel thought she would throw up.

"Let's not forget this one, shall we?" Calliope said, as Angel watched one more scene.

Jerrod was tucked into an alcove. She saw the momentary alarm on his face before a bomb went off near him. All she saw afterward were the bottom of his legs sticking out from the rubble.

"What do *you* think they will do now? They have possibly lost eight more. Do you *really* think they will make *another* attempt after this? You have already cost them too much. If it were me, I would cut my losses."

"That's the difference between you and us. We *never* leave a man behind," Angel said through her tears.

"You did at Black Rock," the demon pointed out. "You left Rachel *and* Jessssse behind. Did you not?"

"I did," Angel admitted.

"And then you fought with the others on whether to go back or not," Calliope reminded her. "Do you honestly think they will be jumping at the chance to come after you again after all of that? If it were me, I would just be happy you are finally not my problem to deal with anymore. You *do* know you are nothing but trouble, right?"

"I'm sorry," Angel said, shaking her head, remembering those on the team who weren't moving. The scenes continued to flash in the cloud as it slowly dissipated. Once it was gone, Angel admitted, "I didn't want anyone to get hurt."

"Pain and stress seem to follow you. Neither the A.N.G.E.L.s, nor the archangel, know what to do with you. But *we* do. You want to be a great leader, right?"

"I want to lead where *God* wants me to lead," Angel countered.

"You cannot lead as an A.N.G.E.L., though. The archangel already overruled that by placing Josh and Jon in charge," Calliope reiterated. "You know I am right. Tell me I am wrong. Go ahead. Just tell me that the archangel has the utmost confidence in you and I will leave you alone."

"He-he gave the team to Josh and Jon," Angel admitted.

"You are a *complete* screw up! What makes you think they will want you back? You were not even able to rescue Liliya by yourself," Calliope went on. "But, *we* know just how strong you *really* are."

Resolve setting in once again, Angel narrowed her eyes. "I am strong enough to fight you."

"Really?" Calliope gestured toward the now dead angel across the cavern. "Do you not think one of God's angels is strong enough?"

Unable to come up with an argument, Angel just shook her head.

"Get it out of here," Calliope ordered the demon. "I will continue to work with her to allow her to see the truth."

Grabbing the dead angel under the arms, the demon dragged the angel out of the cavern. When they were out of earshot, the angel turned into another demon. "How wasss that?" the demon who was the angel asked the other.

"Brilliant! Now, what are we going to do with the *real* angel?" the other demon asked.

"That isss up to Cassiusss. And personally, I would *not* want to be that angel," the demon said, and then let out a cackle of laughter, as the pair went down the tunnel, delighted that their plan worked.

2 Corinthians 11:14 – And no wonder, for Satan himself masquerades as an angel of light.

Chapter 4
The Lord Is Near The Broken Hearted

"What do we do now?" Jacob asked, as he and Amarina finally made it back to the Jeeps out of breath. Grabbing the side of one of the Jeeps, they did their best to get deep breaths of air.

"We go after them," Nico said, matter-of-factly. "Jacob, how many more explosives do you have?"

"I don't…" Jacob shook his head as his voice trailed off.

Placing his hands on Jacob's shoulders, Nico leaned down so he was eye-to-eye, and said, "Your explosives didn't do this. They figured out a way to use them against us. We *need* you to be clear headed, and to make sure there are enough that if we need to blow a hole through the caves to get to them, that we can do that."

Pained, Jacob tried to explain, "I don't want anyone to get hurt, though."

"Jacob, you were given a gift. You were led to this team for a reason. We *need* you right now. Your team needs *you*, Jacob Armstrong, to be the man God created you to be. We need you to see the angles. We need you to possibly blow more so we can get to the others. We can*not* do this without you. We need you."

"I've been listening," Cori's voice came over the radio. "Jacob, this is Cori."

Taking the radio from Amarina, Jacob said, "I know. And, I'm here."

"You didn't do this. Nico is right. We need you. We need ya to be on your toes. We're watching from here, but there's too much time going by with no one moving. You need to have a clear head, yeah?"

"Um," Kai scooted Cori over a bit. Taking the microphone from her, he said, "You got company. They're coming from the south."

"How many?" Nico asked, taking the radio.

"There are at least three vehicles coming your way. They look like open bed trucks, and they're full. You should be able to hear them shortly. We can't tell if they are friendly or not."

"Copy. We'll just pray for friendly," Nico said, as they all anxiously looked to the horizon.

"Please?" Jacob begged. "Please just let at least *one* thing go right today?"

In a matter of moments, the group heard the vehicles in the distance.

"Let's hope that's the cavalry, and not the other side," Nico said nervously running his fingers through his hair.

"Afraid we can't distinguish who is who," Kai reiterated. "You all look like green blobs of light on our screen. All we can see are heat signatures."

"Right-oh," Nico sighed. "Are there heat signatures where chaos occurred?"

"Yes. But there are only five," Kai said, and Delaney gasped. "Don't panic. Once they entered the cave, we haven't been able to track Derek's, Jesse's, *or* Val's heat signatures. Jerrod tucked into a cave too. We couldn't see his before the chaos erupted either. The cave is blocking them."

"Still not making me feel any better, mate," Nico said in a sigh.

"Who *is* that?" Joe asked, looking toward where the trucks were barreling down the road toward them.

"We don't have either of those who know if they're from the other side," Nico grumbled, resting his right hand on his gun.

"Hide behind the Jeeps," Amarina suggested.

As everyone took a spot, hidden from anyone driving by, three trucks came bounding into the area. Old, and in rough shape, the three vehicles were packed with eight people in each, some on top of others in order to cram into the trucks.

A mixed group of Aboriginal and Australian men climbed out of the Jeep. "Amarina!" one guy called. "Where are ya, love?"

"That's my pop!" Amarina came out of her hiding space and shouted, "I'm here!"

As the others slowly stood, they were pleasantly surprised to find twenty-four men with guns, shovels, and axes in their hands. "Boy, are we glad to see you!" Nico grinned.

"We heard explosions, so we come faster," Kalti said, coming out of the center of the group. "We know this is not normal. This is not the same as last time either."

"No. It wasn't," Nico agreed. "This wasn't us. We were caught by surprise. There are five that we know of who are alive…we think."

"We were given dreams to start coming last night," Kalti explained. "When we hear explosions, we come faster."

"There are some alive!" Kai's voice came over the radio. "They're not moving very well, but some are moving."

"Who is that?" Kalti asked, wide-eyed, as the group of Aboriginal men suddenly talked amongst themselves at once.

Holding the radio up, Nico explained, "It's our people. They have satellite. No worries."

"Okay," Kalti said. "What do you want us to do?"

"Here's our problem. We haven't left yet, because we need people here to watch the vehicles. We don't want to leave them unattended. If we do, those who have Angel could come and take out the Jeeps. Then we would have to walk out. And, that's *not* an option."

One of the guys said something in Aboriginal to Kalti, who turned back to the A.N.G.E.L.s, and translated, "He said to leave five of our guys here to watch the Jeeps and trucks, and the rest will go with you to find the others."

"Sounds good. Who will stay?" Nico asked.

When Kalti asked the group, five men hesitantly held their hands up. They all wanted to help.

"I will stay to help Delaney translate for those here," Amarina volunteered.

"You need the muscle more than a mouth," Delaney said, referring to her gift of languages. "Kalti can translate for you out there."

"I want to go this time," Joe said adamantly. "I want to help."

"It's settled," Nico agreed.

After they made a plan, five Aboriginal men, along with Delaney and Amarina stayed with the seven vehicles, while the others made their way to where the team was last known, with guidance from the Haven.

*   *   *

Shoving some rock out of the way, deep inside the collapsed cave system, Jesse struggled to sit up. "Val? Derek?"

"I'm here," Val moaned. "Hurt, but here."

"Derek?" Jesse called out. When there was no response, Jesse climbed out of the pile of rocks that landed on him. With cuts and scrapes all over him, he made his way over to Val's location. "All right. What's hurt?"

"My leg," Val said. "I think it's broken."

"Is that all?"

"Pretty sure a rib is broken too. It hurts to move or breathe."

"Well, don't stop breathing. That would be bad," Jesse said with a smirk, using his off-color sense of humor to keep Val calm. Grunting, he moved a couple large rocks off Val.

"What about Derek?" Val asked.

"Don't know yet. I figured I would get you loose, and then you can help me. Since you can't move very well, it looks like that theory is shot. I still want to get you out from under these rocks before I go looking for him."

"You're going to have to set my leg."

Jesse looked at him, dumbfounded. "I'm gonna what?"

"You have to set my leg, or it won't heal right. We have to splint it too. Is there any wood around here we can use?"

"One thing at a time, eh?" Jesse chuckled nervously. "I *need*," he grunted, picking up a heavy rock, before shoving it to the side, "to get you released." Once he got the large rock off Val's leg, he cringed. Val's leg bone was protruding from the skin and the hole it created in his lower jean leg.

"It's the tibia," Val groaned in pain, as he dropped his head back on the rock wall. "Ugh! You're going to have to set that, and it's *really* going to hurt."

"Want me to set it now or get the other rocks off first?"

"I'm in immense pain right now, so it really doesn't matter. Chances are, when you set it, the pain will knock me out for a bit."

"Hmm, let's get the rest of the rocks off first. I may need you when I get to Derek. Let me do this before you pass out on me. I need you to tell me what to do. You're the only one in here with significant medical training."

Deciding to concentrate on Jesse to deal with the pain, through gritted teeth, Val asked, "Okay. Tell me what's hurt on you?"

"Mainly bruised. Head got hit too, but I'll be okay. Pretty sure all of us were knocked unconscious, but I don't know how long we've been out."

"Can you tell if there are any from the other side near us?"

"There are," Jesse said hesitantly.

Furrowing his brow, Val asked, "What is it?"

"They're here, but they still haven't moved from where they were."

Val closed his eyes, while Jesse continued to pull rocks off him. In his mind, he saw several demons huddled in a cavern with blood on the floor. "What did the cavern look like where they held Angel?"

"Don't know. I wasn't inside. Jon was inside when they came in the first time. Why?" Jesse asked, tossing another rock aside.

"I don't think Angel's here. I think they left several here to make sure we came in here...as bait."

"So, the whole thing *was* a trap?" Jesse grumbled, as he tossed another large rock to the side. "Sneaky buggars!"

"Pretty sure. I think they moved her before we got here." Val nodded. "I see them in a cave where there's a puddle of dried blood on the ground."

"Must be where Danny was taken out."

"Not comforting at all." Val frowned. Shaking his head, he said, "Angel's not here."

Suddenly the tunnel was filled with a bright, white light. "Hello," the archangel said when the light calmed down.

Jesse stood. "What happened? Where's Angel?"

"She was moved."

"Do you know where she is?" Jesse asked, as Val struggled to sit up at the appearance of the archangel.

"I do. She had an angel with her, but that angel has since gone silent. My job is to be with you right now."

"What about the others? Pretty sure this caught everyone by surprise."

"Not everyone," the archangel clarified. "This did not take God by surprise."

"Where is Angel?" Jesse asked again.

"Worry about that later. Derek needs you," the archangel said, shining a light from his hand onto Derek.

Lying face down in the dirt, Derek lay there unconscious, covered in rocks. Some of the rocks on his back were large. There was dirt and blood all over him, as he lay there motionless.

Coated in blood and dirt as well, Jesse's heart sunk at the state of his mentor. "Is he alive?" Jesse asked, afraid of the answer.

"He is for now." The archangel nodded. "There are some angels going after those in the cavern. You should be able to feel them disappearing."

"I am," Jesse confirmed. "I'm more concerned with Derek and Val, though. What about the others? What about my Dad, Jon, Sasha, and Josh? Are Jerrod, Amarina, and Jacob okay?"

"There are angels with the four. Nico and some from Amarina's clan are on their way here with Jacob and Joe. It will take time to get here, though. Amarina, Delaney, and the rest of Amarina's clan are watching the vehicles."

"And Jerrod?"

"He is alive," the archangel confirmed.

Jesse sighed, shaking his head before going over to Derek. He did a quick assessment of the rocks on Derek's back. After moving some of the heavier ones, he then moved to the lighter. Once he finally cleared the rock and debris off Derek and the surrounding area, he crouched down and lightly tapped Derek's face. "Derek? Are you there?" When he didn't answer, Jesse looked to the archangel for help. "Why are you just standing there? Help him!"

"I am not God," the archangel pointed out.

Standing, Jesse got in his face. "Help him!" he shouted, as the anger mixed with adrenaline. Jesse felt like a volcano ready to explode.

"I am here with you."

"*Help him!*" Jesse yelled, pointing to Derek. "He is one of *your* A.N.G.E.L.s! He has given *everything* for God! He has put his life on the line many times for the Kingdom!"

"And, he will be rewarded for his faithfulness."

"Help him!" Jesse said, throwing his arms in the air in exasperation.

Moaning was heard from Derek. Jesse turned back to the archangel, and said, "Thank you." Kneeling down next to him, Jesse asked, "Derek? Can you hear me?"

"I can, but...I can't feel anything."

"What do you mean?"

"I can't feel my legs."

"His back is broken," the archangel clarified.

"His back is...*what?*" Jesse's heart raced. "What do you mean his back is broken?"

"Um, pretty sure he means Derek's back is broken. Kind of like my rib and leg. He couldn't say that any clearer," Val said from his spot. Otherwise not moving, he sighed, laying his head back on the rock wall, working through the immense pain throughout his body. "At least he's alive," Val pointed out.

"What do I do?" Jesse asked.

"Don't move him...at all," Val cautioned. "You could make it worse. We can't move from this position without help."

"You're serious?"

"Yes. If you move him, you may cause further damage. You will have to immobilize my leg in order to move me. But, with a broken rib too?" Val shook his head. "Probably not wise to move me either. I could puncture a lung if I'm moved wrong. It feels like the rib is pressed against it as it is."

Reaching to the other side of Derek, Jesse knelt beside Derek and took Derek's gun from the holster. Dropping the magazine, he examined the gun. He then popped all the bullets out of the magazine onto the ground before he put it back in empty. Then he cocked the gun and dry-fired it. Jesse refilled the magazine with the bullets and replaced the magazine into the gun. "Looks okay. Val, I'm going to leave this with you," he said, handing it to Val.

"Where are *you* going?" Val asked, stunned, accepting the gun.

"I'm going to find us a way out of here."

"You need to stay here, Jesse," the archangel cautioned. "You need to stay with them."

"What good am I going to do by staying here? I need to get them help."

"You will be able to help them when they need you," the archangel explained.

Jesse shook his head. "With all due respect, is that the best you got?"

"Wait," the archangel said when Jesse turned to leave. "I will wait with you."

"Don't know if I want you here," Jesse snapped.

"Jesse!" Val scolded. "You are speaking to an archangel of the Lord God!"

"I know!" Glaring at the archangel, he questioned, "Why didn't you warn us?"

"I am not all knowing," the archangel responded.

"But you know the One who is."

"I got here as fast as I could. I was in a battle when they removed Angel from here. Then one of the other teams needed my help. I, along with some other angels, went to help them. When I returned, she was gone. I was on my way to find out where she went when the explosions went off. God had already sent an angel to Amarina's clan to warn them you would need help. Once they took off, I hurried her clan to get here faster. As I stated earlier, that is the group on their way here from the vehicles. There was already a plan in place. God does not do surprises."

"I get that. What I *don't* get, is if He knew she was already gone, why didn't He warn us?"

"Did Cori not warn you that she may not be here?" the archangel asked, confused.

"She did."

"But, you decided to continue forward with the plan?"

"We did."

"Jacob also told Josh something wasn't right when he placed his explosives, but Josh dismissed him."

Crossing his arms, Jesse took a deep breath, hoping to keep his emotions under control.

"Jesse, your team had doors closed in front of them, but continued to push forward. You cannot be angry with me or God because you chose to ignore them."

Jesse sighed, looking toward Heaven as he struggled inside.

"Why are you blaming the Lord and me?"

"I-I don't…" Jesse's voice trailed off as he shook his head.

"If Val looked for her with his spiritual sight, it would still show her in a cave. She is still located in a cave. That has not changed," the archangel explained.

"Then, you *do* know where she is?"

"Yes. However, there are more pressing issues at hand," the archangel reminded him.

Putting his hands on his hips, Jesse looked up at the archangel, he said, "You have to understand my frustration."

"I do."

As Jesse's body suddenly stopped tingling, leaving only the adrenaline rush for him to fight through, he mentioned, "The last of the demons in these caves are gone."

"See. I *am* helping," the archangel explained. "The demons here are gone for now. There are none in this area at the moment. The angels took care of them. I tried to get here sooner, but I can only be in so many places at once. You and the others did not heed the warning when Cori played the recording. Josh did not take Jacob's warning seriously. You all pressed on with the plan. I am sorry you felt abandoned, but you have to understand that you are not my only team."

"You *do* know where Angel is, though, right?"

"Yes."

"Where is she?"

"She is further into the Outback."

"Further? This land is pretty much as out here as it gets. How much further could they take her?"

"I'm afraid much deeper."

Sighing, Jesse shook his head. "Are the others okay?"

"Do you want me to leave to find out?" the archangel asked.

"I want to know. I know God is near the broken hearted, but I don't want to be anymore brokenhearted than I already am. I know there's nothing I can do to help, but the not knowing is killing me. It's bad enough that we lost Danny. I don't want to lose anyone else."

"Especially Derek?" the archangel asked knowingly.

"Yes," Jesse admitted. "Derek *or* my dad, Jon…or pretty much anyone else on the team. Look, I know my dad is out there with Jon in that mess. I need to know if they're okay."

"They are alive," the archangel confirmed.

"You're cryptic messages are frustrating. Why couldn't you just say yes or no? Why can't you just simply say if they're okay or not? Why do you have to beat around the bush?"

"Angel says the same thing," the archangel said with a smile.

"Whatever!" Jesse snapped. "Just help me take care of these two…please?"

"Now *that* I can do. I thought you would never ask."

Kneeling in front of Val, Jesse took hold of Val's ankle. "Ready?" Jesse asked.

"Noooo," Val moaned, knowing the tremendous pain and agony he was about to face.

"Too bad," Jesse said, and yanked on Val's ankle, pulling the bone back into the leg. Val let out an ear-piercing scream. "Just a sec," Jesse said, feeling the bone, struggling to find the correct position.

"Here," the archangel said, amidst Val's shrieks of pain. The archangel took only a moment to get the leg into place. Then he took another moment to shift the bones in the rib back into place again. "I would advise you not to move."

"No….problem…I…" Val moaned before going unconscious.

"Well, I guess that's one way to get him not to move," Jesse said with a shrug. "What about Derek?"

"Do not move Derek."

"You'll help him though, right?" Jesse asked, nervously.

"It is not my place."

"What does *that* mean?"

"It means that while I can ease his pain, his back will remain broken."

"He can't walk!" Jesse shouted angrily.

"I understand. It is part of the Lord's plan."

"How is *that* a part of His plan?" Jesse stood, fists balled at his side.

"It is not my place to say."

"Are you kidding me? You're going to leave him paralyzed? Are you serious right now?"

The archangel stood. "I am afraid this is true."

Narrowing his eyes, Jesse crossed his arms. "Let me see if I understand you correctly. You are *refusing* to help him?"

"You are not correct. I will ease his pain."

"He-can't-feel-anything!" Jesse enunciated through gritted teeth.

"Yours is not to always understand the plan, only to follow it."

"If I wasn't a Christian, I would give you a major piece of my mind right now!"

"While I am sure of this, it does not change the outcome. Derek will be paralyzed from the waist down."

"You're serious right now?" Jesse crossed his arms, matching the archangel's stance.

"Yes. And, there is nowhere for you to run. You need face this," the archangel said knowingly, as Jesse looked for an exit to get away from the archangel.

Tightening his crossed arms, Jesse sternly warned, "You need to leave right now."

"No. I do not. My job is to stay here to look after all of you."

"But you *won't* help him," Jesse pointed out, exasperated.

"Your place is to understand."

"I need some space," Jesse said, as he thumped his body against the wall. Sliding down the wall to the ground, Jesse dropped his head onto his knees, praying to God for understanding.

"Very good, Jesse."

"Shut up," Jesse growled, glaring at him. "I need you to be quiet right now."

"A soft answer turns away wrath."

"I'm saying it softly, so I don't pass my wrath onto you. I am, however, asking you to shut-your-mouth…*with* all due respect."

"I will grant this. I need to tend to Derek."

Jesse continued to glare at him as the archangel walked over to Derek. With so much rage inside him, he knew he and God had to have a serious conversation.

*   *   *

"How much longer?" Kit asked Kai, as she paced the cyber cave.

"Looks like they're nearing the area," Kai confirmed. "Here's the group," he pointed out. "Mark and Jon are here, and up here are Sasha an' Josh."

"They haven't moved very much," Casey pointed out.

"The fact that they're moving at all is a good sign," Charlie encouraged.

"This must be anxious for you," Katia said to Charlie.

"Not being there to help is *not* a good feeling," Charlie agreed.

"You are where you're supposed to be," Kit said, nibbling on her nails.

"As are you," Charlie said knowingly.

"I know. It could be worse. I could be –" she was cut off by her cell phone ringing. "Hey, Caleb," Kit said, answering her phone as she moved closer to the door of the cyber cave, but was still able to keep an eye on the screen.

"Mum, what's the status?" Caleb asked.

"They're getting help."

"Good, because there is no way we'll be able to get there in time to be of any help. Willow told me where you wanted to send them, but that's too far away. The only other option is to call Alice."

"No. I don't want ya to call Alice Springs," Kit said, shaking her head. "There'll be too much to explain."

"You may still have to if they're injured bad enough," Caleb warned. "Would it not be more prudent to get the help on the way?"

"Just a sec," she said, and covered the phone before she called to Kai, "Kai, can ya ask Nico if he wants Caleb to call Alice for search and rescue?"

"Yep." Going over to the computer, he leaned over in front of Cori, and said into the microphone, "Haven to Eagle One."

"This is Eagle One," Delaney answered the radio.

"Where's Nico?"

"He's under Eagle Two," she said. "They're on their way to the others."

"I'm right here," Nico said into the radio, as they were making their way to the site.

"The station is requesting to know if you want us to contact Alice for Search and Rescue?"

"Negative for now. If we need it, I'll let ya know."

"Copy," he said, and then turned to Kit.

"Not right now," Kit said into the phone to Caleb. "I'll call if we need it. We're hoping we don't."

"I hope ya don't either, but I have a bad feeling you will."

"Okay," Kit said in a sigh. "Stay near the phone."

"Will do. Love you," Caleb said.

"Love you too," Kit said, and hung up. Resuming her pacing, she kept an eye on the screen as well.

Chapter 5
Trust In The Lord With All Your Heart

"Dad?" Jon called out to Mark. "Dad? Where are you?"

Mark only moaned in response.

A sharp pain jetted from Jon's left shoulder. Grabbing it, he noticed that his left arm was limp. "Great!" Jon sighed, and then jumped with a groan. "Just what I need. A dislocated shoulder."

"Jon?" Mark moaned.

"Dad?" Jon called out. "Dad!"

"Here," came a quiet voice to Jon's left. When Jon went to move toward his dad's voice, the rocks shifted under him, taking him down another ten feet on the hillside. Jon let out a yell as the rocks caused more damage to his right wrist in the slide. "Ahhhhhh!" he shouted. He grabbed his right wrist as it rolled under him and a rock at the same time, hearing a crack. "No more! Please!" Jon begged. His body had multiple cuts and bruises all over it, including a massive cut on his forehead, causing a small river of blood trailing down the side of his head. Looking up, Jon calculated that they rode the rockslide for at least fifty feet from their original position. "Dad, when I moved, it caused me to slide again. Don't move!"

"I won't," he heard his dad's voice even further away than it already was.

"Great! What do we do now?" Jon asked, looking toward Heaven. "Help?"

Suddenly four streaks of light appeared in the sky. There were two angels each at Mark and Jon's positions within seconds. "Do not move," one of the angels instructed Jon.

"Already did," he groaned. "When I did, I slid another ten feet."

"I know," he said. Looking over Jon's body, he turned to the other angel, and said, "Broken right wrist, dislocated left shoulder, and an obvious concussion. Wrist is already set in place, but the shoulder…" he shook his head.

Kneeling next to Jon, the other angel warned, "You are not going to like this."

"I know. Just do it," Jon grumbled.

Laying one hand on Jon's shoulder, he tenderly took Jon's wrist with his other hand, and then shook his head. "I am afraid this will hurt."

"Just do what you have to do," the other angel said curtly. "We have to get them out of here before the other side shows up."

Grabbing ahold of Jon's forearm, the angel then pulled up on Jon's left arm. As he pulled up, he also pushed on Jon's left shoulder. As the angel put Jon's shoulder back in place, Jon shut his eyes in pain and agony, as he let out a yell.

"What was that? Was that Jon?" Mark asked, trying to sit up.

"Do not move!" the angel with Mark ordered, as several rocks slid out from under Mark. When the explosion occurred near he and Jon, the ridge they were on collapsed, cascading down in a torrential river of dirt, rocks, and boulders "There are two others with Jon. He will be fine. If you move, you will cause more damage, or worse, slide further down."

"Is he okay?"

The angel nodded. "He will be." Looking toward the other angel with them, he asked, "How far out are those coming to help?"

"They are close. They should be here in a minute or two."

"Good. He needs them," the angel said, concerned.

*   *   *

"What was *that*?" Josh asked, hearing Jon's yell in the distance.

"I do not know, but I hurt in ohhh so many places," Sasha groaned, about twenty feet from Josh.

Four streaks of light shot from the sky, two landing near each of them. "Do not fear. We are here to help," an angel said, crouching down next to Josh.

"I'm not afraid. I'm in pain," Josh groaned, holding onto his mid-section. "Pretty sure my knee took a beating, as well as my ribs."

"Do not move. What about the other?" the angel next to Josh asked.

"I will find out," he said, and disappeared. Appearing right next to Sasha and his angels, he asked, "How is he?"

"Nothing broken. Just concussion. He has bruises and cuts. There are a couple I am concerned about that I cannot stop bleeding. How close are the others?"

"They should be coming in a minute. They have reached the other two now."

"Mark and Jon? How are they?" Sasha asked.

"Not good, but they will be okay. The archangel is with those in the caves."

"Are *they* okay?"

"No. They are conscious, but not okay. None of you are okay."

"Go back to Josh," the other angel ordered.

Disappearing in an instant, the angel reappeared next to Josh. "They should be arriving any minute."

"Josh?" Nico said, running up to Josh and the two angels, with four from Amarina's clan behind him.

"Dad!" Josh said, grateful to see his Dad. "They blew without warning."

"I know. It wasn't Jacob. Trust me," he assured him.

"I know. We need to get outta here. We don't know where the other side is, or when they'll be back."

"There are angels, along with others here to protect us. We *do* need to get ya outta here. It's because of the injuries, not in fear of the other side," Nico explained.

"How are we getting outta here?"

"One thing at a time. We need to first get you all fixed. What are your injuries?"

"Here," Josh pointed to two bleeding sections on his head. "And here," he said, still holding his ribs. "My knee took a beating, but I can still move it."

"Can you stand? Can you walk out?" Nico asked.

He nodded. "I can with a little help."

Nico helped him up, and then passed him onto one of the Aboriginal men to take back to the Jeeps. "Be careful with him," Nico warned, as Josh limped off with the Aboriginal man.

The guy mumbled something in his native language in response, while he accepted Josh. He had Josh's arm around him, holding Josh up as they made their way back.

"Next?" Nico asked.

"Sasha is over there," the angel that was with Josh pointed to Sasha's location.

"Right-oh," Nico said in a sigh, and then they headed toward Sasha's position. When he got there, he knelt next to Sasha, and asked, "Where are you hurt?"

"I am in pain, but I think I am okay enough to get out of here."

"Good," Nico said, helping him up. "Leave this on the side of your head with pressure," he said, putting a piece of gauze from the medical bag he grabbed from the Jeep, onto an area bleeding on Sasha's head. He then wrapped it with more gauze, to hold it in place. "Now, be a good boy, and go with him to the others." Nico sent him off with another Aboriginal. When he left, Nico turned to the angels there, and asked, "Next?"

The angel shook his head. "You cannot help the other two."

"Why not?"

"As those with you have already found out, if they get too close to Mark and Jon, they will start another landslide."

"Great! What do we do now?"

"The angels with them will help them."

"And those in the caves?"

"The archangel is with them."

Taken aback for a moment, Nico gulped. "That bad?"

"It is not good," the angel confirmed.

Getting on his radio, Nico said, "Eagle two to Eagle one and the Haven."

"Go ahead," Delaney said into the radio.

"We're here too," Cori said over her radio.

"Josh and Sasha are on their way back to the vehicles. Be advised, they will need medical attention."

"Where's Jerrod?" Cori asked.

"Jerrod?" Nico asked, pale.

"Yeah," Delaney said. "He was supposed to be somewhere between Josh and Sasha, and Amarina and Jacob's location. If you've reached Sasha and Josh, then you've already passed him."

Looking toward where he should have been, Nico saw an area that was decimated by the bombs. "Bloody hell!" Nico said into the radio. Turning toward the angels, he asked, "Where's Jerrod?"

Nico, along with all four angels, took off in a sprint toward the area where Jerrod should have been, and fanned out.

"Eagle two? What about Jerrod?" Cori asked into the radio again.

"Searching. Do you have anything on the satellite?"

"Stand by," Cori said, and then turned toward those in the cyber cave with her, and asked, "Anything?"

"What's this?" Rachel asked, pointing out a small fragment on the screen. Going over to the microphone, she asked, "Dad, is there a tiny alcove or cave near you?"

"There are a couple. Why?"

"Because I think I see his legs."

"Where?" Nico asked.

"Go about six yards to your left."

"This way," an angel said when he saw a foot.

When they ran up to the alcove, Nico said into his radio, "Got him."

"Is he alive?" Leah asked into the microphone.

"Stand by," Nico said, and then got on his hands and knees next to Jerrod. "Jerrod, hey mate. Are you in there?" When Jerrod didn't answer, Nico put his hand on Jerrod's neck for a pulse. Relieved to feel one, he announced into the radio, "He's alive, but unconscious. He'll have to be carried out. Looks like he was in the area where multiple ones went off. He hid in this alcove from the explosions, but not before it looks like one may have gone off a little too close for comfort."

"Thank you, Lord," Rachel said, relieved.

"Mark? Is your radio working?" Nico asked.

"Yes," Mark mumbled into the radio.

"Mark!" Casey said, excited to hear his voice. Running to the microphone, she said, "Mark, are you okay?"

"I will be soon. I have help. What do you need, Nico?"

"Can you send some of those blokes over here? We need to make a stretcher to get Jerrod out."

"Copy," he said, and then looked up toward the ridge to see Kalti, Joe, and Jacob, along with multiple other men looking down at them. "You need to send some guys to make a stretcher to get Jerrod out."

"Where is he?" Joe called down.

"I know," one of the angels with Mark said. In a split second, he was up on the ridge with the others. He escorted Joe and five other men over to Jerrod and Nico's location.

"Now for you two," the angel left with Mark said.

"How are you going to get us out? If we move, we slide. That's already happened once with Jon," Mark pointed out, and then groaned in pain. "Ahhh! This hurts!" he said through gritted teeth.

"Jon is with two angels. We will get you up one at a time," the angel explained. Looking up at the others on the ridge, he said, "Make a stretcher, and then send it down here. I will secure him. Then you can pull him up."

Jacob only nodded in response. He, along with five others disappeared, leaving Kalti, along with a couple other guys staying there to keep watch.

"Now, what is hurt on you?" the angel asked Mark.

"Right arm is broken," Mark said, showing the angel where his radius and ulna were sticking out from his shirt of his right arm. "My left ankle is broken. My head got it pretty bad too."

"I will need to set these," the angel warned.

"Go ahead."

"Please send down a medical bag," the angel called up to Kalti.

"Nico has it," Kalti explained. "What do you need?"

"I have to reset his arm," the angel said. Resting a hand on Mark's ankle, he then added, "And his ankle is broken. It is fractured. It is still together, so I do not have to rest it, but I do have to brace it."

"Okay, just a minute," Kalti said before he turned to the others and gave them instructions. They split up into groups and disappeared into the brush. "They will find. They will be back in a minute," Kalti called back down to the angel.

"Do you want me to set it now, or wait?" the angel asked.

"Can't you set it, and do some magical thing to make it better?" Mark asked, worried, knowing there was immense pain in his future.

"I cannot make it better, but I *can* set it. Things were set in play, which cannot be reversed. You all must walk down the path we are on the way it plays out."

"How are we going to get Angel if we're in this shape?"

"You will have to trust the team," the angel said matter-of-factly. "You will work as an advisory role from the Haven. You are still an A.N.G.E.L., but one that is retired, as you say. You understand that, yes?"

"Yes," Mark grumbled.

"Good," he said, and took Mark's right arm into his hands. "Now, tell me again just how upset you are about having to stay at the Haven while the younger A.N.G.E.L.s rescue Angel?"

"Honestly?"

"Honestly."

"I think this…AHHHH!" Mark yelled, as the angel pulled on Mark's arm.

It took the angel a moment to get his bones close to the correct position.

"Ahhhh! STOOOOP!" Mark roared, as the angel pulled it back out to get it in the exact position it needed to be placed. "Stop-it-now!" Mark growled, seething, as the angel set Mark's arm down on his chest.

"There."

Mark was unable to speak due to the immense pain he was experiencing. He just gritted his teeth and growled in response as he glared at the angel. Taking deep breaths, he struggled to get the pain under control, as his face was red with anger and strain.

"We have it," Kalti called over the side to the angel.

"Send it down, please."

They sent down a bundle wrapped in one of the aboriginal's over shirts, leaving him a t-shirt. The pack had pieces of tree branches, along with long strands of grass to use for a rope.

"What is this?" the angel called up to those on the top of the ridge.

"Broom wattle is the branches to use to brace," Kalti explained. "Triodia to use for rope. Need to tie it together. There is no other here."

"Good enough," the angel said. Covering Mark's head, the angel protected Mark from a couple rocks that bounded down the hillside when they were knocked loose by the pack coming down.

Once the pack reached him, the angel began his work. Untying the pack, the angel pulled out multiple branches. He broke them to size, and then proceeded to tear the shirt into strips to use as a tie.

The man whose shirt it was objected before Kalti yelled at him. The man immediately shut up. "Go ahead," Kalti said to the angel.

The angel just nodded, as he quickly, but gently bandaged Mark's arm and ankle. Just as he finished, Jacob and those with him arrived with the makeshift stretcher. "Coming down," Jacob called, as they lowered the stretcher made of tree branches and shirts.

The angel had to cover Mark again as more rocks loosened from their position and bounded down the hillside toward them. Once the stretcher reached the pair, the angel slid Mark onto the stretcher, and then tied him in with the remaining shirt pieces. Once Mark was secure, the angel nodded for the others to pull him up. When he reached the top, four guys proceeded to carry him out, back to the Jeeps.

Turning their attention to Jon, they called down to find out how to get him up. The angel with Jon helped him carefully stand. With the angel's help, Jon stood. The angels braced him to stop him from falling again, as more rocks slid out from under him. Once the angels got him stabilized, they each stood on a side to help keep him balanced.

Jon asked, "Okay. Now, how do I get back up there? When we move, the rocks will slide me further down."

"Once Mark is up, toss the rope back down," the angel called to those on the ridge.

After they finished pulling Mark up, the group tossed the rope down to Jon. It was about twelve feet short. "Great! The amount I fell," Jon sighed, shaking his head. "Can anything go right today?" Turning to the angels with him, he said, "I can't go down. The rocks will beat me up worse than they have already done. I can't go to the side, because I'll slide again. And, the rope is too short to reach. What do we do?"

"Oh, ye of little faith," the angel sighed, glancing at Jon sideways.

Jon watched in amazement as the rope slowly crawled down the remaining twelve feet to Jon. "How in the…?" Jon asked.

"If you have faith as small as a mustard seed, you can say to this mulberry tree, 'be uprooted and planted in the sea,' and it will obey you," the angel reminded him by quoting Luke 17:6.

Jon sighed, shaking his head. "God never ceases to amaze me."

"You only need to trust Him with all your heart, Jon."

"Thank you for the reminder," he said, picking up the rope. "Uh, little issue. This isn't a faith issue by any means, but I have a sprained wrist, and you only reset my shoulder a little bit ago. Can I have a little help?"

"You only need to ask," the angel said with a smile. Tying the rope around Jon's waist, the two angels helped push Jon up the hill, steadying his feet when he went to slip as the rocks periodically washed out under him.

After several tense moments, Jon finally reached the top. "Praise the Lord!" Kalti said, giving him a hug.

When Jacob hugged him, he said, "I'm so sorry. That wasn't me. I didn't blow those."

"Do you know what happened?"

"Remember when I went to Josh before they went in?"

"Yeah."

"I told him the dirt had been moved, but he said it was probably just from people going in and out. It turns out that it wasn't just traffic."

"There was no way for you to know. You did your best," Jon said, much to the relief of Jacob. Putting his arm around him, he gave Jacob's shoulders a gentle squeeze, and said, "Don't worry about it. Mistakes happen, and this wasn't yours."

"Thank you," Jacob said, relieved.

Looking around at the devastation surrounding where his teammates were, still holding his broken wrist, Jon said, "We need to get to the others."

"No. You need to get back to the Jeep," an angel who was with Jon corrected him. "You are injured. There are more than enough people and angels here to get to the others."

"I can't leave them. I can still use this arm," Jon objected, referring to the one the angel put back into place.

"Go to where Jerrod is, and then go back to the Jeep with them," the angel said sternly.

"Fine," Jon said in a sigh. Together, those who were left headed over to where Nico, Joe, and Jerrod were located. "How's Jerrod doing?" Jon asked Nico once they got there.

"Not good. Can't get him to wake up," Nico said, as they loaded him onto a makeshift stretcher. "How are you?"

Jon glanced at the angel with him as he said, "Injured, so I need to get back to the Jeep. I'm under orders."

Snickering, Nico said, "I see. I would listen to them if I were you."

"Here's Mark's radio," Joe said handing it to Jon. "You'll need it. We only need one here."

"Actually, we're going to keep it," Nico said, taking it from Jon. "If we can get it to those in the caves, it'll be easier to communicate with them," he pointed out.

"Good idea," Joe agreed.

Kalti said something to four men, who each took a corner of Jerrod's stretcher, and started walking off. "Go with them," he said to Jon.

"Yes, sir," Jon said, and jogged to catch up to the men as he tightly held his arm so it wouldn't move.

"How do we get to the others?" Nico asked the angels still there.

"Just a minute," an angel said, and disappeared into the cave with the trio of men and the archangel. "The others have been rescued, and are on their way back to the vehicles. How do we get these three out?"

"Very good. Val and Derek are not getting out on their own," the archangel explained. "Jesse can, but he is not leaving without the other two."

"Absolutely not," Jesse said, still on the ground, glaring at the archangel.

"I see," the angel said in understanding, noting Jesse's demeanor. "Then we will need to blow a hole through the cave wall," he suggested.

"Yes. It is where you need to set the charges that is the problem," the archangel cautioned.

"We can protect them," the angel said confidently.

"It will not be pleasant."

"I understand. None of this is. It is our duty, though. And, we do it willingly."

The archangel nodded. In an instant, the angel disappeared and reappeared next to the group. "Jacob, you will need to set charges here," he said, pointing to an area. "And there," he said, pointing to another. "The rest of us need to go shelter the three in there, while those out here hide from the blast."

As soon as he said it, the angels with him, stood at attention. "Yes, sir!" they said in unison, and disappeared.

"If the angels try to protect them in there, they may end up under a load of rock and dirt," Jacob objected. "I can't promise no one will get hurt."

"There are others from your team severely injured inside," the messenger angel pointed out. "Those angels, along with me, will protect them from further damage."

"You don't understand. Everyone who is in that cave will get buried alive if I place them where you want me to," Jacob explained. "I can't imagine the tunnels are that wide? Setting them that close to the cave wall will more than likely cause a collapse."

"It will, but it is what is needed to get to them. These are orders from the archangel," the angel explained. "Now, set the charges. I must return to the others. The rest of you need to take cover. The explosion will be vast."

With that, the angel disappeared from the group, and reappeared in the cave with the others. "Jacob is getting ready," he informed the archangel.

"Take your positions," the archangel ordered.

Four angels positioned themselves over Derek's body and spread their wings. Meanwhile, three more covered Val's, and the messenger angel and the archangel went over to Jesse.

"Don't touch me," Jesse snapped when the archangel knelt next to him.

"Jesse," the archangel said, resting his hand on Jesse's knee. Jesse just bore a hole into the archangel with his eyes, otherwise not moving a muscle, as the archangel continued, "I was there when you were born. I have watched you grow into the strong young man you are now. I would not do anything to hurt you."

"No, you just won't do anything to *help* either," Jesse said flatly.

"Jesse, Jacob is going to blow his explosives any moment. I need to protect you. *You* are the one who is to save Angel. You cannot do that if you are hurt."

Narrowing his eyes at the archangel, Jesse asked, "Is that true, or are you just telling me that to get me to do what you want me to do?"

"I have already been told that you will lead the team who will ultimately find her and bring her home. I need you to be healthy in order to do so. Please let us protect you?"

"I don't –"

Before he could object any further, the explosives went off. The messenger angel and the archangel both dove on top of Jesse. The archangel spread his wings over both the messenger angel and Jesse in order to protect them both, as the cave wall blew in toward them before collapsing on top of them.

When the ground shook around them, Jesse felt fear mix with his anger, and instinctively curled up into a ball to protect himself. There was no time to pray. There was no time to think. All he could do was hold his breath at the amount of dirt that clogged the air around them, while the ground rumbled and shook.

C.J. Peterson

Chapter 6
You Will Find Me When You Seek Me With All Your Heart

"Please just let me sleep?" Angel begged the three demons that would scream and screech every time she even attempted to close her eyes for the last few days. Drained, weak, exhausted, and bleary-eyed, she did her best to cover her ears with her arms, since her hands were above her head. "Just stop!" she pleaded.

When Cassius walked in, the demons stopped and backed away from Angel. "Hello, preciousss," he hissed, gently lifting her chin with his fingers, so she would look at him.

"I am *not* your precious," Angel snapped.

"I will bet you are hungry. Would you care for sssomething to eat, preciousss?"

"Again, I am *not* your precious!"

"Go get her some water," Cassius instructed one of the demons.

"B-but…sssir?" the demon stammered, confused.

"If we do not give her more water, she will die," Cassius pointed out. After the demon left, Cassius turned to another demon, and ordered, "Find her some good food."

"Sssir?" the demon cocked his head to the side, bewildered.

"She needs to eat."

"At what cost?" Angel narrowed her eyes at Cassius, as the demon left to do his bidding.

"No cossst," Cassius said, innocently.

Glaring at him, Angel said, "Just so you know, I *will not* give into you. I will *never* deny Christ."

The first demon returned with the water. Cassius helped her slowly drink it. Then, when the second demon returned, Cassius released her from her restraints, and allowed her to finally sit on the ground. "Eat, preciousss," Cassius encouraged.

Having difficulty even lifting her hand to her mouth, she kept her independence, refusing to be held. While she ate, Angel kept an eye on everyone in the cave with her.

It wasn't until she finished eating, and drained the water from the third bottle that Cassius reached down and picked everything up. After handing the dish and bottles to a demon, Cassius sat down with her and said, "I am sssorry for your treatment."

"I *highly* doubt that," Angel said, with her arms dropped onto her legs, otherwise motionless.

"Look, the troublesss you alwaysss ssseem to find are connected to the archangel. Where doesss the archangel sssay he getsss hisss authority?"

"He gets it from the Lord God," Angel said, not sure where Cassius was going.

"Have you ever *heard* the Lord give him thisss authority?"

"I have heard the Lord."

"Are you *sure* it wasss the Lord?" Cassius pressed.

"Of course I'm sure!"

"No, you are not," Cassius challenged. "You have never actually heard the Lord. You are not sure the Lord even sssent the archangel. As a matter of fact, I challenge that the archangel really isssn't an archangel. Perhapsss it is a fallen angel?" he posed.

"You cannot be serious!" Angel said, stunned. "I believe and trust in the Lord. I *know* the Lord sends the archangel! I *know* and *trust* in the Lord *and* His missions. We help people!"

"Like you helped Aden Knight?"

"That was *your* doing!" she accused.

"How would we know how to find him with only a firssst name?"

Taken back for a moment, a smile slowly crossed Angel's face. "You messed up. You have the other half of the list. You *did* have his first name. You only needed to watch us until we led you to him. Nice try, Cassius, but I'm not biting. The Lord *did* send the archangel to us for missions. He also sanctions and leads us, protecting us from the likes of *you*! You might as well kill me, Cassius. I'm *not* bending."

"Ssstring her back up. Do *not* let her sssleep!" Cassius hissed, as he stormed out of the cave with the sound of Angel's crazed laughter filling the cavern around him.

*   *   *

"We *need* to get extra help!" Josh insisted over the radio. "This can*not* be taken care of by just us!"

"We can't explain this. What are you going to tell the authorities that happened?" Nico demanded, as he and the others came out of hiding in their place near where Jacob blew the caves.

"With the amount of explosions that have happened, I wouldn't be surprised if –" Josh was cut off by the sounds of a helicopter coming in from a distance. "Never mind," Josh said into the radio. "They're here."

*   *   *

Amongst the rubble of the blown cave, the archangel was the first to move. "Jesse?" the archangel asked, with his wings still covering them. "Jesse, are you okay?"

"Y-yeah," Jesse said, slowly sitting up. Looking at the wings that covered him, he asked, "What happens if you move your wings?"

"There is a lot of debris," the archangel admitted.

Noticing the strain on both the archangel and angel's bodies and faces, Jesse asked, "Is it possible to move and the debris not cave in on us?"

"At this point, I am afraid not." The archangel shook his head. "If any of us move without help, it will come down."

"Jesse?" crackled over the radio in Jesse's lap.

Looking down, Jesse picked it up. "Nico?"

"What's your status?"

Jesse looked to the archangel, who said, "All are alive."

Into the radio, Jesse said, "We're all alive."

"Stay put," Nico said. "We'll get in there as soon as possible." Hearing a helicopter land near the Jeeps, he added, "Pretty sure we're about to get some help."

"Praise God!" Jesse said, relieved.

"I wish," Nico groaned. "It's search and rescue, probably from Alice Springs. We have some explaining to do."

*   *   *

"So, you have no idea where the explosives came from?" the officer asked Nico.

"No sir. We were all on a hike, and were exploring, when it suddenly blew up all around us!"

"You seriously expect me to believe that?" the officer raised an eyebrow, as Jerrod and Mark were loaded onto a helicopter. Two other ambulances, along with three police cars pulled up while they were talking.

"I'm hoping," Nico admitted with a sheepish grin.

"Sullivan, I know many who work on your station," the officer said, leaning on his car. "I heard stories from long ago about things that happened on your station. They're kind of legendary. Is that stuff going on here too?"

"Off the record?" Nico asked.

"Off the record," the officer agreed.

"Yes."

Standing, stunned, the officer leaned in and asked, "You're serious? That stuff's real?" When Nico nodded, the officer said, "Noooo, what's your game?"

"I'm very serious. It's the truth!"

"Really?"

Nico only nodded in response.

"How am I gonna put this in a report?"

"Make something up?" Nico offered. "I can't tell ya how to do your job, but right now we have to get the others out of the caves."

"Right-oh," the officer said, "Let's go."

Multiple men loaded up their gear from the rescue truck before they followed Nico back to the caves. Several hours later, under the portable lights, there was suddenly a shout, "Over here!"

Nico, Joe, and Jacob ran over to where Delaney and four rescue workers were feverishly tossing debris. "Who is it?"

"Derek," Delaney said. "And, it's not good."

Moving the last of the rocks from his body, they found an unconscious Derek. He seemed to be in a cavern. The way the debris fell, it looked to the rescue workers that he was just lucky enough to have a debris bubble around him.

"Jesse, we found Derek," Nico said into his radio.

"Careful how you move him. His back is broken," Jesse said. As the lights pierced the darkness around him, the angel and archangel disappeared. "I'm here!" Jesse shouted from his little bubble as well. "Careful how you move the rocks."

"The third one is over here," another rescue worker called out.

It took them about an hour to safely dig them out. Once all were out, they life-flighted Derek and Val to the hospital in Alice Springs, while Jesse went via ambulance.

*   *   *

Well, welcome back to the real world," Mark said, as Jesse woke in his hospital room. Mark was released a few hours earlier. After stopping to check in on the others brought in from the team, Mark settled in Jon and Jesse's room.

"Dad?" Jesse asked, as his mind slowly cleared, allowing him to focus on the hospital room around him. The beeping of the monitor was already starting to annoy him, and the strong scents were giving him a headache. He wasn't looking forward to eating hospital food either.

"Welcome back to the world, brother," Jon said from his bed on Jesse's left. Jon's one arm was in a cast, and he had a sling on the other, along with a bandage on his head. When Jesse looked at him, Jon mentioned, "Yeah, the wrist is broken on this arm. The shoulder had gotten dislocated on the other. They said something is torn in there, and it will take a bit to heal, but they wanted me to have the use of at least one arm," he said, wiggling the fingers on his casted right arm. "I can't lift my arm above shoulder level until it's healed. I should recover in a few weeks. I refused to leave, though, until you were ready to go with us."

"Who all has been discharged? How long was I out?" Jesse asked, confused.

"You've been out for three days. Seems you had a concussion. You scared your mom. When they finally got you out, you looked at Joe and said, *'Angel's further into the Outback'*, and then went unconscious. You're mom's still spinning from the fact that Angel wasn't in there, and then when you wouldn't wake up..." Mark shook his head. "Anyway, as far as who has been discharged? Well, it looks like Derek's going to be in here for a while. He has another surgery scheduled for today in a few hours. Jerrod finally woke up yesterday. That was *not* a good wake up. If Josh, Sasha, Joe, and Jacob weren't in the waiting room, it could have gone ugly real fast. He didn't know where he was, and started to choke out a nurse before another one ran for help. The guys ran in and restrained him so the nurses could calm him down. They didn't want to knock him out again. They were afraid he would wake up the same way. I guess his PTSD was rearing its ugly head again. I think I have an idea on how to help him, but he'll have to wait until he gets back to Nevada. Anyway, he completely lost it, and is currently under sedation. They're going to wake him later tonight when we can get as many of us as we can in the room with him so he remembers us, and hopefully won't freak out this time. Jon, you coming this time?"

"Yep. They can let me out now," Jon said sitting up. "I just wanted to be here when Jesse woke."

"They also wanted to keep you here for observation. You really don't think you have control over when they let you go, do you?" Mark asked, raising an eyebrow. "Do you *really* think you staying here was *your* choice?"

"A guy can hope." Jon grinned, lying back in the bed. Then he added, "I really do want out. When is the doc coming for rounds?"

"Should be here in about a half-hour," Mark said, looking at his watch.

"Dad?" Jesse said, gesturing for him to go on.

"Oh! Sorry," Mark apologized. "Okay, so Derek's back is broken. I'm sorry, Jesse. The doctor said him walking again is a long shot. It's pretty bad. His back is broken in multiple places. A couple of his vertebrae are shattered. They had to piece them back together."

"The archangel said he won't walk again," Jesse said somberly.

"At least he's still with us," Mark pointed out.

"True. Who else?" Jesse asked, hoping to not dive into that subject just yet.

"Well, my arm is broken," Mark said, holding up his casted arm, "Along with my ankle. Sasha came out the best out of all of us."

"What about Val?" Jesse asked. "He was hurt pretty badly too."

"He has a couple broken ribs, along with a broken leg."

"Can you tell me who is still good enough to go get Angel?" Jesse pressed, visibly frustrated.

"Well, you can in a few days. Then there's Delaney, Joe, Jacob, Nico, Sasha, and Katia said she was coming this time. Rachel said depending on when we try again, she may be able to help."

"No. I don't want her in the field until she's ready. You didn't mention Josh. What's his status?"

"His knee is injured. He needs a few weeks."

"We don't have weeks," Jesse insisted. "Angel doesn't *have* weeks."

"Let's get those who can, back to –"

"Dad, they can't fly until cleared by medical," Jon cut him off.

"It's been three days," Mark pointed out. "We're not going anywhere until I know Derek's status, so that'll be at least another week. I may send some back to the Haven, though, in order to save on money. They can regroup and come up with a plan there."

"When can I go?" Jesse pressed.

"In a few days," Mark said. "The doctor will want to keep an eye on you for at least another day. You just woke up."

"I feel fine. I need to get to Angel. I'm the one who will lead the team in. The archangel already told me that."

"Look, we've had to get creative during this. After what happened to Danny, and now this, we have *a lot* of authorities sniffing around," Mark said sternly. "We need to go at this cautiously. We can't push."

"Dad, Angel's been in their trenches by herself for over a week! That's *way* too long!"

"Trust me! It's *my* daughter! I get that!" Mark snapped. Taking a breath to calm himself, Mark more calmly said, "Angel's my daughter and your sister. She is strong in the Lord. She can do this. She *will* come through this…one way or another. She only needs to continue to seek Him with all her heart."

Dropping his head back onto the bed, Jesse sighed. After doing a mental tally, he said, "So, you're telling me that I have Delaney, Joe, Jacob, Katia, and Sasha to do this?"

Mark nodded. "Sounds about right. Josh's knee is messed up, so he said he wouldn't be of any use to you in the field right now. He's going back to the Haven with the others when they're ready. The injured will be making their way back as soon as Jerrod's ready to go. I'm staying with Derek until he's ready to come home. I don't want to leave him."

"Well then," Jesse said in a sigh.

"What's wrong with that crew?" Jon asked. "We've done more with less."

"We've done more with less *trained* people," Jesse corrected. "Delaney, Katia, and Sasha aren't trained. Do I at least get Nico and Charlie?"

"That's up to them." Mark shrugged. "Nico's been a volunteer since this started. Charlie and Katia are currently on their way back here, so you'll definitely have them. They've already landed in Sydney. They take off on a non-stop here in about fifteen minutes, and should land in Alice Springs in about three and a half hours. At that point, Nico will pick them up and bring them here."

"That's a long flight," Jon pointed out. "Aren't they going to want to get a shower?"

"They said they'd rather see everyone first," Mark explained. "I need to go call your mom and let her know you've finally woken up."

"Tell her I love her," Jesse said. As Mark went to leave in a wheelchair, Jesse asked, "When can I see Derek?"

"He's already down in pre-op. You'll have to wait until tomorrow at the earliest, but even then I don't think he'll be in a good place."

"What do you mean?"

"He can't feel his legs. His mind is not in a good place right now."

"He's alive," Jesse pointed out.

Closing the door to the hall, Mark wheeled back over to Jesse's bed. Thinking for a moment the best way to word it, he said, "Jesse, you have to understand. He was whole, and now he no longer feels whole."

"What do you mean?"

"He has been independent and active his entire life. And now, he's going to have to be dependent on someone or something for the rest of his life. He's used to saving people, and now he knows that won't happen anymore. He doesn't know his purpose. He can no longer control things around him. He has to rely on others, and hope they make the right choices for him."

"His purpose is to serve the Lord."

"He has to find a new way to do that. He has to start over. He has to learn how to live life again…a new way."

"He's strong. He can do it."

"He may need to borrow your strength in order to get through this. He feels weak. He feels compromised. He feels worthless. He no longer feels like he's a valid part of the team. He feels like he's too old to start over again."

"He can't be serious?" Jesse said, stunned.

"He is very serious. He needs a lot of prayer. As a matter of fact, this entire team needs a lot of prayer. We need to refocus on the Lord and how God wants this to work."

"What do you mean?"

"Jesse, take a hard look at the team with me for a moment."

"Okay," Jesse agreed.

"Derek feels defeated. He doesn't know if he'll ever be able to be a functioning team member again. Nico feels useless. He had to stand by and watch everything happen in front of him. Charlie lost his best friend. I haven't been able to rescue my own daughter from the clutches of the underworld…twice. Jon really doesn't have the use of both of his arms."

"I have limited use of my left," Jon pointed out.

"Which can be used in the field how?" Mark challenged.

"Good point. Carry on," Jon conceded.

Turning back to Jesse, he continued, "Rachel has had to stand back and watch her team fall over and over again, without being able to do a thing. She also lost one of her mentors in Danny. Josh lost Danny as well. Josh also made a critical error in the field. Jacob told him that something wasn't right. He dismissed Jacob, and told him he was paranoid. Had he listened, this whole thing may not have happened. Had Nico, Derek, and I taken Cori and Kai's warning to heart that Angel may not be there, we also wouldn't be in this mess." Shaking his head at the disaster around them for a moment, he said, "Then there's Jacob. He feels responsible because the other side used his explosives to make this mess. He also feels angry because Josh didn't listen to him. Then there's you."

"Me?" Jesse asked, wide-eyed. "What's wrong with me?"

"Tell me you're not angry," Jon challenged.

"Shut up! I hate your gift," Jesse grumbled.

"Even *I* can feel your anger," Mark pointed out. "Don't think for a moment that God and the archangel aren't aware of your anger."

"Oh, they are," Jesse assured him. "I made that pretty clear."

"You need to get a handle on that, before it swallows you. The other side will use that against you."

"I know. What about the rest of the team?" Jesse asked, changing the subject.

"Delaney, Katia, and Sasha still need to be evaluated as to their abilities, but you don't have time for that," Mark said. "Jerrod's questionable on his physical condition, but after his last wake up, pretty sure his emotional and mental need to have a serious moment or two with Jesus. Joe and Jacob are the *only* two that I can see who are actually stable."

"How are we supposed to get to Angel with all of this extra baggage?" Jesse asked. "This seems like an impossible task."

"Luke 1:37 reminds us that, *'For with God nothing will be impossible.'* You already know that God doesn't call the qualified," Mark said.

"No, He qualifies the called," Jesse finished.

"And, in Jeremiah 29:13, it says, *'You will seek Me and find Me when you seek Me with all your heart.'* Right?" Jon said.

"Yes," Jesse agreed. "Mom taught us that verse when we were five. That's one she hammered into our brain."

"Why do you think she did that?" Mark asked.

"Because she wanted to make sure we focused on God, and not the situation around us."

"Here's the situation," Mark started, "You have Nico, Charlie, Sasha, Katia, Jacob, Joe, and Delaney, along with all the support the Haven can give you to get your sister out. Along with all of them, you also, and most importantly, have God and the archangel on your side. The archangel knows where she is. He'll help you get to her."

"In other words, look at what I have, not what I don't have?"

"Yes. Once we have Angel and everyone back at the Haven, only then will we look at all those heart issues we talked about earlier. The priority is getting Angel, and getting everyone back to the Haven."

"Yes, sir," Jesse agreed.

"Good." Mark patted Jesse's leg. "Now, get some rest, pray, and get right with God. You're going to need Him."

"He's the *only* way you'll get her out," Jon added.

"In the meantime, I –"

"G'day," the doctor said, coming into the room with a nurse behind him, cutting Mark off.

Mark shook the doctor's hand. "Hello, Doc."

"How are you doing today?"

"It was a rough wake-up," Jesse admitted.

After doing an assessment, the doctor agreed to release Jon, but wanted to keep Jesse for another night, much to his irritation. This, however, gave him a chance to make a plan. With Katia and Charlie coming in, he would need to figure out who would need to stay, and whom to send to the Haven.

*   *   *

"Good morning, young Angel," Calliope said, coming into the cavern. Turning to the demons, she said, "Cassius is looking for you." As they left, leaving one just outside the cave entrance, Calliope turned back to Angel, "How are you feeling today?"

"Why do you care?" Angel grumbled, exhausted beyond caring anymore.

"Oh, why do you think I don't care?"

"Is that a trick question?"

"Angel, honey, I really do care about your wellbeing. I just think you are slightly misguided, and are in need of an advisor. I feel I can be that for you. Cassius just wants to take care of you. Even Korax is worried for you. You're not eating. You're not sleeping."

"And, whose fault is that?" Angel shot.

"Honey, your nightmares are getting worse. We need you to calm yourself, and focus on getting better."

"And, how am I supposed to do that when you have those demons screaming at me night and day?"

"You want to rest, you only need to close your eyes."

"Oh, so your minions can keep me up screaming and showing me more images of my teammates blowing up, and seeing images of Danny dying over and over again? No thank you."

"You're looking at this all wrong. Here," Calliope said, reaching past the cave doorway. She pulled Allen into the cave with them, "even Allen is worried for you."

"Angel, I really want to help you. From one human to another," Allen said, setting his hand on her shoulder.

"Get your hands off me! You are *not* a person!" Angel snapped, as she wiggled away from him. "You gave up your humanity when you turned your back on the Lord."

"Angel, honey, you are on your own. That little angel who was with you has been taken out. Obviously, your so-called 'team' has abandoned you after not one, but *two* failed attempts. Trust me, they are *not* going to go for three."

Angel narrowed her eyes. "We *never* leave a man behind!"

"Really? Because from what I hear, you did. It's my understanding that *you* left Rachel and Jesse, *your brother,* behind in Black Rock."

"That was a different situation."

"Really? Because you *are* being held by us in our new Black Rock. The rest of the team was safe, and now has been put into dangerous situations – twice – coming to get you. This has led to the *death* of one, and there is another who is in a dangerous position. This sounds just like the situation at Black Rock…if not worse. Do you *really* think they are going to come after you again? And if so, *when* do you think they are going come? And with whom? You have no idea how many of your teammates are in the hospital. And, once they are out, there are not many who are not injured in some way or another."

Angel swallowed hard as she processed what Calliope said. In a way she was right. Shaking her head, she insisted, "No. My team, my *family*, will *not* give up on me! The *Lord will not* give up on me. I will continue to seek Him with all of my heart. In turn, He will never leave me, nor forsake me. That is a promise!"

"Angel," Allen started, but Angel shook her head to stop him.

"Allen, I can see the torture in your eyes. The one speaking is not your human portion. I'm not exactly sure *what* you are right now, or what form you are going to be, but you are *not* human. You sold your soul to the wrong side. I *will not* follow suit!"

"We shall see, young Angel. We shall see," Calliope said before leaving, with Allen on her heals.

"We get to have fun once again," the demon said, walking back into the cave with three others.

They proceeded to periodically scream horrific shrill shrieks near her ears. She couldn't think. She couldn't focus. She had no memory she could focus on in order to stay sane for very much longer. To her, this was worse than the physical torture she endured. At least there was an ending to that. This was a never-ending, ear-piercing, constant barrage of insanity. The visions of death that continued to permeate her mind were undeniably a twisted version of the truth.

Begging and pleading for God to rescue her mind, and protect her heart and soul, Angel continued to resist with everything in her, in hopes of making it through with her soul still belonging to the Lord.

Chapter 7
I Will Give Thanks To The Lord
With All My Heart

With Derek still in the hospital, those injured returned to the Haven, with the exception of Mark who stayed with Derek at the hospital. Those team members still able to remain, went to Alice Springs, and regrouped in a hotel.

Once landed, Mark set up for Jerrod to go to Pennsylvania to get a service dog. It would be a six-week program, but he would have to stay in Pennsylvania to complete the program. Once he graduated, he would have a service dog in order to help him wade through the nightmares. It would also become so in tuned to Jerrod, it would wake Jerrod from his nightmares when he slept. The dog would be an extra pair of eyes for Jerrod. If he was in public and started to feel anxious, the dog would help him by easing his anxiety there as well. The dog would also be alert when they were out in public, giving Jerrod the assurance of knowing someone else had his back. They would be inseparable. Mark knew many military members who were helped with these blessed canines. Between God, a counselor, and the dog, he had confidence that Jerrod would finally be able to start to conquer the nightmares.

*   *   *

In Alice Springs, Delaney and Katia shared one room, while the remaining guys split between two rooms. Joe, Jacob, and Nico were in one, while Jesse, Sasha, and Charlie were in the other.

Meeting in Jesse's room, the team wasn't sure what direction to head. Finally, Jesse took control of the meeting. "Right now, this is all we have left to find and get Angel." Objections were heard through the room, until Jesse finally got everyone calmed down by putting his fingers to his mouth and letting out a sharp whistle. "Thank you," he said, relieved that the conversations finally halted. "Look, we are stronger than you think. We have Jacob and his presents. We have Nico and Charlie's experience. We have mine and Sasha's strength. And, we have Joe and Delaney's minds. We also have the gifts each one of us possesses from the Spirit. God won more with less. He helped Gideon defeat the Midian armies with only three hundred men. If we let Him be our guide and strength, then we can't lose. We *will* get her out this time. The other side thinks they won. They think we will give up, but we will *never* give up. We *never* leave a man behind."

"Where is she?" Joe asked. "Does anyone have an idea of where to start?"

"Well, I have been praying, and –"

Jesse was cut off by the sudden appearance of the archangel, along with four others, one in each corner of the room. "This room is now sealed and protected," the archangel explained. "We need to have a serious conversation regarding your status."

"Our *status* is that we are going to go get Angel," Jesse said, daring the archangel to disagree.

"I agree," the archangel said, knowing he would have to tread carefully with Jesse until Jesse could work through his emotions. "It is how you are going to do it that is in question."

Crossing his arms, Jesse asked, "Okay, what's your plan?"

Pulling a map out of a tube that rested on his back, the archangel laid out a map of Australia on the table. "We are here," he pointed. "She is here."

"*Where?*" Charlie asked shocked, as he looked in closer at the map. "You *do* realize that is almost three hundred miles to the south west? There is absolutely *nothing* there."

"*Angel* is there," the archangel simply said.

"And *how* are we going to get out there? That's so far into the never-never it is not even funny!"

"You will make it."

"I understand you think this is a simple hike, but this makes the journey to Tanami seem like a walk in the park. This is seriously out there," Charlie said, trying to make the archangel understand.

"Do you not have faith?"

"I do," Charlie said. "So, I'm going to ask you how it is you are going to get us out of there once we get Angel out?"

"That will be up to the Lord."

"*Will* we make it out of there?" Jacob asked.

"Again, that is up to the Lord," the archangel reiterated.

"Will we get Angel this time?" Delaney asked.

"Yes," the archangel responded. "This is not in doubt."

"Will she be *alive*?" Sasha asked.

"You have many questions that I cannot answer," the archangel responded.

"Have to say you do not share much comfort," Katia huffed, crossing her arms. Walking over to the archangel, she stood before him, and said, "With all respect, Angel let the others, including my sister, escape. A.N.G.E.L. Danny gave his life to help the others escape. We have many still seriously injured while trying to help her escape a second time. Why is it that you cannot give us encouragement, and help us understand?"

"Frankly, I don't want to lose more. It'll be rough enough for us to lick our wounds and push forward after all of this," Jesse explained. "I feel like we've been through a war."

"You are in a war every day," the archangel explained. "As I explained to you in Russia, you need to stand firm. You need to put on the armor of God in order to win these battles. The Lord has armed you with special gifts for a reason. I have been instructed to share 2 Chronicles 20:15 with you. It is to remind you, *"This is what the Lord says to you: 'Do not be afraid or discouraged because of this vast army. For the battle is not yours, but God's.'"* This battle is not yours. Satan and his minions have declared war on the Lord God Almighty, and The Lord *will* win. This is promised to you in Revelation."

"The war is the Lord's," Jesse said. "And as His soldiers, wouldn't it be wise to share the plan with the troops?"

"I do not know the plan."

Narrowing his eyes as he crossed his arms, Jesse challenged, "How can *you* not know the plan? We're working under you. Wouldn't it be wise for the Lord to let *you* know the plan?"

"Mine is not to question the Lord," the archangel said in his defense.

"Wow. This is getting really frustrating."

"Yours is not always to know the plan, just to follow the path. You know the One who knows the entire journey. Yours is to trust in Him, and to take the first step. That first step starts with you going here," the archangel said, pointing to the same place on the map.

"*Here,*" Nico pointed to the place on the map, "is no man's land."

"Exactly. Why would you think the other side would place themselves in the middle of civilization?" the archangel asked.

"I wouldn't, but this place is…" Nico stopped. "Okay, do we know right now if she's still alive?"

"Yes. She is."

"And, you know this because of the angel with her. Correct?"

"No. He is no longer."

"No what? No longer with her?"

"No."

"*Where is he?*" Nico demanded. "He's supposed to be beside her, encouraging her to keep focused on God."

The archangel put his head down in response.

"Okay," Nico said, taking a deep breath. "But, you know for sure that right now Angel's still alive?"

"Yes," the archangel said. The words hung in the air for a few moments before he went on, "You need to get to her. I will be going with you."

"Really?" Jesse asked, surprised.

"Is it because it's that much more dangerous, or because you don't think we can do it?" Joe challenged.

"I have the utmost confidence in all of you. You were all chosen for a reason," the archangel explained. "Each one of you has a gift given to you for this very reason. It is not the quantity of soldiers, as much as it is the *quality* of the soldiers. Jesse already pointed this out in regards to how the Lord won the battle for Gideon."

"Well, we're going to need the Lord even more in order to remotely pull this off," Jesse pointed out.

The archangel nodded as he crossed his arms. "*That* is the plan."

*   *   *

"Good morning, sunshine," Mark said jokingly to Derek, as he rolled into the room.

Derek woke a while ago from the surgery, and they recently transferred him back to his room. "Hey," he mumbled, and then dropped his head back onto the pillow, groaning.

After the staff got Derek settled into bed, Mark maneuvered his chair beside the bed. "So, wanna hear some interesting stories?"

"Sure. Why not?"

"Well, there *was* an angel with Angel, but it has since passed. She is now alone."

"She's strong, Mark. That stubborn tenacity that often irritates you, will help her pull through this."

"It will. The question is, what shape will she be in once she's rescued?"

"Better than me, I promise you."

Sitting back in his chair, Mark studied Derek. "Wanna dump some of that?" he asked.

"No."

"You're going to have to eventually. I'm not going anywhere. Besides, you have a few more weeks here before we can go back to the Haven. Might as well get it out now."

"Seriously?"

"Yeah. There's no running from this one."

"Poor choice of words, brother," Derek said in a sigh.

"Just talk to me. There's nothing you can say that will make me think less of you."

Derek cocked his head to the side. "Is that good or bad?"

"Depends," Mark said, taking a sip of his coffee, "are you going to be honest, or do I need to wrestle it out of you?"

"See, this is what I am angry about." When Mark gestured for Derek to go on, he explained, "I'm a soldier. I'm strong. I have always held my own. I have survived some of the most horrific things only to end up like this!" he said, slapping his legs. "I remember all those rescues in Iraq and Afghanistan. I remember all of our missions. I remember –"

"You remember your strength is forging documents, right?"

"While it is, I still went on missions."

"For the most part, yes. However, your skills are still valuable. And, what you can teach Delaney will be invaluable to her and the team. That's not even mentioning what you have done for Jesse through the years. It would have crushed him if you died. It would have also been another massive hit to the A.N.G.E.L.s, who are already spinning from the loss of Danny."

"I don't care about the A.N.G.E.L.s right now!" Derek shouted.

He went to object, but instead Mark took a deep breath, letting Derek go on.

"I care about the fact that I can't feel my legs! I care about the fact that I can no longer function the way I am used to functioning. I care about that fact that I feel useless, worthless, and less than. I feel…" Derek stopped and looked toward the ceiling, letting out a breath of air. Calmer, he explained, "We trained to face every type of battle on the field except this. This is…" he looked back down at his legs, "this is something I cannot train for."

"You are still a valuable member of this family."

Glaring at him, Derek said, "I *have* no family! It's *yours*!"

"Tell that to Jesse!" Mark challenged.

"Jesse would be so much better off not with the A.N.G.E.L.s. He's a graphic artist," Derek shouted. "He should be creating artwork, not painting the names of dead people on a rock! Do you not understand how much it guts him every time he has to paint a name?"

"Of course I do! He's my son!"

"Then why would you put him through that? Why did you let *all three* of your children do this? Why would you let them put their lives on the line?"

"It was their choice. They each chose to answer the call."

"A call that you trained them to follow."

"What are you saying?" Mark asked, stunned.

"That you groomed them to do this."

"I did not!" Mark snapped. "I let them make their own choices. You can't seriously tell me that someone can tell Angel what to do. Have you *met* her?"

Glaring at him, Derek crossed his arms.

"Where is this coming from?" Mark asked. "This is something we have all answered the call to. Our call is higher than anything the world can offer. We are servants of the Lord Almighty. We answer to Him, and assist His people whenever and wherever we can. You know this! You've helped train people for this!"

"I have."

"Are you going to tell me that you felt forced to do this?"

"No. Never. I made my choices of my own free will."

"Then," Mark challenged, "why do you think my children would do any less? Why do you think *you* are any less?" Softening his voice, Mark maneuvered to sit on the side of the bed. Once settled, he said, "Derek, you are my brother. You may not be blood, but you *are* my brother. You are an uncle to our children. You are the godfather of Jesse. He thinks of you as a second father. What do you think would have happened to him if you died?"

Taking a moment, he finally answered, "He wouldn't have recovered."

"Exactly! It's bad enough that he paints names of those lost on the rock, but could you imagine him having to paint *your* name? While he does it in honor of those we've lost, painting yours would shred his innermost core."

"It breaks his heart every time he has to do it. You know this, right?"

"I know it does. How did we get on Jesse from you?" Mark asked.

"There's a lot I have held in over the years," Derek admitted.

"I'm surprised Jon hasn't called you on it."

"I'm that good."

"And, you are *still* that good…with or without the use of your legs."

Taking a moment to collect his thoughts, Derek continued, "I understand that. But, do you understand that I'll have to learn how to walk again?"

"While I don't mean to discourage you, Doc said your back is too broken. He *and* the archangel said you would not walk again."

"Great!" Derek threw his hands in the air in exasperation. "Even the archangel is against me."

"Derek, your strength is not in your legs. It's in your hands and in your mind. Yes, you were helpful in the field, but seriously, what you have in that head of yours is far more valuable."

"I'll have to learn how to even go to the bathroom again, or take a shower. Even getting out of bed will be a new challenge. You get that, right?"

"You're strong."

Tears brimming his eyes, he admitted, "Even strong people sometimes need help."

"That's why I'm here, brother. You're *not* going through this alone." Resting his hand on Derek's leg, Mark went on, "I am not leaving this place until you're ready to get on that plane. I'll be here through your physical therapy. I'll be here to bring you in contraband for food when they try to make you eat that stuff that they attempt to call food."

"I don't know if I can do this."

"You can, and you will. You have been there for me through the years. Let me be here for you now. Let the family help and guide you. Let us carry you when you don't think you can go on."

"I have never had to ask for help from anyone besides God," Derek admitted.

"Now is not the time to play the super hero. You have a lot you're going to have to work through, but I promise you that I will not leave. I give you my word that only the Lord God will be able to pull me away. Deal?" Mark asked, sticking his hand out for Derek to shake.

Looking at his hand for a moment, Derek said, "I'm going to get angry."

"So would I."

"I'm going to get frustrated."

"So would I," Mark said, his hand still in the air.

"I'm going to break down," Derek said quieter.

"So would I," Mark said, and instead of shaking his hand, he hugged Derek, who broke down in sobs.

"I don't want to do this. I'm not strong enough for this."

"You are, or God would not have given this to you. He gives the toughest battles to His strongest soldiers," he said, as Derek wiped his face off, and Mark moved back to his chair.

"There are days I wish I wasn't so strong."

"Those who you've rescued or helped over the years are grateful you're so strong," Mark countered.

"I may yell at you."

"Bring it on, brother," Mark said with a smile. "We've been through worse."

"You're not going to let me out of this, are you?"

Shaking his head, Mark said, "Not a chance."

"Fine," Derek said in a sigh.

"Remember, our motto: '*Blood doesn't make family, love makes family.*'"

"All right," Derek relented, "Let's start with you finding me a cute nurse to help me out."

Laughing, Mark said, "Now, *that* I can do."

*   *   *

Back at the Haven, the injured finally arrived to a hero's welcome. During the party that Casey, Kit, Rachel, Leah, and Liliya set up, Liliya pulled Jon aside.

"What's up?" Jon asked, as they went out to the back deck, away from the noise from inside.

Sitting on the bench beside Jon, Liliya said, "Katia trusts you."

"That's a good thing, right?" Jon asked, leaning against the railing.

"She does not trust easily."

Watching her nervously fiddle with her napkin for a moment, Jon finally asked, "What's on your mind?"

"A lot."

"I can feel the anxiety and stress. While I can feel the emotions, I don't have the benefit of knowing what's causing them."

"When Angel and I talked, she made the story of Jesus clear. I understood what I was praying for."

"Good."

"Being in the caves, it became more real than I imagined."

"Yeah, I can see that. Seeing real angels and demons for the first time is a terrifying thing," Jon agreed.

Snapping her fingers to come up with the right words, she finally admitted, "I do not know how to say this."

"Just do your best. We'll sort through it."

"How do I go on from here? I know Jesus died for me. I know He rose from the grave on day three. I know from deep inside that He did it for me. I just do not know if I did it because I did not want to go to hell, or because I truly believed. When I talk to Katia, it seems more…what's the word? Oh! Personal."

"That's because it's not a religion, it's a relationship. It's great that you know all of what you know about Jesus here," Jon pointed to his head, "But do you know Him here?" he asked, pointing to his own heart. "The biggest difference between religion and relationship is eighteen inches."

"How do I move from here," she asked, pointing to her own head, "to here?" she asked, pointing to her own heart.

"Let's walk through this."

"Okay," Liliya said uneasily.

"Relax," Jon chuckled. "You'll be just fine."

"Okay," she said, a little more relaxed.

"Who is Jesus?"

"He is the Son of God."

"Can you go a little deeper?"

"He came from Heaven to be a sacrifice for all of us, so when we die, we do not have to go to hell."

"Good. When you say He was a sacrifice, what does that mean?"

"There was a raid in a garden."

"The Garden of Gethsemane," Jon filled in for her.

"Right," she said, grateful. "After that, He was innocent, but they put Him on trial. Even though He was not guilty, the people demanded He die on the cross."

"Do you believe that?" Jon asked.

"Yes."

"Romans 10:9 tells us, *'If you declare with your mouth, "Jesus is Lord," and believe in your heart that God raised Him from the dead, you will be saved.'*"

"Right. I did that with Angel in Russia."

"Well, in Matthew 16:24-26, it says, *'Then Jesus said to His disciples, "Whoever wants to be my disciple must deny themselves and take up their cross and follow me. For whoever wants to save their life, will lose it, but whoever loses their life for Me will find it. What good will it be for someone to gain the whole world, yet forfeit their soul? Or what can anyone give in exchange for their soul?"'* This isn't a one-time decision, and then you just keep living your life the way you did before you asked Jesus to forgive you of your sins, and for the eternal life granted to you by His sacrifice. It's a relationship with Jesus Christ. It's a daily walk with Him. Just like you want to talk to Katia all the time, He wants to have that same relationship with you, only deeper."

"Deeper than my sister?" she asked, surprised. "How is this possible? Katia has been here my entire life."

"He's not only been with you for your entire life, He was there before you were even in the womb. He knows you better than you even know yourself. He also knows what it's like to live this life as a human. He knows what it's like to be tempted. He suffered when He came to Earth. He also lived and loved His friends. He's walked this path. He wants to help you walk it successfully. The only way to do that is to have a relationship. Without that relationship, you won't know when the Spirit is trying to talk to you."

"I see."

"You have a fresh start here in the States. No one knows of your past. Even we don't know it all…only what you tell us. Take this opportunity to make changes in your life – changes that will bring you closer to God. You asked how to make it personal, like Katia has? You do it by taking the steps to *make* it personal. I'll tell you what, let's start with baby steps."

"How do I take these baby steps?"

"You have a Bible, right?"

"Yes. Casey gave me one when I came here."

"Good. In the table of contents, it lists the books of the Bible, along with their page number. Look up a book called Proverbs. There are thirty-one chapters in this book, just like there are thirty-one days in the longest months. Read the chapter that coincides with the date. Each day you read, pick out a verse that stands out to you. Then write down why it stands out to you."

"I do not have a notebook."

"I'll have Mom get you one. She homeschools the wonder twins. I'm sure there are notebooks all over this place."

"Okay."

"When you finish, take some time to talk to Jesus."

"How?"

"Remember when you prayed with Angel?"

"Yes."

"Just like that."

"But, how do I do this each day. I do not know what words to say."

Jon shrugged. "Say what's in your heart."

Liliya shook her head. "I do not know."

"What *do* you know?"

"I know we are back to from here," she pointed to her head, "to here," she pointed to her heart.

Jon nodded in understanding. "Back to where we started." Praying in his head for the right words, he said, "Do you love your sister?"

"Yes."

"When you say that, I don't feel anything from you."

"That is because I do not feel."

"Well, you *do,* it's just not always a good feeling."

"Not usually," Liliya agreed.

"You don't feel deep emotions?"

"I was not allowed to in the orphanage."

"I can see that. I have a feeling that's where we should start. If you can't feel with all of your heart, how are you supposed to have a healthy relationship with anyone?"

"Good question."

"Let's see if we can work on getting a good answer."

Chapter 8
May He Give You the Desires Of Your Heart

Driving through the Outback with extra gas cans on their vehicles, the team was spread between three Jeeps. This left plenty of room for supplies spread between the Jeeps as well. Jesse, Nico, and Charlie were the drivers. They were divided with Jesse, Delaney and Joe in one; Charlie, Jacob, and Katia in the second; and Nico, Sasha, and the archangel (dressed in khaki clothing, with his sword still on his hip) in the third Jeep.

"I must say this is definitely a different experience. I've never chauffeured an archangel before," Nico said in a chuckle.

"This is not new for me. I have been in a vehicle before," the archangel said, watching three kangaroos hopping through a field, heading for a partially dried up waterhole.

"Deep in the sweltering heat of the Outback?" Nico asked.

"I was out here with Kit at one point, if you recall," the archangel reminded him.

"Too true, but if I remember right, Kit said you were riding a horse."

"I was. This is just another form of transportation."

"Have to ask," Sasha said, "If you are the archangel of God, why do you not just go in and get Angel?"

"This is a part of Jesse and Angel's journey they must walk."

"I see. Are we all to take this journey with them?" Sasha asked.

"You all are part of each other's journey," the archangel clarified. "Each one of you has a journey. Each journey will lead you down the path the Lord has for you. Each path that your team members take will intertwine with each other, making you a stronger team."

"So, that is a yes. Now I understand why people get annoyed when they converse with you," Sasha said in a sigh. "You are frustrating."

Chuckling, the archangel just shook his head.

Letting out a slow breath of air, Nico commented, "This is going to be a long drive."

*   *   *

Calliope walked into the cavern that held Angel. "Good morning, darling."

Looking up, Angel was too exhausted to speak by that point. Barely getting a wink of sleep over the last several days, she was hearing and seeing things, and wasn't quite sure if anything she saw at that point was real or not. Half the time, it seemed things were not real. She didn't trust her own mind and wasn't sure how much more she could take.

Along with the lack of sleep, the continuous screaming and screeching of the demons assigned to watch her and keep her awake, and the limited food and water, Angel's body continuously shook beyond her control. They would also show her visions of her fellow A.N.G.E.L.s dying over and over again, along with various other visions of her teammates doing nefarious actions, to the point that she questioned her own memory.

"Go ahead and cut her loose," Calliope ordered.

As soon as they released her, Angel collapsed onto the ground, kicking up the dirt around her. When her head hit the ground, she inhaled the dust. Coughing, she slowly sat up. She would have brushed the dirt off, but she struggled to even sit up. She did have the energy to glare at Calliope with distain. That was something she knew she would never be too tired to do.

Crouching in front of Angel so she was eye-to-eye with her, Calliope explained, "Guess what today is?"

Angel just shook her head in response.

Raising Angel's chin to make sure Angel was looking at her, Calliope sneered. When Angel tried to pull away from her, Calliope grabbed her chin, forcing Angel to look at her. "Tsk, tsk, young one. I come to bring you good news," Calliope explained. "You should be grateful, not the spoiled brat you have become. You see, your so-called friends are coming to get you, and they're bringing that annoying archangel with them. Cassius has decided to release you."

Cocking her head to the side, Angel tried to figure out Calliope's angle.

Crossing her arms, resting them on her knees, Calliope went on, "It seems your teammates have been through enough. *And*, it seems, so have you. Cassius feels that you may still –"

Calliope was cut off by Jesse running in with Nico and Sasha behind him. Grabbing Angel, Jesse scooped her off the ground, and immediately placed a knife to her throat, while Nico and Sasha held the others at gunpoint.

"Jesse?" Angel asked, wide-eyed and frantic.

"Because of your antics, Danny was killed, and Derek was paralyzed! I've had *enough*!" Jesse growled.

Angel took a deep breath. Looking toward heaven, she heard Ephesians 1:17-18 go through her mind, *"That the God of our Lord Jesus Christ, the Father of glory, may give to you a spirit of wisdom and of revelation in the knowledge of Him. I pray that the eyes of your heart may be enlightened, so that you will know what is the hope of His calling, what are the riches of the glory of His inheritance in the saints."*

Angel closed her eyes. The anger built up inside her to the point that she thought she would explode. Opening her eyes, she glared at Calliope, and shouted, "NO MORE!"

"No more, what, dear?" Calliope asked innocently, with her hands in the air.

"I SAID, NO MORE!" Angel roared, at the top of her lungs. Throat dry, lips parched, she formed the words, as tears crawled down her cheeks. "NO MORE!" she shouted again. "NO-MORE!"

Right before her eyes, Nico, Jesse, and Sasha dissipated. As the ash drifted slowly to the ground, Angel balled her fists at her sides, not backing down.

"Calm down, sweetheart."

"I am *not* your sweetheart!" Angel yelled.

Putting her hands in front of her to block Angel from coming at her, Calliope took a couple cautious steps back. The anger toward her was overpowering.

Keeping an eye on the two demons with Calliope, Angel centered on taking Calliope out. She had enough!

As a demon took a step toward Angel, Angel spun toward it, growling, she then repeated, "NO MORE!"

The demon looked at Calliope, who shook her head for it not to do anything. The demon just put its hands in the air, taking a couple steps back, giving Angel space.

Angel walked toward the entrance of the cavern. Stopping at the threshold, she turned, daring the trio to make an attempt to stop her. "No more," she said sternly.

The demons looked to Calliope for direction. Calliope, keeping her hands in the air, shook her head again, signaling them to not challenge Angel. Calliope recognized that they had pushed her beyond her breaking point. What Angel was capable of at that moment, remained to be seen.

Taking brave steps forward, Angel made her way through the cave system. As she passed each group surrounding the fires, no one moved. Stunned at seeing her walk freely, yet as rigid as she moved, fists still balled at her sides, no one challenged her.

Walking out of the entrance of the cave system, the cool, fresh, night air hit her face, stinging her parched lips. Her bare feet didn't even feel the rocks below them, as she took each brave step forward. Turning back to make sure she was not followed, she continued out into the wilderness, unafraid at that point. Nothing else could be as bad as what she just went through.

*   *   *

Sitting with the group around the night fire, Jesse flipped a coal back into it.

"You know, it doesn't take Jon's gift to see and feel how angry you are," Delaney pointed out.

Jesse just looked at her, rolling his eyes.

"Really?" Joe crossed his arms. "I understand you're angry, but –"

"But nothing!" Jesse stood. "Because of her actions, Danny is dead, and Derek is paralyzed for the rest of his life."

"Technically, Derek is paralyzed because your team ignored the signs we were sending for you to not go in," the archangel corrected.

"You!" Jesse pointed to him. "I don't want to hear another word from *you*!"

"Jesse!" Nico stood, getting between the archangel and Jesse, as the archangel just sat calmly in his place. "That is extremely disrespectful!"

"He knows why I'm angry at him," Jesse said, crossing his arms, almost holding himself.

"Do we need to take a walk?" the archangel offered.

"I don't want to go anywhere with you."

Turning to the archangel, Nico asked, "Can you alert the Haven to have Rachel call Jesse's phone?"

"I can do that," the archangel nodded. He disappeared for a brief moment, before reappearing back to his original position, sitting on the ground with his legs stretched out in front of him. "She will be informed to contact you in a minute," the archangel said to Jesse. "I highly suggest you speak with her in a lot nicer tone than you have us for the last few days. She does not tolerate disrespectful behavior at all."

"I know Rachel just as well as you do," Jesse pointed out.

"I doubt that. I have been around her since the day she was born."

"Keep it up!" Jesse warned.

"Go take a walk, but don't get lost," Nico said. When Jesse didn't move, Nico added, "*Now!*"

"Fine," Jesse said, and slowly walked away from camp. Keeping an eye out in every direction, he finally rested on a big rock about fifty yards from the campsite, waiting to hear from Rachel.

*   *   *

"Rach?" Kit said, gently shaking Rachel.

"What? Who? What's going on? What time is it?" Rachel asked, groggy.

"Shh! Don't wake Leah," Kit whispered.

"What time is it?"

"Five o'clock in the morning."

"*Why* are you waking me up?" she asked. Then a thought hit her that quickly sobered her. "Did something happen to Dad, Josh, or Jesse?" As her eyes adjusted, she noticed who was standing next to her mother. "Is that an angel?" Panicked, she asked again, "Did something happen to Dad, Josh, or Jesse?"

"Shhhh!" Kit hushed her. "No. Now, please quiet down before you wake –"

"Forget it, Mum. I'm awake. Please go with her, Rach, so I can go back to sleep?" Leah asked, cutting her mom off.

"Let's go downstairs," Kit suggested. "I'm going to have to wake Kai too."

"I would wake Cori. Kai is *not* a morning person," Rachel said, grabbing her robe as they headed out the door. "Cori is a lot more pleasant. Just don't irritate Charm."

As Kit went to get Cori and Charm, Rachel and the angel went downstairs. "What's going on?" she asked the angel.

"I have been sent with a message for you to call Jesse."

Furrowing her brow, Rachel asked, "Why? Is he in trouble?"

"He is regarding his heart. His mind and heart are full of anger," the angel explained. "Cori will need to do her work so you may speak to him."

Hearing shuffling on the stairs, and the jingle of Charm's collar, Rachel looked over to see Cori and Charm come down the stairs with Kit. "Give me a few minutes," Cori said, walking straight through the living room as if she could see, straight to the door of the basement.

"I don't know how she does it," Kit commented, stopping at the couch.

"I count the steps," Cori said, heading down the stairs to the cyber cave. "Remember, no matter how quietly you talk, I can still hear you. I'll have him on the line in a few minutes, luv," she said to Rachel.

"I'll be there shortly," Rachel said. Turing back to the angel, she asked, "Is there anything I need to know before I get on the phone with him?"

"As I stated, he has a lot of anger in his heart," the angel explained.

"Think about it, Rach," Kit said. "Losing Danny? Having to watch Derek suffering in a cave, not being able to do anything to help him? Then, finding out he'll be paralyzed for life? That's not to mention all those we have here who are wounded. And, all of this could have been avoided if Angel had included everyone in the team in trying to rescue Liliya, instead of taking matters into her own hands. He has a right to be angry."

"While he does, the Lord is the One who is in control," the angel reminded them. "The Lord is never caught by surprise by a person's actions."

"At this point, I think the consequences to Angel's actions are more what is on his mind," Rachel pointed out.

"Which is the point of the call," the angel explained. "He cannot have a clear mind to rescue Angel with all of that anger in him."

"Not to mention to whom it's directed," Kit added. "I understand he's taking it out on the archangel."

"Right-oh," Rachel said, slowly standing. Still a little tender from her healing ribs, she made her way down to the cyber cave, just as Cori dialed Jesse's phone.

"Hello?" Jesse answered from deep in the Outback.

"Jesse?" Cori asked, while Rachel took a seat next to her.

"Yes. Cori?"

"Yeah."

"The archangel said Rachel would be calling."

"I'm here, mate," Rachel said. Turning to Cori, she asked, "How do I hang up?"

"Just click this, and then close all the windows. I will warn you that you will be limited to ten minutes," Cori cautioned.

"After that, certain alarms may go off, and it might get traced. So, be off in eight."

"Gotcha," Rachel said, taking note of the time. "Go back to bed."

"Thanks, luv," she said standing to go. "C'mon, Charm," she called to her black lab.

With that, Cori left the basement for upstairs, and Rachel was alone with Jesse. "Jesse?" Rachel asked. "What's going on?"

Taking a deep breath, Jesse slowly let it out. "You have no idea how good it is to hear your voice."

"Oh, I have a pretty good idea," Rachel countered. "I had t' watch you get caught in a cave-in from the explosions. Then, pray as Jacob blasted you out. That's not to mention that I haven't been able t' talk to you at all."

"Calm down," Jesse said, hearing the stress in her voice. "I understand."

"No. I don't think you do!" Rachel said, anxiety taking over. "I've had to sit here, doing abso-bloody-lutely nothing but praying, while I watched and heard all of you going through what you went through. I felt absolutely helpless!"

"Rachel." Jesse couldn't help the chuckle that escaped him. "You're supposed to be talking *me* down."

"Now you're bloody laughing at me!"

"Watch it. I know you're crew doesn't like that kind of language."

Slowly letting out a breath of air to calm herself, Rachel said, "You're right. Mum and Pop would both reprimand me."

"That's better."

"Well, getting woken by Mum and an angel didn't help matters. I wasn't sure *what* was going on."

"I'm sure that was a shock," he said, chuckling again at imagining Rachel's face when she woke.

"Stop laughing at me!"

"I can't help it. This is the first time in days that I *have* laughed."

"Where's your mind been?" Rachel asked.

"Not in a good place," Jesse admitted.

"Talk to me."

"I don't even know where to start, but I'm pretty sure it'll take more than the ten minutes we have."

"Seven and a half," Rachel corrected. "You have to be focused enough to get Angel. Now, tell me your thoughts on Danny and Derek?"

"While it *is* about Danny and Derek, the bigger part of it is actually Angel herself. She fought her team for days before she finally overruled them and got us all into this mess."

"Pride goes before the fall," Rachel said in a sigh.

"I agree. However, because of her actions, there have been multiple injuries. Some are serious, critical, and even fatal. She's going to have to answer for those."

"While she does, it may have to be by someone not as biased as you," Rachel pointed out.

"Then Josh, Jon, and Val can't either. They're the ones she fought."

"Agreed."

"But, she *will* have to answer for them. She can't be going around doing whatever she wants, whenever she wants. This is a team. It's a unit. She's not operating with that thought in mind."

"I agree."

"I am *so* grateful I'm in your unit," Jesse sighed.

"So, what's your plan to get her out?"

"Not sure. The archangel's with us right now. He's been traveling with us."

"Seriously?" Rachel asked, stunned.

"Yep. In khakis and everything…complete with his sword at his waist." Jesse chuckled again. "It would be almost comical if we weren't in the situation we're in." When Rachel laughed, he continued, "Seriously! He sits in the back of the Jeep with his arms stretched out on either side of him as if he's the king, while Nico drives. Imagine it! Right now he's sitting in front of the fire with his legs sticking out in front of him.

You would think he was a regular human…until you catch sight of his wings, the sword, or he opens his mouth."

"Wow! I know this is big, but this must be *really* big."

"This *whole thing* has been really big! What she did has worldwide ramifications. It not only affected her team, but also the retired folks, the Australian unit, and our team as well. Danny Hawk was taken out because of her actions. Do you understand that?"

"Jesse, Danny was *my* mentor," Rachel reminded him. "That would be like Derek being taken from you. I, along with Josh, *fully* comprehend the loss of Danny."

"You're right. I'm sorry."

"You're going to have to get a grip on your emotions until you can deal with them back here at the Haven."

"I know. That's why I'm talking to you. It seems I snapped at Delaney –"

"You snapped at *Delaney*?" Rachel asked stunned, cutting him off. "That's like snapping at a puppy!"

"Trust me, I actually made Joe mad."

"You made *Joe* mad? I didn't think that was possible! You *really* need to get a grip! You upset the two people I didn't think was possible!"

"Again…why do you think I'm on the phone with you?"

"Jesse," Rachel said, calmer, "you were trained to be an A.N.G.E.L. since you were young. You know what comes with the territory. You chose to answer the call from the Lord with a 'yes.'"

"Okay, tell me something I don't know."

"I know your heart. I also know this isn't you. You are strong, but you have a forgiving spirit."

"Everyone reaches their breaking point."

"Can you not imagine that after everything she has been through, that she hasn't learned her lesson? When you *do* get her out – and you will – I can't imagine what shape she'll be in. It couldn't have been a picnic for her."

"No, I would think not."

"Liliya's still having nightmares. Angel's probably been in survival mode since she was taken."

"I've just seen her get away with so much growing up. This is big. I want her to have to face this."

"I'm sure you do. Let's get her home to the Haven before we attempt to hold her accountable for her actions. There's a ton of heart work going on over here. There's anger, hurt, even betrayal."

"Betrayal?"

"Josh, Jon, and Val feel that as their leader, she betrayed the team."

"Wow. I never thought of it that way."

"Trust me. There's a lot going on in everyone's mind. First and foremost is the safety of Angel."

"I just don't want people to overlook her actions in response to her actually being back."

"Trust me. That will *not* be a problem," Rachel said. "Looking around here, it looks like everyone's been through a battle…which they have. This battle, though, goes deeper than the physical. The emotional battles raging will all need to be addressed if we are to become united teams once again."

"All right," Jesse agreed.

"You can do this," Rachel encouraged.

"Just keep praying for us. Pretty sure we're going to need it. This crew is half experienced, half inexperienced."

"To say the least. And, you always have my prayers."

"I would say I wish you were here, but I don't think it would be good for you."

Rachel chuckled. "No. Not yet."

"I love you, Rachel."

"I know. You know how I feel about you too."

"I do."

"Good. Now, go get your sister, so you guys can all get back here safely. We're nearing our time limit."

"Okay."

"Be safe."

"Thank you," Jesse said, and hung up. Looking toward the group, he knew he would have to apologize before anything else was said, but at least he knew his heart was finally in the right place.

*   *   *

"What are you still doing up?" Rachel asked, coming up stairs to the living room after shutting the computer down.

"I thought we should talk," Kit said, patting the seat next to her on the couch. "Since the zoo is currently asleep, we have the place to ourselves," she said, lovingly referring to the crowd of injured A.N.G.E.L.s from the two units, along with the others who lived there. There had also been several A.N.G.E.L.s from throughout the world who started arriving the day after Danny's death. They were fortunately staying at a hotel in Reno. They would come over during the daytime hours to help out with all those injured, as well as cooking and cleaning. Kit was glad she came. Casey would definitely have had her hands full without help!

"What do you want to talk about?" Rachel asked, settling down next to her mom on the couch, wrapping up in a blanket.

"Well, let's start with Danny."

"Let's not," Rachel pleaded.

"Rach, he was close to our entire family. He was as close to family as any of the station hands…and you *know* they are all treated like family."

"I do," she said, wrapping her arms around her legs, as she dropped her chin onto her knees.

"He, Ethan, and Charlie trained all four of you. He poured his life and experience into you."

"Mum, with all due respect, please stop. I don't want to have to work through this right now."

"Okay, then what about Jesse?"

"What *about* Jesse?" Rachel sat up, taken aback by the turn of the conversation.

"You know you are in love with each other," Kit pointed out.

"Mum," Rachel rolled her eyes, "I can't have a relationship with someone on my team. The others may think I'm biased."

"Pretty sure they already operate as if you two are together. They're not blind, sweetheart," Kit said, resting her hand on Rachel's hands.

"No, but I have been keeping him at arm's reach. We haven't crossed any lines."

"Why not? It's obvious to everyone that you two should be together."

"Mum, I *really* don't want to do this right now."

"Why not? It's just the two of us."

"Because we have way too much going on around here to deal with it right now."

"Honey, God wants you to have the desires of your heart. Why can you not lead a team and have a relationship at the same time?"

"Because I would feel compromised! Besides, what if it doesn't work?"

"You practically live together! Obviously, there are others with you, but you get what I'm saying. You would know by now if it wasn't going to work. None of the personalities on the teams are enough to push you to potentially break up," Kit pointed out.

"What if we don't have chemistry? It would be extremely awkward."

"Have you two touched yet?"

"Yes," Rachel admitted, blushing.

"Have you, um, kissed yet?"

"No!" Rachel looked up, stunned. "I would never!"

"Why not?"

"Mum!"

"You two are young and in love. Why not?"

"Because I am team lead. I can't have my mind distracted."

"Oh, honestly, Rachel! I almost lost your dad with that line of thinking. You need to seize the moment!"

"I'll think and pray about it."

"Code for no?"

"Not necessarily. I'll leave that up to God," Rachel said, resting her head on the back of the couch as she yawned.

"The sun is coming up already," Kit observed out the back glass door. "Want to go out onto the back deck?"

"Sure."

As the two made their way outside, they sat down on a couple of the deck chairs turned toward the rising sun, wrapped in blankets. As the moon said goodbye, the majestic colors of light blue, bright magenta, and orange appeared on the horizon, before exploding into rusty colors of peach and gold. As the moments passed, and the sun came up over the mountains, shifting the colors to red, before turning a royal gold. As the sun came up, and the night faded, the brighter it got around them.

Kit sighed, "I do miss watching the sunrises."

"You get up early on the station," Rachel pointed out.

"Not really. Willow usually sets a plate aside for me, and when I get up, I eat."

"You never slept in before."

"I've been a bit more tired lately."

Looking at her mother, she noticed Kit a little more pale than usual. "Are you feeling okay?"

"Not really," Kit admitted.

"Is there something you want to tell me?"

"Not really," Kit said again.

"Mum?" Rachel asked, heart racing. "What's going on?"

"I've not been feeling well lately. That's all."

"Do Leah and Willow know?"

"Yes."

"*What* do they know?" Rachel pressed.

"They know I've been making a lot of extra trips to the doctor lately."

"For what? And, does Pop know?"

"Your dad knew I had some blood work done."

Sitting up in her chair, Rachel stiffened. Sternly, she insisted, "Mum, what is going on?"

Looking out at the sunrise, Kit admitted, "The doctor had me take some tests the day before I left Australia to confirm what a couple other doctors have said. I didn't want to tell your dad, because I wanted him to focus on getting everyone home. I heard from my primary doctor yesterday."

"And?" Rachel pushed.

"Well, at first they thought I was a touch anemic, but it turns out I may have inherited something from my mother."

"Mum, your mum died of leukemia."

Kit just looked up at Rachel, whose face registered understanding almost immediately as she went pale.

Rachel gulped. "Leukemia?" she squeaked out.

"The doctor wants me back home. He wants to begin treatment immediately."

"What does he think about recovery?"

"He has high hopes for remission, but that will be entirely up to the Lord," Kit said. "I will fight this. If I make it through, great! If I don't, I will see you when you join me later in Heaven. I know where I'm going, and I'm okay with going, whenever the Lord decides I'm done here on this earth."

Tears brimmed her eyes, as Rachel's bottom lip trembled. Shaking her head, Rachel begged, "Please tell me this isn't true?"

"Rachel," Kit rested her hand on Rachel's shoulder, "you are a strong young lady, or God would not have chosen you for this position. Having said that, I want you to be happy. I want to face this, knowing you are happy in what you are doing, and confident in your decisions. If you are tortured on whether or not to pursue things with Jesse, then you are not happy. You may have to rethink your current course. God wants you to have your heart's desire. So do your father and I."

"I know." Rachel sniffed, wiping away the tears. "This just isn't fair! I am giving myself to work for the Lord. Why would He do this now?"

"Rachel, His timing is not our timing. We may not always understand His timing either."

Standing, Rachel wrapped the blanket tighter around her body. "This isn't right! This isn't fair!"

Kit stood to give Rachel a hug, but Rachel took off into the house before she could grab her. Sighing, Kit sunk back down into her chair, and wrapped back up in her blanket. "Help her, Lord. Help her to understand that it is Your will, not mine, and that my soul rests in You…no matter what."

Chapter 9
Create In Me A Pure Heart

Stumbling with bare feet through the cold night air of the Outback in the silver sequined dress she put on that afternoon so long ago in Russia, Angel struggled to see clearly. Suffering from lack of food, water, and sleep, she only knew she wanted to put as much distance between her and the caves of the other side as possible.

Having no idea of what direction to head, she looked up toward the heavens and asked, "Lord, You clearly got me out of there. How about some direction?

Looking out at the vast expanse before her of desert lands, a chill went down her spine. *Could she have survived weeks of torture just to die in this godforsaken desert?*

"Please let me hear your voice?" Angel begged, shuffling through the desert in an inch of rocks and pebbles that cut her feet with each step. She stopped being able to feel them a few hours ago. Dropping to her hands and knees, she grasped handfuls of dirt. Throwing it away from herself, she screamed at the top of her lungs in frustration.

* * *

"What was that?" Katia asked, alarmed.

"That is not a normal sound out here," Charlie pointed out.

"Was that a big cat of some kind?" Jacob asked. "Do they have them out here?"

"*That* was Angel," the archangel simply said, slowly standing. Dusting himself off, he added, "Looks like she has been rescued after all."

"Did I hear you say that was *Angel*?" Jesse asked, finally rejoining the group.

"Yes."

"What direction did that come from?" Joe asked, not wanting to acknowledge that the scream sounded terrifying.

"Angel!" Everyone started yelling, as they went away from the fire.

"Shhh! If we're all shouting, we won't hear her," Jesse pointed out.

*   *   *

Hearing shouts in the distance, Angel's ears perked. Standing, she wavered in her place as she looked further ahead…and saw a fire in the distance. Unsure of how far away it was, she slowly stumbled forward, closing the gap as she focused on the fire. Not caring that the rocks were still cutting the bottoms of her feet, she pushed on. Her salvation, she hoped, was a short distance away!

*   *   *

"Okay, go for another round," Jesse instructed.

As they went a little further from the fire, the group shouted as loud as they could for a moment before listening again.

*   *   *

"I can't yell!" Angel cried to God, tears pouring from her eyes. Pushing, she prayed the group of people would not stop shouting. As long as they continued to shout, she knew she was still alive. She knew if they heard her, it wasn't fake…at least she prayed it wasn't another fake moment from the other side. At that point, she wasn't sure what was real, and what was not. If she made her way to the fire, and this wasn't real, she knew she would probably lose it completely!

*   *   *

"That way," the archangel said, seeing a wobbly figure in the distance. "I'll go get her," he said, and disappeared from the group.

*   *   *

Appearing in front of her, the archangel looked at her for a moment. "Angel?"

Seeming to study the archangel for a second, Angel slowly nodded. "Are you real?" she asked, unsure.

"Yes. Can I take you to the others?"

Looking in the distance, Angel's heart raced. "I want to, but I don't want to."

"I do not understand."

"I want to get out of here, but I know I royally messed up."

"For that, you *will* have to face the consequences. However, there are many people who just want you home. You are in desperate need of medical, hydration and nutritional assistance."

"I know. I just…" Angel said, and then collapsed.

The archangel barely caught her before Angel hit the ground. Scooping her up in his arms, he disappeared from their current position, reappearing next to the fire. "Angel is here," the archangel announced, as they were on the ground. Tapping her face, he asked, "Angel?"

Everyone spun around, facing him. Unsure of what they were looking at, Jesse asked, "Is she…?"

"She is alive. She is in need of water, food, and medical attention."

"We have two choices." Charlie suggested, "We can go to my clan, where she can get the attention she needs, or we can take her to the hospital in Alice Springs, where they can take care of her as well."

"And answer more questions?" Jesse shook his head. "How far out is your clan?"

"About two hours by Jeep from here."

"Done. Let's load up. Charlie, you lead," Jesse said decisively. "We don't need anymore attention."

*   *   *

Curled up on her bed, hugging her pillow, Rachel quietly cried to herself.

"You know, if you keep that up, we may never get any sleep," Leah finally said, breaking the silence.

"Did you know?" Rachel asked, wiping her face as she sat up in bed.

Rolling toward Rachel, Leah explained, "We had an idea, but Mum confirmed it yesterday. It was our fear, especially knowing it's in the family history."

"How am I supposed to help Jesse with his anger, when I have some of my own?"

"Why are you angry?" Leah asked, moving over to the side of Rachel's bed. "I would think you would be more upset than angry."

"I'm angry, because I am giving possibly the last years I will have on this earth with my mother to fight for the Lord. I would *think* that would garner a little favor in keeping my family safe."

"We are never safe." Leah shook her head. "We live in Australia, where everything is trying to kill you."

"This is true," Rachel said, laughing and crying at the same time. Wiping the tears from her cheeks, she shook her head. "I don't want to lose Mum."

"Who said we were going to lose her? The doctor is optimistic about her prognosis."

"I'm sure he told her that to be kind."

"Oh no." Leah shook her head. "Trust me. I made sure to grill him. He showed me the charts and tests. I had Mum get testing done at a couple different doctors in order to make sure it was accurate. Her primary doctor called yesterday with the final conclusion."

"Has she heard back from all of them?"

"Yes. They all said the same thing."

"That's unique," Rachel said, tongue-in-cheek.

"That's how I know it's accurate."

"I see," Rachel said, straightening the covers. "I guess I have some heart work to do with God."

"You, and just about everyone in this house. Then there's the Outback crew. There's no telling what's going on out there right now."

"I'm sure Kai or Cori will get ahold of them later to find out. In the meantime, why don't we head downstairs and get breakfast going?" Leah suggested. "Casey's got her hands full around here."

"And with more coming in the next few weeks, it's only going to get busier. It's a good thing I'm feeling better."

"Just don't push yourself," Leah warned. "If you do, it may take longer for you to get back out to the field."

"I don't know if I'm going back out."

"What?" Leah looked at her, stunned. "What do you mean?"

"If Mum's really sick, I don't know if I can go out into the field right now. I feel like my place is with her at the station."

"We can handle it."

"I don't doubt that, but she's my mum too."

"You have a higher calling. Mum understands this. We do too. You and Josh got the call. We didn't."

"I don't care right now. I care about Mum! I care that she may potentially die, and I may not be there. I want to be there for her."

"This is a long journey. And, it's just beginning. What if I keep you updated? What if I make sure you know what's going on, and if things seem the least bit scary, I'll let you know?" Leah offered.

"I don't know." Rachel shook her head. Pulling her knees up, she wrapped her arms around them, and dropped her chin onto her knees. "All I know is there is a lot going on in my brain and heart, and I don't know if I can do this right now."

"This sounds like a crisis of the heart."

"This *is* a crisis of the heart."

"I think you have a lot of praying to do," Leah said, getting off the bed. "Do you want a distraction, or do you want some time to yourself?"

"Probably some time. Do you know when Mum's leaving for Australia?"

"I don't, but I can find out."

"Please? In the meantime, I think I just need some time alone. If there are any updates from the team, please let me know as soon as possible."

"Will do," Leah said, sliding into her slippers while putting on her robe. Then she left for the kitchen.

Rachel took a deep, cleansing breath. Looking toward Heaven, she said, "Father, we need to chat."

*　　*　　*

Even deeper in the Outback than they already were, the three Jeeps pulled up to an open area, cluttered with makeshift houses of wood, mud, and thatch. Several men poked their heads out of their homes, as it was around midnight.

Charlie threw his Jeep in park before jumping out of the driver's seat. Gesturing for everyone to stay in their seats, Charlie ran over to the group of men from the clan. Talking in their own language, Charlie explained the situation to them.

"Looks like the men are going to get some women to help with Angel," Delaney said quietly to Joe, as she continued to strain to listen.

"I love that you can understand what everyone is saying," Joe said with a smirk.

"There are times where it's a curse," she admitted. "By the way, thank you for standing up to Jesse for me."

Joe shrugged it off. "Anytime."

"Well," Delaney looked down for a moment before she glanced back up to Joe, and said, "I've never had a guy stick up for me like that."

"Then, you've run into the wrong guys, darlin'," Joe said, resting his arm across Delaney's shoulders. When she nudged into him, he gave her a squeeze. "Charlie's coming back," he said, seeing Charlie jogging back over to the Jeep.

"In order to not wake the entire clan, we need to park over there." Charlie nodded toward another open area with vehicles. Pulling over to the area with the other two Jeeps behind, Charlie shut his off, and ran back to Nico's Jeep. "Will you follow me with her?" he asked the archangel.

"Yes."

While he got out, Charlie said to Nico, "Keep everyone else over here. I'll come get you once I get Angel settled."

Nico nodded in response as he shut his Jeep off as well. With all three Jeeps shut off, Nico sat for a moment trying to wrap his brain around what actually happened.

After Charlie, the archangel, and Angel left for one of the homes, Nico gathered the others together. "We need to wait here for Charlie," he explained.

"I don't mean to be cruel, but Angel looked *really* rough!" Jacob pointed out.

Delaney shuddered. "Yeah. It looks like she has hundreds of cuts all over her. That's not even mentioning that she's skin and bones, and she looks like she hasn't slept in weeks. I can't imagine what all she went through."

"She is strong," Sasha said confidently. "She will make it through."

"She will make it through in body, but will she make it through in heart?" Katia asked.

"That's a question for the Lord," Nico said. Glancing at Jesse out of the corner of his eye, he said, "You've been mighty quiet, mate. Wanna tell us what's going through your mind?"

Jesse leaned against the Jeep. Crossing his arms, he responded with a, "Nope."

"Fair enough. You'll have to eventually."

"At this point, she's getting the help she needs. That's all that matters."

"That is not *all* that matters," Katia disagreed. "*Your* heart matters too."

Silence hung in the air after that, until Charlie returned. "Okay. Who wants to sleep?"

"Is that a serious question?" Delaney asked.

"There are a few families shifting around. Give them about thirty minutes, and we'll be able to sleep."

"Great!" Delaney said, stretching and yawning. When she finished, she asked, "What did they say about Angel?"

"She is in bad shape," Charlie admitted. Jesse snapped his head up at hearing that. "She's severely dehydrated. She hasn't eaten a whole lot since she's been taken. She also has cuts and bruises all over her body, along with some broken bones."

"Broken bones?" Katia asked, astonished.

"She has broken ribs, and a broken wrist," Charlie explained.

"I see," Katia said, and went over next to Jesse, leaning on the Jeep. Leaning over, she quietly asked, "Do you want to talk?"

"No," Jesse said. "I think I'm going to take a walk."

"Just be careful, mate. Australia is known for animals that like to kill humans. We have nine out of the ten most deadly snakes in the world here," Nico pointed out.

"And, that's just the snakes," Charlie added. "Take a torch."

"A torch?" Jesse asked.

"Flashlight," Nico said, tossing him one. "There's no cell out here, so don't get lost."

"I'm just going away from camp a bit," Jesse said, and left the others to talk amongst themselves.

Walking out into the openness, the silence almost felt suffocating. With each step, the darkness encased Jesse even more. Feeling the heaviness around him, he wandered just a bit further. This allowed him the opportunity to not be heard from the village, but to still see it.

A million thoughts flew through his mind. The visions of the events since they left for Ireland slammed into his brain, getting worse with each one. Saying good-bye to Rachel at the airport ripped his heart out. Realizing the position that Angel found herself in made him sick to his stomach. Grabbing the limp body of Danny Hawk from Jon, brought Jesse to his knees. Then, when he didn't think he could handle anymore, the scenes from the cave-in hurled toward his mind at lightning speed, sending him into a prostrate position.

"Why?" Jesse shouted, fist rose toward Heaven. Body strained, he let out a growl that ended in a yell of, "ENOUGH!"

Isaiah 41:10 played slowly through his mind. *"So do not fear, for I am with you; do not be dismayed, for I am your God. I will strengthen you and help you; I will uphold you with my righteous right hand."*

"You say that," Jesse said loudly, pointing toward Heaven, "but all that stuff still happened. Where were you when Danny was dying? Where were you when Derek had a massive boulder crush his spine? Where were you when Angel was taken?"

Tears poured down Jesse's cheeks when Jesse heard Psalm 34:17 and 18 in his mind. *"The righteous cry out, and the Lord hears them; He delivers them from all their troubles. The Lord is close to the brokenhearted and saves those who are crushed in spirit."*

"I am crushed! I am broken!" Jesse sobbed. "Let mercy come and wash away everything within me! The anger is powerful! It's taking over everything inside me. I don't-I don't know what to do, Lord." Quieter, Jesse admitted as he continued sobbing, "I don't know what to do, Jesus. I just don't know what to do."

Proverbs 3:5 and 6 crept through as an answer, *"Trust in the Lord with all your heart and lean not on your own understanding; in all your ways acknowledge Him, and He will make your paths straight."*

Jesse nodded in understanding. "I understand You want me to trust you, but my heart is ugly right now. I don't feel worthy. I don't even feel kind right now."

"You are always precious in His sight," the archangel said, appearing behind Jesse.

"I don't want to talk to you right now," Jesse snapped. "I came out here to be alone."

"Your anger is not directed toward me. Your anger is directed toward The Lord, but you do not feel it is right to be angry with Him."

"No. I already told Him I was angry with Him. I'm angry with you too."

"Because human anger does not produce the righteousness that God desires," the archangel reminded him of James 1:20.

Jesse only glared in response.

"In your anger, do not sin: Do not let the sun go down while you are still angry, and do not give the devil a foothold," the archangel quoted Ephesians 4:26 and 27.

"I'm afraid I've already let the sun set on my anger. The question is: How do I get it out of my heart?"

"Ask."

"What do I do with the feelings? They're still there."

Kneeling next to Jesse, the archangel put his hand on Jesse's shoulder. Jesse felt a rush of peace as the archangel explained, "You will have those feelings, but the team needs your strength. Derek, Angel, and the others will look toward you for leadership until the others are back up on their feet. There is more than just you to think about. The team is battered and bruised. They need your strength. You need to be up to the position."

"They can lean on Nico for a bit."

"No. They cannot."

"Why not?"

"Because Nico has to take care of Kit."

Alarmed, Jesse asked, "What's wrong with Kit?"

"She has leukemia."

The words hung in the air for a moment, before Jesse asked, "Does Rachel know?"

"She just found out this morning, after your phone call."

"I see."

"There is much going on that you do not know. Nico is not aware of Kit's condition. They suspect, but he does not know the results of the testing."

"Shouldn't you tell him?"

"That is not for me to tell. An angel spoke with Kit this morning. It was her request that she be the one to tell Nico."

"I understand." Jesse nodded. Looking up at the archangel, he asked, "Will she live?"

"That is not for me to decide."

"Is it for you to *know*?" Jesse asked, irritated.

"I do not."

"With all due respect, do you truly understand how frustrating it is working with you at times?"

Chuckling, the archangel explained, "I am not the Lord Almighty. I have limits to what I can and cannot do. There are times as a team, where working with you is frustrating as well."

"I can see that."

"I do know it is worth it." When the archangel said that, Jesse's heart softened. "There you go," the archangel encouraged. "There will be many situations and scenarios you will go through as an A.N.G.E.L. in this realm. In doing them, there will be a vast amount of emotions you will have to face. Anger will be only one of many. You will face sorrow, heartbreak, and even betrayal, but you will also face true joy, exhilaration, and even love. In facing each of these emotions, you must also be able to continue to do the work before you."

"I *know* what I signed up for. I'm struggling with continuing to do it. I don't know if I can keep doing this knowing I'll keep losing my friends and family."

"You will never truly lose those who are His. You will see them once again when the Kingdom is united."

"I understand that. In the meantime, I have to live with the hole in my heart."

"Then lean on the One who has faced it all as well. Jesus faced everything when He walked among you. He even faced death, and the betrayal from those He held dear – those from His inner circle."

"I understand that. What I don't want to do though, is to go through this for my entire life."

Quoting Matthew 16:24-26, the archangel reminded him, *"Whoever wants to be my disciple must deny themselves and take up their cross and follow me. For whoever wants to save their life, will lose it, but whoever loses their life for Me will find it. What good will it be for someone to gain the whole world, yet forfeit their soul?"*

"I know the verse."

"Then live the verse. Are you willing to lose your life for Him?"

"I am. It's other's lives I'm struggling with."

"That is their own choice. If you chose to leave the A.N.G.E.L.s, that does not mean anyone else will make that choice as well. You may still lose them."

"I understand."

"Life will knock you down regardless if you are an A.N.G.E.L. or not."

"That's comforting."

"You were called, but you always have a choice."

"I know."

"What choice will you make today?"

"That's what I am not sure of."

"Then you need to be sure." Standing, the archangel said, "Let me know your decision. You have until Angel is ready to return to the States."

Still on his knees, Jesse only nodded in response. As the archangel walked back to the others, Jesse looked toward Heaven. With his hands in his lap, feeling defeated, tears streamed down his cheeks. Jesse begged, "Create in me a clean heart, oh God. Show me the direction and plan you have for me. Please forgive me for my anger, resentment, and frustration. Please help me to control my anger. Help me to see things as You do. Help me to make the right decision. I don't think I'm strong enough for this, but obviously You do. You created me. You have a specific plan for me. Even though this looks like it's more than I can handle on my own, I know with You, all things are possible. I know I don't have to be strong enough, because You are strong enough for the both of us. I give up. I've tried doing a lot of this on my own, with you assisting. I now know it is You Who is the One in charge, with *me* assisting. Take over, Lord. Once again, I am Yours. Send me."

Chapter 10
The Lord Looks At The Heart

"She will have a long journey ahead of her," Charlie said, translating for the others as his Chief spoke. The afternoon after bringing her in, the group stood off to the side under a cluster of Boab trees near the village. "She has been through a lot both physically and mentally. We will need to heal her physical injuries before we can heal her mental needs. This will take time."

"Time is something we don't have," Jesse said. "We need to get back to the Haven to the others."

After Charlie explained to the Chief what Jesse said, he responded, and Charlie explained, "The others will understand. Your mother went through the same thing."

Jesse furrowed his brow. "How do you know my mother?"

"He said his father was the one who helped her when Jackie took her captive and tortured her."

"The scars on her back." Jesse nodded in understanding. Thinking for a moment, he then responded, "Do what you need to do. We'll wait."

"That could take a long time," Charlie cautioned.

"It will take as long as it takes," Jesse said sternly. "We will wait."

"Are you sure, mate?" Nico asked. "This could take a while."

"You can go back. I understand. But, I'm waiting."

"I am too," Joe said, taking a step forward.

"Me too," Delaney said, taking her place next to Joe before grabbing his hand. Feeling Joe give her hand a gentle squeeze, they both looked at Jesse, and nodded in agreement.

"I'm not leaving until my team does," Jacob said firmly, as he leaned against a tree, arms crossed.

"I will stay," Katia agreed.

"Me too." Sasha stood next to Katia. "We will wait."

Turning back to Nico, Jesse said, "We understand your family has needs. Maybe more than you know."

"What do ya mean by that?" Nico asked.

"You need to return to the station," the archangel instructed Nico. "Kit is already on her way back."

"Why? What happened?"

"Charlie, will you please escort Nico home?" the archangel asked, ignoring Nico's question.

"Do I not get a choice here?" Nico asked, confused.

"You need to return home," the archangel said sternly.

"I should not be the one to take him home," Charlie disagreed. "I need to be here to be the go-between." Then looking at the group, he added, "And to help train."

"Then, I will take him home," the archangel agreed with Charlie. "We will leave momentarily. We do not need a Jeep for transportation."

"What do you mean train?" Sasha asked. Jacob dropped his head and shook it, as he groaned. Sasha asked Jacob, "What is this train? Why does it disturb you?"

Jacob looked up at him, and explained, "You're going to have to learn to see what is not there."

"To feel what cannot be readily felt," Jesse continued.

"And to learn to anticipate the enemies movements before he can even make them," Charlie finished. "You will learn to rely on the word of God to get you through what you do not think is possible to endure. You will learn the Challenger/Aggressor game. You will learn to shoot with deadly aim. You will learn to throw knives, and fire a bow and arrow, hitting the center with 90-95% accuracy. You will also learn to find a strength within yourself that only comes from combining your strength with the Lord. He will carry you, as He has carried Angel. You will learn exactly what it means to be on Team A.N.G.E.L. in the Lord's Army."

*   *   *

Over the next few days, while learning to throw knives and shoot bow and arrows, the group heard Angel screaming off and on. As disturbing as it was, knowing her strength, they couldn't imagine what she went through to trigger that from her.

"Can we see her?" Delaney asked Charlie at lunch.

"Who?" Charlie asked.

"Just me and Katia."

"Jesse?" Charlie asked. "Do you want to see her?"

"Not at the moment," Jess said, taking a bite of his sandwich. "Let the girls go."

"She may need a woman to talk to," Katia explained, glancing at Jesse who looked tense.

"I'll talk to the women and see," Charlie said, and left the group.

"Are you going to want to talk to her any time soon?" Joe asked Jesse when Charlie was out of earshot.

"What business is it of yours?" Jesse snapped.

"She's your sister," Delaney said. "How can you be so angry with her, knowing all she went through?"

"Because she *caused* most of it."

"You can't be serious!"

"I can," Jesse simply responded.

"Jesse, I have a dream that you will forgive her," Sasha said. "It will take time, but it will be in that house."

"I don't know about that. It could be awhile," Jesse admitted. "She and I have a *lot* to work out. As a matter of fact, I'm not planning on talking to her until we get back to the Haven."

"You're really going to wait until we get back to the Haven?" Delaney asked, stunned.

"Knowing what we've been through to get everyone rescued – including her – do you seriously not think I have a reason to be angry?" Jesse said, frustration evident. "Danny is dead, Derek is paralyzed, and Jerrod has to work through his nightmares again. Thankfully Jerrod and Derek are getting help, but that's not the point. And, you know, that's not *even* mentioning all of the broken bones, and other injuries sustained by others through all of this. She didn't listen to Josh, Jon, Val, or even the archangel when they tried to tell her she was going the wrong direction. She decided to take matters into her own hands. She decided she knew better than all of them. Do you know if she's even asked forgiveness from the Lord yet? Do you know if she even has the slightest bit of remorse for her actions?" When everyone shook their heads, Jesse went on, "I don't either. What I *do* know is that we need to take the time we have to get you all ready. Katia, Delaney, if you feel the need to go talk to her, be my guest. It's only going to aid in her recovery."

"I would *think* talking to her only family member, her *brother* who is here, would go much further in aiding her recovery," Delaney pointed out.

"This is the part of her journey where she's going to have to pull up her big-girl panties and walk on her own," Jesse said before taking a drink.

"That sounds so callous," Delaney argued.

"Look," Jesse slammed his drink down on the table, "she got herself into this. Jon and I have been cleaning up her messes for *years*. If she wants to lead her team, she will have to do the work herself. I will be waiting in the end, praying for her to make it through."

"I think she would appreciate you standing beside her more," Katia disagreed.

"I'll forgive her later, but I don't think me being around her right now is a good idea. She will have to go through this with the Spirit, Jesus, and God."

"Oh, I am sure she will. Family does need to be there too," Katia pushed.

"No man left behind," Jacob simply said.

"You all have not lived with her all her life. You have no idea what we had to do in order to keep her out of trouble," Jesse tried to get them to understand. "You have only seen her in the capacity she has been in for a short time. Jacob's seen what her messes create."

"I have, but I'm still not abandoning her," Jacob said.

"Really? Then why are you on Rachel's unit and not hers?" Jesse challenged.

"Because I feel Rachel is a better leader. I also get along better with her."

"Because Rachel listens to her team. Rachel sees the entire team as a unit," Jesse explained.

"Yes," Jacob said, "but I also know Angel would do anything for anyone. She proved that in the caves. Jon told me she had the opportunity to get out. She could have been rescued first, but she chose to let the others, Liliya included, to be let go first. You cannot tell me she didn't know what that would cost her."

"I'm sure she did, but that doesn't negate what happened because of her original choice."

"She has hundreds of little cuts all over her body!" Sasha stood, exasperated. "Her mind is gone! The entire ride over here, she talked in her sleep. The pain and agony all over her face was unmistakable! You cannot tell me that you have *never* made a mistake?"

"I have," Jesse agreed, looking up at Sasha.

"Matthew 7:1 and 2," Joe said, tugging Sasha back down to his seat. *"Do not judge, or you will be judged. For the same way you judge others, you will be judged, and with what measure will you use, it will be measured to you."* Folding his hands in front of him, Joe went on, "We all have made mistakes. We all have created problems. Granted, those had less drastic consequences, but some of us are a little more stubborn than others when it comes to learning our lessons. Obviously, Angel is one of those."

"Why did Danny and Derek, and the others, have to pay for *her* mistake?" Jesse asked, his body shaking from adrenaline.

"We are all human. We all make choices. We all have sinned. We all here at this table have been forgiven by Jesus...Angel included," Delaney said. "This isn't the first time one of us has had to suffer massive consequences as an

A.N.G.E.L., and it certainly won't be the last. I *do* know this, though, if I made the choices Angel did, and the consequences are what happened? I would *definitely* want as much support as I could find."

"That is what makes us different from the other side," Katia added. When Jesse looked at her, she explained, "Josh said we are a family. We make mistakes. We ask forgiveness. We love. Love covers an abundance of sin. It is also what binds us."

"What is the difference between being an enabler, and forgiving time and time *and time* again?" Jesse challenged.

Katia answered simply, "Blood of Jesus."

After a heavy moment, Jesse got up from the table and met Charlie about halfway between the table and the house he had just walked out of. "After lunch, train them. I have to go talk to Angel."

Charlie raised an eyebrow. "I am aware, but is that safe?"

"Yes. Wait. What do you mean when you said, 'I am aware'?"

"Go knock on the door. The women will let you in. They are expecting you."

"How did you know?" Jesse asked.

"The Spirit told me you were coming. What? You think you are the only one with Spiritual Gifts?" Charlie asked, a grin across his face. "Go. I have a team to whip into shape. The rest of the team is down. This crew needs to pick up the slack."

"Thank you." Jesse patted Charlie's shoulder before he headed over to the house. Standing in front of the door, he looked toward Heaven. "If this is a test, I ask You to help me pass it, because I *know* I can't pass this on my own."

"What's he waiting for?" Jacob asked Charlie when he got over to the table.

Turning to see Jesse still standing at the door, Charlie turned back to the group. "He is waiting for back up. Here," he said, putting his hands out. As each team member stood and grabbed a hand, Charlie prayed aloud, "We stand here together, hearts united, as one team for You, Lord. You know the struggles each of us face. We know You are the only One who can break the chains that bind us. Jesse needs You to put Your blessed, strong arms around him, showing him Your power and grace. He needs You to help him fly free in the freedom only You can give. He needs You to help him forgive, and recover. We ask that he be covered and protected by the blood of Jesus. In the precious name of Jesus..."

With their eyes closed, Joe declared, "I see the locks opening up that connect the chains around him. I see each chain drop to his feet, one after another."

Katia opened her eyes and looked over to see Jesse raise his hands to Heaven.

"I see the saints standing around Jesse," Joe continued. "I see them encouraging him to continue his race, to take off the weight that is holding him down."

Katia saw Jesse drop to his knees, with his hands on his knees, and his head bowed.

Joe continued, "I see Jesus breakthrough the crowd, making His way to Jesse. He puts His hand on Jesse's shoulder, letting him know He is there with him."

Tears poured down Jesse's cheeks, soaking his shirt.

"The Lord kneels next to Jesse, putting His arm around him," Joe went on. "As Jesse stands in the faith and strength of the Father…"

Jesse stood. He wiped the tears off his face. Taking a deep breath, he looked toward Heaven one more time before he knocked on the door.

"…Jesse takes the bold step forward in the grace and mercy of the Lord. With the Lord's strength, he *will* make it through this," Joe declared. "With the Lord's power and might, he *will* forgive and move on. With the strength and forgiveness of family, Angel *will* recover."

Katia turned to see Jesse walk through the threshold.

*　　*　　*

Stepping into the dark home, lit only by lanterns, Jesse headed down the hallway to one of the rooms off the main room. There, he saw his sister on a bed. The cuts that covered her body were coated by an herbal mixture that was thick as mud, mixed by the two women watching over her. "Angel?" he whispered.

Slowly opening her eyes, tears immediately stung them when she saw Jesse standing at the foot of her bed. Lifting her arm, her eyes blurred as the tears freely flowed down her cheeks. "I'm sorry," was all she could squeak out.

Taking her hand, Jesse sat down on the side of the bed. The struggle within him resumed, but he pushed it aside, knowing he already asked God to take that battle from him. "You're safe," he said.

Nodding in understanding, she asked, "The others? Danny?"

Jesse shook his head as tears continuously flowed. Taking a deep breath, he looked toward the ceiling in an attempt to control his emotions as he wiped his face.

"I'm sorry, Jesse," she apologized.

"That's not all."

"I don't know what is real and what isn't," Angel confessed.

"Her spirit is in torture," one of the women explained.

"You speak English?"

"Little," the woman admitted. "Charlie help me."

"I see," Jesse said, before turning back to Angel. Holding her hand to his chest, he asked, "Do you want to know who all is here in Australia with us?"

"Yes."

"Delaney, Joe, Jacob, Katia, Sasha, Charlie, and me. Nico had to go to Kit at the station."

"Did something happen?" Angel asked confused.

"Kit has leukemia."

Angel gasped. "Oh no."

"Yeah." Jesse nodded. "The others not here were injured when we tried to do a second rescue."

Taking a staggering breath, Angel's heart raced. "Did-did anyone die?"

"Danny Hawk is the only one who didn't make it. The others are injured."

Shaking her head, Angel couldn't control herself anymore, and she started sobbing uncontrollably.

"Derek is-Derek is still alive, but he's paralyzed from the waist down," Jesse explained.

"No," Angel whispered through her tears. "I'm so sorry! I didn't mean for any of this to happen!" Partially sitting up, Angel grabbed Jesse's arms, and begged, "Please forgive me! I didn't know! I didn't know any of this would happen!"

"I know. We'll deal with that later. Right now, you need to get healthy. We're not going anywhere until you do. Charlie and I will train those here until you can return to the States with us."

Angel released Jesse, and slowly dropped back onto her bed. Covering her eyes, her tears rushed out of control. She sobbed, unable to speak.

"Angel, I can't begin to understand what you went through, but I understand you went through a lot. I'm sure the emotional turmoil is worse than the physical. That will take longer for you to recover. Know this, though, you *will* get through it. And when you do, you'll be stronger for it. You'll be a better leader, a better friend, and a better child of God. And through it, we will be here with you…*I* will be here with you."

When she continued to cry, Jesse leaned down and hugged her. When he did, a heavy feeling overcame him of love for his sister. Hugging her tighter, he said, "Forgive me for being angry with you, please?"

Angel only nodded in response. She understood she was the one at fault for all the damage done to the A.N.G.E.L. teams, along with the loss of a legend. She was cognizant of why Jesse was angry with her, and knew it would take time for him to trust her in the future. She would take forgiveness where she could get it.

Pulling away, Jesse gently laid her down. Looking toward the women, he asked, "When will she be able to come outside and see the others?"

"May be too much." The women who spoke a little English explained. "She needs to get better first."

"Thank you," Jesse said. "Mind if I send them in two at a time?"

The woman nodded. "Is better idea, yes."

"Thank you," Jesse said to her before turning back to Angel. "The team wants to see you, so I'll send them in for breaks to see you."

"When will you be back?" Angel asked.

"I will later." He stood. "In the meantime, do your best to get better." He gave her a kiss on her head, and headed toward the door.

"I love you, Jesse," Angel called to him as he went to leave.

With his hand still on the doorknob, Jesse looked toward Heaven. "I love you too, Angel," he said, and quickly walked out. Outside the door of the house, he leaned against the wall of the front of the house, and slid down, tears streaming down his face. "I don't know if I can do this Lord. The struggle is difficult. You have to help me through this. When I see her, I want to love on her and protect her, but I also see all of the damage she has done, and the anger comes flooding back. Help me, Lord!"

*   *   *

"Kit!" Nico said, relieved to see her come down the terminal at the airport. Running to meet him, Kit threw herself into his arms. "I'm so sorry! I didn't know. Pete told me when I got home." Looking up, he suddenly noticed Rachel and Leah walking down the terminal as well. "What the…? Why are they here? I thought they were staying with Casey?"

"Oh, there's no way they were going to let me come home without them," Kit said, holding onto Nico's arms to keep her balance. "Besides, Rachel's got another assignment."

"Is she well enough for that?"

"Yep," Kit said confidently.

"Daddy!" Rachel ran over and hugged her dad, closely followed by Leah.

"So glad to see you alive and well," Leah added as she hugged him.

"C'mon, Pete's waiting to take us home. You can tell me about your assignment," Nico said to Rachel as they headed over to the luggage claim area.

*   *   *

"So, you're going to be heading out in the morning?" Nico asked when Rachel finished, as they turned down the road to the station. "I don't think your nieces and nephews, *or* your siblings *or* the ranch hands are going to be too happy about that. They haven't seen you in quite some time."

"I know, but Angel needs me. Besides, I'll be back for the wedding," Rachel said, winking and nudging Leah.

"You have no idea how happy I am that you'll be here. And, that you'll be my maid of honor." Leah grinned. "It wouldn't be the same without you."

"Well, we have about six weeks until Christmas and the wedding, since the wedding will be on the twenty-second. I'll be back by then, whether or not Angel's ready," Rachel promised. "A Christmas wedding! How beautiful!"

"Going to have to get your dress ordered before you leave in the morning. You'll have to go next door to Willow's mom's to get measured."

"What color are they?"

"Red."

"Oooo!"

"Yep! We're going to have these deep red and white roses, called fire and ice roses," Leah said, dreamily. "They'll be in bouquets with pine boughs and green foliage, along with miniature pine cones, and holly. We're also going to decorate the house with the Christmas tree, garland, and all while lights. We're actually getting married under an arch just outside the main house. It will be decorated the same."

"Beautiful!"

"Thank you!" Leah said, as they pulled onto the station.

When they drove down the driveway toward the house, they could hear cheering, as the station hands ran toward the main house to meet them there. Practically getting mobbed upon stepping out of the truck, Rachel could barely stand. The little family felt happy, grateful, welcomed…and loved.

Chapter 11
That We May Gain A Heart Of Wisdom

After a whirlwind day and a half of traveling, seeing family and friends, and getting measured for her dress, Rachel decided to take it easy for the night. It would be a long, arduous, forty-eight hour drive out to where the rest of the group was located with Charlie's clan. The plan was to drive the fourteen hours to Alice Springs, spend the night, and then Caleb and Pete would take turns driving out to where the others were located, deep in Western Australia.

"Are you sure you're ready for this?" Nico asked Rachel, as they sat on the front porch after dinner with some others, including most of the family members.

"No, but I'm one of the few who understands her position," Rachel explained.

"You don't think she'll be resentful?" Leah asked. "It's my understanding from Val and Josh, that she got replaced by Josh and Jon from the archangel right before she got taken."

"Really?" Rachel asked, surprised.

"I guess that's what triggered her actions."

"Interesting," Rachel said, mentally filing this new piece of information.

"Ohhh, I know that look," Caleb said with a smile. "That furrowed brow…that faraway look. You're trying to put the pieces together."

"She likes a challenge," Willow pointed out.

"She's also good with puzzles," Leah added.

"*She* is still here," Rachel reminded them.

"And, *she* has inherited her mother's wisdom, so I have the utmost faith in *her* abilities," Nico finished.

"Speaking of Mum, is she in bed early again?" Caleb asked. "She looked exhausted."

"Yes. She starts her chemotherapy in a few days," Nico explained. "Can't say I'm not worried."

At the word 'chemotherapy,' the station hands near them listened more intently. "Is there anything we can do to make it a little easier on all of you?" Jarrah, one of the station hands, asked.

"Praying is the best thing you can all do," Nico said. "I'm scared for her, but I can't let her know that. She needs to be around strong people. She'll most of all need the strength of God if she's going to pull through this at all."

"I kind of don't want to leave," Rachel admitted. "I want to stay with Mum."

"I know you do, and she appreciates it. She knows, though, that your job carries a much heavier weight," Nico pointed out.

"I don't want to watch her go through this," Leah said, upset.

"I know, luv," Nico said, pulling her close to him in a hug. "None of us do, but it's part of her journey."

"Well, it stinks!" Caleb said, tossing a rock at a spider, barely missing it as it scurried away.

"Caleb!" Nico said, stunned by Caleb's assertiveness.

"What?" he snapped. "You seriously want to watch her lose her hair? You want to watch her vomit day after day? Watch her drop weight like crazy? Watch her lose her fingernails and toenails?"

"No. No one does, but –"

"But nothing, Pop," Caleb said, cutting him off. "She's too young. I know her mum had it, and that's what she passed from. I don't want her to go yet. I want my children to have her in their life a lot longer. *I* want to have her in my life longer. Call me selfish if you want, but it's the truth!"

"And, to be honest, I want her to meet my children," Leah admitted. "I know we're supposed to be strong, and we're supposed to trust in the Lord through all of this. I also know we're supposed to be at peace through this. I have to tell you, though, I don't want her to go either."

"She won't go unless her work here is done. If God wants her here, then she'll stay. If not, then we'll see her when we get to Heaven," Nico said.

"You cannot seriously be at peace with this?" Caleb asked him.

"Not yet, but I've learned to trust God in all things over the years."

"That's the church answer," Caleb accused.

"I know that's what it sounds like, but it'll have to do until I can process everything," Nico admitted. "At this point, she needs strength and encouragement. That is something I *can* control. The rest?" He shook his head. "I can't."

"Will she be okay until I can get back?" Rachel asked. "We're leaving really early in the morning."

"She'll fight," Nico encouraged. "You're mum is stronger than you give her credit for."

"I know. I just don't think it's fair or right. She's given everything for the Lord," Caleb argued. "She's been through it all. Why does she still have to face this?"

"I swear! Some days, you and your brother are the sons of thunder! I went rounds with Josh on some things at the Haven. I'm going to tell you the same thing I told Josh on the phone earlier…Kit is strong enough to do this," Nico asserted. "She's strong, but when she was younger, she was nowhere near as strong as she is now. God's taken her through what He has, so she can now face this with that strength."

"What happens if her soul is strong enough, but her body isn't?" Leah asked.

"Her soul is always the Lord's, whether she's here or in Heaven. Her soul *is* her strength. And, God gave her a strong one."

*   *   *

After a long day of driving to the hotel in Alice Springs, Rachel lay down in her bed, while Caleb and Pete shared the other queen bed. "I don't know about you blokes, but I'm exhausted!" she complained.

"I'm just glad to finally see you," Caleb said. "While you're gone, we only get communication through that weird email address you guys have set up."

"It's the best we can do," Rachel said. "Of course, with Cori and Kai, there are other ways we can communicate now. They have ways I never even heard of. I was thrilled when we were able to talk to those in the field in the middle of nowhere when everything cut loose at Tanami."

"No doubt! That sounded like a mess!" Pete said. "I honestly don't know how you all do it."

"God," Rachel responded.

"Rach, are you *really* okay with all of this?" Caleb asked.

"Could you be more specific? I've kind of had a long week."

"Are you okay with leaving while Mum goes through this?"

"Not really, but I'm going to trust God. He hasn't let me down yet."

"How can you leave? I'm only going for a few days. You'll be gone for weeks…again."

"Because Angel needs me."

"Mum does too," Caleb pointed out.

Rolling over, as she lay on her pillow, Rachel explained, "God gave me an assignment. I am to help Angel through this. I *could* turn Him down, but I won't. I respect and honor Him too much to do that."

"What about Mum? She needs you too."

"She does, but Angel's my priority."

"How can you separate yourself from your feelings?"

"I have to. Practice, I guess. I can't separate myself completely. I still have feelings. I just need to get through the situation, and work through the feelings later."

"What will you do if she dies while you're in the field?" Pete asked.

"I will mourn for her and go to her funeral, but I will see her again," Rachel explained.

"Seriously?" Caleb challenged.

"It's the best answer I can give right now."

"What are you going to do to help Angel?" Caleb asked, changing the subject.

Rachel shrugged. "I'm going to do what the Spirit tells me to do."

"Will she be okay?"

"I don't know. That'll be up to God."

"You look tired," Pete observed.

"Very much so," Rachel said, as she stretched and yawned.

"Take your medicine, and get some sleep," Pete said, tossing the pill bottle to her as he got a bottle of water from the cooler. "It's going to be a long drive tomorrow."

"I know, but at the end of the drive are the A.N.G.E.L.s," Rachel said with a smile.

"Speaking of the A.N.G.E.L.s," Caleb started, "what's going on with you and Jesse?"

"How did you hear about Jesse?"

"You're kidding, right?" Caleb laughed. Pete chuckled as well. "When you all came in from Black Rock, blind Freddie could have seen it!"

"Seen what?" Rachel challenged.

"That you two are in love with each other. Are you really going to challenge that?"

"No, but I can't do anything about it," she said, and then took her pill. After she chugged the water, she sat up until the medicine kicked in.

"Why not?" Pete asked.

"Because I'm in charge of the unit. I can't have a relationship with someone on the team I am leading. That could cause favoritism."

"So, no one on your team knows you like each other?" Caleb pushed.

"They do," she said hesitantly.

"Then, what's the problem?"

"I don't want to make people feel uncomfortable."

"Have you talked to them about it?"

"No."

"Then, how do you know?"

"I don't."

"Have you prayed about it?" Pete asked.

"I have."

"Have you gotten an answer yet?"

"Not yet."

"Keep praying. In the meantime, we need to work on going to sleep," Pete said, and rolled over, facing the wall, leaving Caleb and Rachel to talk.

"How did you know it was okay to go out with Willow?" Rachel asked after a moment.

"I really liked her at first. The more I got to know her, the more I wanted to know her."

"She's a great woman."

"She is. Did you know her parents wanted her mum to have an abortion?"

"I know her real mother is her sister, and that her parents are actually her grandparents."

"Yeah. Her real mother was fifteen when she got pregnant."

"Right."

"Her parents wanted her to have an abortion. She didn't want to, so she called Mum and Dad for help."

"Really?"

"Yeah. Mum and Dad literally saved Willow's life."

"Wow!" Rachel said, amazed.

"Yeah. If her parents had their way years ago, Willow wouldn't be here. I wouldn't have my wife or children."

"I'll bet they're happy they changed their minds now."

"Oh yeah! We've talked about it. Two wrongs don't make a right."

"What do you mean?"

"Well, Anna got pregnant without being married. Her parents wanted her to have an abortion, so her life wouldn't be ruined. Both of those are wrong. They tried to use a wrong in order to correct another wrong. That doesn't work."

"I agree."

"So, tell me what you like about Jesse?" Caleb asked, realizing Rachel shifted the subject on him.

"Hmmm," Rachel said, thinking. "He's sweet. He's always looking out for others. He's incredibly talented. He's also cute," she said with a smile. "Most importantly, though, he's a good Christian man, who puts what God wants first. He's as honorable as he is adorable!"

"Hmm, sounds like you really like him."

"What's not to like?"

"Okay, then, what's the problem?"

"Again, I lead the team."

"If you weren't leader, would you go ahead?"

"More than likely. We're like a couple of magnets – always drawn together."

"What if *he* were leader instead?"

Rachel narrowed her eyes at Caleb. "Ooooo, you've been taking lessons from Mum."

Caleb shrugged. "Just making a point."

"I get it. I need to pray about it some more," Rachel relented.

"Fair enough," Caleb agreed. Then he asked, "Has the medicine hit yet?"

"It's starting."

"Good. Get some rest. I love you, Rach."

"Love you too, Caleb. And, thank you."

"Anytime. I'm here for you," he said, turning off the light.

"I'm here for you too," she said, and rolled over, going to sleep.

*   *   *

Finally arriving at the village after two and a half days of travel, Rachel was exhausted. As they pulled in, the A.N.G.E.L. team sitting at the table under the tree, stood.

"Who is that?" Jesse asked Charlie, who suddenly had a grin on his face when he recognized those in the vehicle.

"Pete!" Charlie said, excited. Pete is Charlie's brother-in-law. He is married to Charlie's sister, Victoria. Charlie has two sisters, Victoria and Grace.

Jacob squinted to see better. "Is that…?"

"Rachel!" Joe said, excited.

"Rachel," Jesse whispered, stunned, as he watched her get out of the Jeep. "Rachel!" he shouted, and ran over to her, swinging her in the air, setting her down as gently as he could.

"Glad to have you back," Jacob said, as he and everyone else gave her a group hug.

"You must be Caleb," Katia said, shaking his hand as the group separated. "You look exactly like Josh."

"Yes. I must be. You are all going to have to introduce yourselves. I've heard the stories, but it'll be nice to put faces to the names."

Just then they heard a shrill, ear-piercing scream. Looking toward the house, wide-eyed, Rachel asked, "What was *that*?"

"Angel," Jesse said. "Go," he pushed her toward the house, "she needs you."

As Rachel jogged over to the house, the front door flung open. A woman ran out toward Charlie, rattling off in Aboriginal.

Rachel slowly pushed the door that was left ajar, open, and then closed it behind her. The house was dark, except for the dim sunlight that struggled to get through the thick curtains on the windows. With each step, her heart raced faster.

Hearing another scream, Rachel covered her ears as she continued to search the house. The scream seemed to come from every corner. Wandering down the hall, she was finally able to take her hands off her ears when Angel's scream ceased.

Walking into the dark room, Rachel was barely able to make out shapes in the room. She saw the dresser and three twin beds. Then another shape caught her eye. Huddled in the corner, shaking, looking like an abused animal…was Angel. "Angel?" Rachel asked, stunned. "Angel, what happened to you?"

"No more," Angel whimpered. "I don't want to do it anymore."

"Do what?" Rachel crouched in front of her. "What happened?"

"Th-they w-wouldn't st-stop," Angel stammered. "Bombarding with memories…or thoughts…or…I'm not even sure…is this real?"

"Angel, honey," Rachel said, reaching out to her. When Angel pulled away, Rachel said, "I'm sorry. Will you please tell me what happened?"

Studying her for a moment, Angel asked, "Are you real?"

When Rachel nodded, Angel reached out and touched Rachel's face. "Yes," Rachel said, resting her hand over Angel's. "Yes, I'm real. You're safe."

"I'm *never* going to be safe. Th-they said they'd find me."

Situating herself into a more comfortable position on the ground, Rachel said, "Angel, you've been through a lot. What if we take this slow?"

"You don't know!" Angel shouted at her, wild-eyed. "You-you don't know what they did to me!"

"You're right. I don't. Talk to me, Ang. I'm going to stay here with you. Through the nightmares, and through the memories, I'm here for you."

"The angel said he would be too, but-but he left."

"Pretty sure that wasn't voluntary."

"They did it right in front of me. How did they see him?" Angel asked, almost paranoid. "Can they see everything? Do they know everything?"

"No. Only God does."

Angel waited a moment before she said, "You know Jesse's angry with me, right?"

"I know a lot of people aren't happy with your behavior, but they love you and are concerned for you."

"They don't know the pressure!"

"I know, but *I* do."

"Right!" Angel grabbed Rachel's arm, desperate. "You do! You understand!"

"I do."

"Then, you'll help me?"

"Help you what?"

"Help me take them out."

"Who?"

"The A.N.G.E.L.s. They're bad people! They hurt people!"

"Angel?" Rachel asked, confused. "What do you mean?"

"They showed me things. Things they did."

"Angel, I have to go talk to Charlie. Can you do me a favor and stay right here until I come back?"

"Yeah. Yeah, I can do that," she said, looking in every direction, as she huddled closer to the corner. "I don't think they can see me here. I'll stay here."

"Have you eaten lately? Do you need something to drink?"

"I'm starving! They starved me!"

"Okay. I'll go get you something to eat and drink. Will you wait here for me?"

"Yes."

"Good. I'll be right back," she said, and left the house, making a beeline for Charlie. "What happened to her?" she demanded.

"Why? What did she say?" Charlie asked.

"She thinks we're bad. She thinks the *A.N.G.E.L.s* are bad. She thinks she needs to take us out. If I didn't know better, I would think she was possessed by the way she was acting."

"What?" Jesse asked, stunned. "She was remorseful last time I talked to her."

"She's paranoid," Rachel explained.

"That goes more with what the women are telling me. They are getting stressed in trying to work with her, and take care of her," Charlie explained. "I wish The Colonel or Danny were still alive. We need them for this."

"We need the archangel," Rachel insisted. Looking toward Heaven, she shouted, "We need you down here…pronto!"

"I don't think he takes kindly to demands," Charlie pointed out.

"This is an emergency situation," Rachel said, on edge.

"What's going on?" Jacob asked, as the others came over at hearing Rachel shout.

"Angel's in trouble. I want you all to start sleeping in shifts. Those who are not sleeping, I want you praying," Rachel ordered.

"We have to train," Katia objected.

"No, we have to save one of our own. This is just as important as training. This is spiritual training. This starts immediately. Delaney, would you mind making a schedule? Training is suspended indefinitely. Praying needs to start...*now!*"

"What happened?" Joe asked. "I've never seen you this nervous."

"There is a battle for her soul in there," Rachel said, pointing toward the house. A few gasps were heard as she looked to Heaven again, and yelled, "Seriously! We need you down here, please?"

Suddenly, there were a dozen streaks of light, with the archangel's being the brightest. "I am not used to being spoken to in that tone of voice," the archangel said sharply. "Despite that, the Lord sent me with urgency. He said Angel is in trouble."

"She is," Rachel agreed.

"Surround this village," the archangel ordered those with him. "No one is to come in or go out without expressed consent from me. Understood?"

The angels nodded, and immediately surrounded the village with flaming swords. As they did, the flames in the swords joined, creating a fiery barrier.

The Chief came over, yelling at Charlie. Once Charlie explained the situation, the Chief calmed down. "They have to hunt for food," Charlie said to the archangel. "If they don't, they will run out."

"They will never run out," the archangel said matter-of-factly. "Their storehouses for meat will always be full while you are here. Their grain bin will never be empty. Their gardens will be fruitful. For their trouble, they will be filled once more before you move on."

When Charlie explained what the archangel said, the Chief agreed, and went to his people to explain the situation.

"The only people I want going in or out of the house with Angel are me, Rachel, and Charlie," the archangel added.

"What about me?" Jesse asked, stunned.

"Not at this time. The struggles within you are not going to help this situation."

"I understand," Jesse agreed.

"Continue your own work. You need to continue to progress," the archangel encouraged Jesse. "This is of the utmost importance."

Grabbing Jesse's hand, Rachel said, "Don't worry. I will take care of her."

"I know you will," Jesse gave her hand a squeeze before going over to the table with the others, while Charlie, the archangel, and Rachel talked.

"Um," Caleb cleared his throat, as he and Pete walked up to Rachel and the archangel, "We need to leave. We're needed on the station."

"Agreed," the archangel said. Getting the attention of a couple of angels guarding the village, he told them to let Caleb and Pete out.

After hugging Rachel, and Pete saying his good-byes to friends and family, the pair left for Alice Springs, to head back to Serenity Wells Station.

Once they were gone, Rachel turned back to the archangel and Charlie, "What happened to her? If I didn't know she was already protected by the blood of Jesus, I would think she was possessed!"

"They cannot touch the soul, so they went after her mind. She is strong, but the battle within is intense," the archangel explained. "They starved her, and when she was almost to the point of too long, they would feed her. They gave her minimal water to keep her sustained. They would not let her sleep for days, while they planted visions in her mind."

"They brainwashed her!" Rachel said, stunned.

"They were able to convince Allen to join their side. They did not count on Angel's strength in the Lord, or her resolve. When she would not bend, they went at her a different way."

"How can we fight this?" Charlie asked.

"Truly I tell you, whatever you bind on earth will be bound in heaven, and whatever you loose on earth will be loosed in heaven. Again, truly I tell you that if two of you on earth agree about anything they ask for, it will be done for them by My

Father in heaven," the archangel quoted Matthew 18:18 and 19. "You were right to instruct the team to pray continuously. Your first instinct was correct. This is why you are a great leader. You know where your strength comes from." As the team prayed around the table, the archangel, and those angels surrounding the village began to glow even brighter. "Prayer is a mighty and powerful weapon. There is nothing stronger than the Lord's saints on their knees."

Several people within the village stopped what they were doing, and got on their knees in prayer. The Chief went over to Charlie and talked to him. Charlie turned to the others and explained, "There are some here who are a Christian. This will cause them to be potential outcasts. Chief says not to worry. He will join them shortly. He is going to talk to the elders, all of whom are Christians as well. When this happens, chaos may ensue. That is why he warned me. Some in the village want to keep to the old ways. They will not be happy to find out that the Chief and the elders are Christians, or that they have agreed to this."

"They will have a choice to make," the archangel said. "Ours will be to stay here and fight for the one who is lost."

"Yes, sir," Charlie said, and went over to the Chief, where he and the elders were talking, leaving the archangel and Rachel.

"Will she make it?" Rachel asked the archangel.

"The battle will be fierce, but she is strong. This will make her stronger. You know the Lord's Word."

"I do," Rachel said. Looking toward the house Angel was in, she quoted Psalm 91:1-4, *"Whoever dwells in the shelter of the Most High will rest in the shadow of the Almighty. I will say of the Lord, "He is my refuge and my fortress, my God, in Whom I trust." Surely He will save you from the fowler's snare and from the deadly pestilence. He will cover you with His feathers, and under His wings you will find refuge; His faithfulness will be your shield and rampart."* Looking back to the archangel, Rachel went on, "She is resting under His protective feathers through this storm. She *will* find refuge. She only needs to see the light."

"You are the light of the world. A town built on a hill cannot be hidden," the archangel quoted Matthew 5:14. "She will see His light in You. You will help bring your sister back to us. The Lord will protect you as you go into battle on her behalf. You can do this, Rachel."

"I know." Rachel nodded, nervous. "I only wish I knew if she were really in there. You should have seen her."

When he rested his hand on Rachel's shoulder, peace emitted from it, washing over her. "You *do* know that she is in there. You also know you will be successful. Claim it. Have the confidence that you do not go in there alone. You go in there with not only the Lord, Jesus, and the Spirit, but with all the saints before you. Charlie wished for Danny and The Colonel to be here. They are, along with all of those who have come and gone before you. They are praying for you," the archangel pointed to the table of the team praying, along with the various villagers. "The team back at the Haven has received word, and is praying for you. Not only are the A.N.G.E.L.s from around the world praying for you, but those who are the prayer warriors of the Lord are in prayer as well. They may or may not know why they are praying, but rest assured they are deep in prayer."

"I know. That *does* make me feel better. I've just never faced anything like this. How will I know what to say and do? I don't want to mess this up."

"Then, it is a good thing you are not going in by yourself," the archangel said, resting his arm over Rachel's shoulders. "Come. Let us go save your sister."

Rachel stopped walking. "Wait! I told her I would bring food and drink."

A young village girl ran over with a plate of food and a drink, and handed it to Rachel.

"Ask, and ye shall receive. See? You are not alone," the archangel said, as Rachel took the food and drink, and the girl ran back to her home. "If you need it, it will be provided…even before you know you need it yourself."

Looking back toward Jesse, Rachel was relieved when Jesse smiled at her and nodded for her to go on before he returned to prayer.

"He is a strong young man," the archangel mentioned as they walked.

"Is it okay?"

"Of course it is okay. You are only told not to be unequally yoked. You are both equal," the archangel pointed out. Then he added, "I must admit that he is a little upset at me."

"Probably not for long. He has a forgiving heart."

"He does. He is more like his mother than his father. He is quiet, but he is wise."

"Wisdom comes with experience," Rachel commented.

"And, you are about to gain much," the archangel said, as he turned the handle of the door to the house.

Remembering a verse her mother taught her, Rachel quoted Psalm 90:12, *"Teach us to number our days, that we may gain a heart of wisdom."*

"Time is short on this earth, Rachel."

"But eternity is forever."

Chapter 12
Hold Fast To Him And Serve Him
With All Your Heart

The house was a home the village used for an infirmary. Normally the lanterns, candles, and oil lamps were lit when in use, except this time. The light was too sensitive for Angel. When she first woke, it was okay, but she continued to ask them to put one out after another until it was completely dark in the house.

After all the lights were out, over the next few days, as Angel got stronger, the women looking after her watched Angel transform into an increasingly paranoid and angry, young lady. When they attempted to feed her, she threw it back at them. After the third time, one woman quit. When she woke screaming for the tenth time, the woman who spoke partial English left, which was just as Rachel pulled up.

With taking care of Angel twenty-four hours a day since her arrival, the women didn't have time to clean up after themselves. Between fighting with Angel to put the mixture on her body to assist in healing the claw marks, cleaning up the food, and Angel barely sleeping, it wore the women out, leaving the place a disaster.

To Rachel, it almost seemed like she stepped back in time. Deep in the heart of the Outback, where there was no electricity, this group of villagers used old methods to treat current ailments. This included herbs drying by being hung over the doorway, or stored in jars on shelves. Some of the herbs drying made an amazing scent as they hung. The herbs, mixed with the earthy smell and medical strength cleaners, created an interesting scent. Rachel wasn't sure if she liked it or not. There were Eucalyptus bunches, along with small bundles of Sweetgrass, Sage, and Lemon Grass, just to name a few. The jars contained various tree barks, tree saps, oils, mushrooms, and grubs, among other things. Rachel opened the jar labeled Melaleuca, and deeply inhaled. She loved the scent of Tea Tree. Putting it back on the shelf, she wandered over to the bookcase located in the corner. It was stocked with books, along with handwritten notebooks containing what Pete called 'recipes.' The mixture all over Angel was just one of many of their recipes. Next to the bookshelf was a small table used by those taking care of patients. It contained folders, along with stacks of papers and notebooks, and a sign-in log.

The two-bedroom home had the bedrooms off the main room. One room was for surgeries, and was kept continuously clean. At this point, it was the only area in the entire house still spotless. It also lacked the dust that coated quite a bit in the home. The second room contained three twin beds to be used for patients. Each was neatly made, with the exception of the one currently in use. The two women did their best to keep the place tidy, but out of sheer exhaustion, they just gave up.

Located just to the left of the front door, was a small woodstove. Next to it was a sink that drained to the outside. There were also shelves above the sink containing multiple glass lab equipment mixed with dishes, along with a couple marble mortar and pestles for crushing the plants and herbs.

Knowing Angel was in the patient room from before, Rachel and the archangel headed in that direction. Standing in the doorway, Rachel quietly asked the archangel, "How do we do this?"

Quoting Hebrews 4:12, the archangel said, *"For the word of God is alive and active. Sharper than any double-edged sword, it penetrates even to dividing the soul and spirit, joints and marrow; it judges the thoughts and attitudes of the heart."*

"Right." Rachel nodded in agreement. "We do it with the word of God. His words are stronger than anything the other side may have planted in her mind."

"Stand firm then, with the belt of truth buckled around your waist, with the breastplate of righteousness in place," the archangel quoted Ephesians 6:14.

"There's also, *Then you will know the truth, and the truth will set you free,* '" Rachel quoted John 8:32 before also quoting Psalm 145:18, *" 'The Lord is near to all who call on Him, to all who call on Him in truth.' "*

"There you go," the archangel said proudly, resting his hand on Rachel's shoulder. "You have learned much over the years."

"Let's hope and pray it's enough," Rachel said in a sigh, as they walked into the room where Angel was still cowering in the dark corner.

When they walked in, she was mumbling, "A hope and a future." Slowly standing, she continued to quickly whisper, "A hope and a future…a hope and a future…a hope and a future."

"What's she saying?" Rachel asked.

"I am not sure," the archangel said, studying her.

While Angel rose from the corner, she kept one hand on the wall to keep her balance. "A hope and a future…a hope and a future…a hope and a future."

"Angel, sweetheart, are you okay?" Rachel asked cautiously. When Angel's only response was to continue to whisper the phrase over and over again, Rachel asked, "Do ya know who I am, luv?"

Looking from the archangel to Rachel multiple times, she finally nodded, but continued to mumble the phrase.

"Angel, I'm your friend. We're leaders on a team called the A.N.G.E.L.s. You remember that, right?"

"A.N.G.E.L.s…A.N.G.E.L.s are bad," Angel said before starting her phrase again. "A hope and a future…a hope and a future."

"No. We're not bad."

"Neither are we," the archangel said, kneeling a couple feet from Angel. Resting his arm on his knee, he said, "Angel, is that a verse you are saying?"

Nodding, she repeated, "A hope and a future…a hope and a future."

"Right!" Rachel said when it hit her. "That's Jeremiah 29:11! *'For I know the plans I have for you," declares the Lord, "plans to prosper you and not to harm you, plans to give you hope and a future.'"*

"Not to harm you!" Angel shouted. Pointing her finger at Rachel, she sternly said, "*Not* to harm you!"

"No. No one's going to harm you here."

"*Not* to harm you!" Angel said, showing them her arms.

"We didn't do that. The A.N.G.E.L.s *didn't* do that," Rachel insisted.

"A.N.G.E.L.s are bad! They're evil!" Angel shouted.

"No. We're not." Rachel explained, "Cassius, Korax, Calliope, and their minions are what's evil."

"I hurt them," Angel said, beside herself. Tears brimmed her eyes as she said, "Danny, Mark, Jon, Val, and Derek – I hurt them."

"No, you didn't. Cassius, Korax, and Calliope hurt them. They're the ones who are bad," Rachel reiterated.

Conversations like these went on for hours. After several hours of this type of conversation, Rachel was exhausted. "I need a break," Rachel said, standing. "At least some fresh air."

"Go ahead. Please send in a couple of the others. It will help to continuously have familiar faces. Do not let it be Jesse." The archangel explained, "His anger will not help this situation. It will take some time to break through these walls. We cannot have her fall back if Jesse snaps at her."

"I agree," Rachel said. When Angel looked at her, wide-eyed, Rachel said, "I'll be back in a little bit. I promise you that I'm not leaving." When Angel nodded, Rachel took the cue and left.

Stepping out into the night air, Rachel took a deep breath. Glancing over at the table, she saw Jesse, Joe, and Delaney in prayer. When she got over to them, she asked, Delaney and Joe to go in for a bit. Once they went into the house, Rachel sat down at the table, dropping her head onto her arms.

"That bad?" Jesse asked.

Glancing up at him, she confirmed, "It's rough." Sitting up straight, she explained, "They brainwashed her."

"Really?"

"She looks like an abused animal. She keeps mumbling things that don't make sense. Well, they do, but they don't."

"What do you mean?"

"She says things, but they're about the other side, only she's saying them about us."

"Like?"

"Like we're bad. Like we hurt people. Like we're deceitful, and we lie, and we are cruel."

Jesse whistled. "Wow. How are you combatting that?"

"Verses, and telling the stories the right way. The way they actually happened."

"Sounds exhausting."

"It is, and I'm sure you'll get your turn."

"Maybe," he said, and looked out toward the village. "The archangel was pretty adamant that I don't go in."

"He's concerned that the anger still has ahold of you. He doesn't want that to cause a potential setback with Angel."

"Oh, I get it." Looking out into the darkness of the night, he said, "I'd ask if you want to take a walk, but we're grounded, so to speak."

"More like protected," Rachel corrected. "We can't do what we have to do if we're trying to keep an eye out for the other side at the same time. We also can't take her home looking the way she looks. Are the others sleeping?"

"Sleeping or eating." Jesse pointed toward one of the homes that had its lights on.

Rachel could see Charlie and Jacob at the table with the family eating dinner. "I see. When do you get to eat?"

"We're eating in shifts." After a moment of silence, Jesse mentioned, "I've missed you."

"Missed you too. I missed the team, and being on the field."

"You're not ready to go out into the field yet. You're still injured. You need to be one hundred percent before you go back out."

"I agree. But, this is a good second." Rachel picked up a small stick that fell off the tree above the picnic table and started playing with it. "Jesse, can we talk?"

"Are we not talking now?"

Rachel smirked. "We are, but I want to go deeper then the weather."

"What do you want to talk about?"

"The elephant in the room, or on the table in this case?"

"Which one?" Jesse asked.

"Is there more than one?" Rachel asked, surprised.

"You've missed a bit."

"Care to clear that up?"

"I've been dealing with major anger issues."

Rachel shrugged. "We all have them."

"I yelled at the archangel…more than once."

"Really? How'd *that* go?"

"Not too well. He was patient and understanding, but I'm still angry with him."

"About?"

Taking a deep breath before he slowly let it out, he said, "When we were in the cave, and the explosions happened, Derek got severely hurt."

"I know."

"What you don't know is that the archangel did absolutely nothing to help him," Jesse explained. As he talked, Rachel could almost feel the anger emitting from him. "He is a supernatural being. He could have come to us at any time and told us to not go in. He could have sent an angel to tell us she wasn't there. When the boulder crushed his back, instead of healing Derek, the archangel just had angels sit with him. He did nothing to help him."

"He protected you when the explosions went off."

"He did. By that point I was already angry with him. He said Kai and Cori warned us, but we didn't listen. He said Jacob tried to warn Josh, but he didn't listen either."

"That is all true. You can't be upset with him because he didn't post a billboard, or slap it across the internet for you guys not to go in. You can't hold him responsible for that."

"Why not?"

"Free will."

"Tsk!" Jesse clicked his tongue. "Sometimes I hate free will."

"Without it, our faithfulness wouldn't mean anywhere near as much." Taking his hand, Rachel said, "You can't hold God *or* the archangel responsible for a choice that you collectively made as a group. God did protect you guys. No one died on this mission."

"But, Danny did on the first one. He gave himself to save the others. That's just not right!"

"It's not, but again, free will. He knew full well what he was doing."

"Why did God let it happen in the first place?"

"God didn't *let* it happen…Angel did this all on her own. Liliya was taken. Angel thought she should be able to rescue

Liliya on her own. She thought she was indestructible, but she's not. Why should God or the archangel clean up messes that we create? Why is it God's responsibility?"

"It's not, but we're doing His work. I would *think* He would step in when we need help."

"He does. You guys needed help, so He sent the archangel and some of His other angels to protect you guys when they blew the cave open to get to you blokes. You can't seriously be angry with Him, are you?"

"I'm not angry with God."

"Yes, you are," Rachel said knowingly. "You are taking out your anger on the archangel, but it's God you're angry with. Be honest with yourself…and Him."

"I don't know if I can. I don't think it's right."

"It's not right to be angry with anyone," Rachel pointed out. "You're using the archangel as a target. He's your emotional punching bag right now. You need to stop it."

"I don't know how. It's like once it started to flow; it took on a life of its own. I don't know how to stop it."

"You have to pray when you start to feel it coming on. One good way to stop it is to actually talk to the archangel about it. You guys need to get back on the same page. We're on the same team."

"I know. I just don't know how to start."

"I'd start with right where you're sitting. Clean up your heart and soul with God, and ask for *His* help. You are first and foremost one of His children – A.N.G.E.L. or not. He loves you and wants to help. Delaney and Joe are in with Angel for now. Jacob and Charlie are eating. Everything is currently quiet here in the village. Take the time to get yourself right with God. When the archangel takes a break, take some time to get right with him as well. You have to before you see Derek. Derek will know you're angry in a heartbeat."

"Oh, I know he will."

Standing, Rachel said, "Take the time to get right with God. You need Him."

"I will." When she went to walk away, Jesse asked, "Rach?"

"Yeah?"

"What was the other thing?"

"Now is not a good time. We'll get to it another day," she said, and walked off.

"God," Jesse started. Looking up toward the multitude of stars that seemed to multiply across the brilliant night sky, Jesse asked, "Can we talk?"

*   *   *

Up in Pennsylvania, Jerrod was in training to get his service dog. For the last week, the guys who were getting the dogs, played with all of them as a group. The trainers watched them through the week to see which dog played with which guy more than another. By the end of the first day, there was one dog that seemed to claim Jerrod, much to Jerrod's delight. The male dog's name was Chief. Jerrod loved that idea, since he was a Chief when he left the Navy.

Chief was a German Shepherd. While he looked dangerous, Jerrod already knew he was sweet and protective. He knew he would be matched with him, because the bond was obvious.

Standing in a line of ten guys, Jerrod was the first in line. Hearing his name called, he prayed with all his might for Chief. Once Chief's name was called out for Jerrod, Chief happily ran to him, wagging his tail. A trainer pulled the pair away from the rest of the group to another area to begin work.

"Seems like Chief took an immediate liking to you," the trainer observed.

Kneeling next to him, Jerrod said, "I really like him. I'm glad he picked me."

"Are you ready for some intensive training?"

"I'm ready for some back-up, if that's what you're asking."

"Okay, let's get started."

After a few hours of training, they broke for lunch. When Jerrod got his food, he went over to a table of four, where there were already three guys sitting. "Can I sit?"

"Sure," one of the guys, Donny, gestured to the chair across from him.

Taking his seat, Jerrod asked, "So, who did you guys get matched with?"

"I got Ranger," Mike said.

Donny finished the bite in his mouth before he said, "I got Scout."

With a grin, Chase said, "And, I got Champ."

"All great dogs."

"Yeah, but yours is a lot more attached to you. It's like Chief zeroed in on you on day one," Mike pointed out. "It took Ranger a few days before he decided to lay claim."

"By the end of this, they'll all be super attached." Donny waved him off. "I'm looking forward to it. To have someone watching your back in public, I think, will help out immensely. Like a personal battle buddy."

"I agree," Chase said. "That's one of the many reasons why I'm here."

"Are the nightmares as strong for you as they seem to be for me?" Jerrod asked.

Mike, who was Jerrod's roommate, said, "Mine are bad, but yours, buddy?" He shook his head. "I hope he can help."

"I mean, I know I'm already never alone, but it will be a blessing to have him as well," Jerrod said, and then took a bite of his lunch.

"What do you mean you're never alone?" Donny asked. "Do you have family?"

"No. Well, sort of, but God is the One who's always there," Jerrod explained.

"Oh, you're one of *those*," Donny said, sitting back in his chair, crossing his arms.

"One of what?"

"One of those religious people."

"Don't know what you mean, brother."

"You know. One of those Bible thumpers…Jesus Freaks."

"Really? You're going to be rude like that? Have I tried to shove the Bible down your throat at any point in time since we've been here?" Jerrod challenged.

"No."

"Then, what would make you call me any of those labels?"

"That's what you are."

"Why label, though? And, to be honest, I am not offended by any of them. I wear them as a badge of honor." When Donny shrugged, Jerrod asked, "When you talk about *your* friends, do I call *you* names?"

"Friends are not a religion."

"Neither is my relationship with Jesus. It's a relationship, not a religion. Look, the Lord has gotten me through many battles. He's Who I cry out to in the middle of the night when those night terrors of real-life situations that happened, try to take over my entire being. He calms my soul."

"Then, why doesn't He just take the nightmares away? Would He take them away if you trusted Him more?" Donny asked.

"I trust Him with everything that's in me. War is not His doing. It breaks His heart," Jerrod explained. "Sin is the reason I have the nightmares. He is only trying to calm my spirit."

"If He's all powerful, then why can't He just take them away?"

"Oh, He can. He can do anything He wants. But sin and free will created war. Sin and free will are the reason war exists. I chose to join the Navy, knowing it may land me right in the middle of war. I chose to be on the side that saved lives whenever possible, not take them. Not saying I didn't take some of my own, but I saved many more than I took."

"That doesn't answer the question of why He won't take your nightmares away."

"Let me think how to phrase this," Jerrod said, thinking for a moment. "You're a dad, right?"

"Yeah."

"As a dad, when you see your child making a mistake, you want to stop them, right?"

"Right. Any good parent would."

"What if they chose not to listen? What if they did it multiple times? At what point would you let your child learn from their mistakes by facing the consequences?"

"I don't know. That's a tough call."

"It's a call God, the Father, has to make every day. You can't judge Him by what doesn't get stopped. He begged every one of us not to fight. He doesn't want war. All of us sitting at this table chose to enlist. We made a choice to put our lives on the line for this country, because we love it and believe in it. Jesus did the same thing. He literally put His life on the line when they nailed Him to the cross by His hands and feet. He chose to still forgive them with His last breath. *That* is the Jesus I choose to follow. He died because He loved and believed in us, the human race. He's Who I cling to every day."

"That's your choice."

"Yes, it is," Jerrod said firmly. "I'll tell you what, if any of you want to talk about it further, let me know. In the meantime, I'm going to eat," he said, and started eating. "We don't have a lot of time before training starts again."

"Agreed," Mike said, mulling over Jerrod's words in his head. He knew he would talk to Jerrod later, but for now, he would eat.

Chapter 13
With All My Heart, I Have Sought You

Angel lay curled on the bed in the room, with Rachel and the archangel sitting in chairs next to her bed. They had been talking to her for weeks, trying to break through the walls she put up for protection during her time in the caverns. The archangel and Rachel had made progress, and Rachel prayed it would continue.

"John 10:10 reminds you that, *'The thief comes only to steal and kill and destroy; I have come that they may have life, and have it to the full.'* Angel, which one sounds like the bad one?" Rachel asked.

"The thief," she responded weakly. "But they said you guys were the bad ones."

"While they had you, did they allow you to live life to the full?"

"No."

"What did they do to you, Angel?" Rachel asked, taking her hand.

For the first time, Angel didn't pull away. "They…they barely fed me or gave me anything to drink. They kept playing visions of horrible things," she said with a shudder.

"But I am afraid that just as Eve was deceived by the serpent's cunning, your minds may somehow be led astray

from your sincere and pure devotion to Christ," the archangel quoted 2 Corinthians 11:3.

"Does that sound like what you went through?" Rachel asked. Angel only nodded in response, so Rachel went on, "In Romans 16:20, it says, *'The God of peace will soon crush Satan under your feet. The grace of our Lord Jesus be with you.'* When you continue to say Satan, Cassius, Korax, and Calliope are right, do you really know what you're saying?"

"They said they would take care of me. They took care of Allen, but I didn't believe them," Angel said. "I'm not sure what to believe right now."

"They tried to convince you by messing with your mind. We're showing you the truth by using the Word. The Word of God has never changed. Do you agree that the Word of God has never changed?"

"Yes. There are translations, but the main books have never changed," Angel said slowly sitting up.

"Do you want to know what it says about Satan in John?" Rachel asked. When Angel nodded, she quoted John 8:44, *"You belong to your father, the devil and you want to carry out your father's desires. He was a murderer from the beginning, not holding to the truth, for there is no truth in him. When he lies, he speaks his native language, for he is a liar and the father of lies."*

"Does that sound like someone you want to follow?" the archangel asked.

"No," Angel admitted.

"Do you want to know his fate?" the archangel asked.

Rachel opened her Bible. Knowing it was a long one, she wanted to also be able to show it to Angel. Looking up Revelation 20:1-3, she read, *"And I saw an angel coming down out of heaven, having the key to the Abyss and holding in his hand a great chain. He seized the dragon, that ancient serpent, who is the devil, or Satan, and bound him for a thousand years. He threw him into the Abyss, and locked and sealed it over him, to keep him from deceiving the nations anymore until the thousand years were ended."*

"That is his fate. Does that sound like someone you want to follow?" the archangel asked again.

"No," she responded.

"Now, let's look at the other side...our side," Rachel said. Quoting 1 John 4:16, she said, *"And so we know and rely on the love God has for us. God is love. Whoever lives in love lives in God, and God in them."* With the Spirit's guidance, Rachel pressed on, "We already know Satan is the father of lies, right?"

"Right," Angel said.

"Now, let's see what else the Bible says about God." Flipping until she found the verse she wanted, she read Titus 1:2, *"In the hope of eternal life, which God, who does not lie, promised before the beginning of time."* Rachel looked up at Angel. "Satan lies, but God does not. Now, let's look at His power." Turning to Colossians 1:16, she read, *"For in Him all things were created: things in heaven and on earth, visible and invisible, whether thrones or powers or rulers or authorities; all things have been created through Him and for Him."*

"But, if He's so powerful, why didn't He stop it?" Angel asked. "Why didn't He get me out and stop what they were doing to me?"

"Be alert and sober mind. Your enemy the devil prowls around like a roaring lion looking for someone to devour. Resist him, standing firm in the faith, because you know that the family of believers throughout the world is undergoing the same kind of sufferings," the archangel quoted 1 Peter 5:8&9. "Lucifer does his best down here, because he knows his time is limited. He also knows his fate, and is doing his best to take everyone down with him that he can."

"How do I stop this? How do I get rid of these images and feelings? How do I know what is right?" Angel asked in desperation.

"James 4:7 tells us, *'Submit yourselves, then, to God. Resist the devil, and he will flee from you.'* When you don't know what the truth is, pray to God to clear it up," Rachel explained. "You have played the games. You know the verses we use to help each other through situations. When you feel confused, or aren't sure, pray for clarity. Ask God to help you."

"You're telling me the truth, though?" Angel asked, unsure.

"Has the Word of God helped you in the past?"

"Yes."

"Has it changed?"

"No."

"You told us that things didn't make sense when you thought about your memories, right?"

"Right."

"Then, follow what you *know* is true. Hold the Words from the Bible close to your heart. Allow God to clear things up for you. Time will be your best friend. What they did to you was inexcusable…in so many ways," Rachel said, holding Angel's hand. "You are my friend. Yes, there are times where we don't get along, but I will always love you as my sister. Family members can fight, but no one goes after another family member. If they do, then they are dealing with the entire family," she said with a smile and a wink.

"Protected," Angel whispered. "I haven't felt protected in a long time."

"Just like I did not let you fall in the wilderness when you passed out from exhaustion, starvation, and dehydration, the family of God will not let you fall," the archangel explained. "You may have thought you were alone, but you were *never* alone. The saints, the family of God, the angels, and most importantly, God, Jesus, and the Spirit cheered you on every day. The other side may have been able to penetrate your mind, but they will never be able to touch your soul unless you give it to them. They know that. Your soul is protected by the blood of Jesus. *Nothing* can take you out of His hands."

"John 10:28-30 reminds us what Jesus told us," Rachel said. Showing Angel the verses in the Bible, she read, "See, it says, *'I give them eternal life, and they shall never perish; no one will snatch them out of My hand. My Father, who has given them to Me, is greater than all; no one can snatch them out of My Father's hand. I and the Father are one.'* You may have felt that you were alone, but you were not. God had you in His protective hands the entire time. He promised in 1 Corinthians 10:13, that *'No temptation has overtaken you except what is common to mankind. And God is faithful; He will not let you be tempted beyond what you can bear. But when you are tempted, He will also provide a way out so that you can endure it.'* He *is* faithful, Angel. When you were to that point, did He get you out?"

"Yes. I told them I had enough, and left," Angel explained. "But, it was too easy."

"Too easy, or did you have Jesus beside you?" Rachel challenged.

"I guess…I don't know. He could have been."

"Who has shown you love?" the archangel asked.

"They said they would."

"They said they *would,* but who has shown it to you already?" Rachel asked. "Who has shown you darkness, and who has shown you light?"

"What they showed me was dark," Angel admitted.

"Come on, Angel, let's do the game. Verses on darkness and light. I'll start," Rachel encouraged. "I'll go easy on the first one. Psalm 119:105, *'Thy Word is a lamp unto my feet, and a light unto my path.'*"

"John 8:12?" Angel offered.

"Good. What does it say?" Rachel asked.

"When Jesus spoke again to the people, He said, "I am the light of the world. Whoever follows Me will never walk in darkness, but will have the light of life." But, it *was* dark."

"If it was dark, you would have lost your way," the archangel said. Then he quoted Psalm 119:130, *"The unfolding of Your words gives light; it gives understanding to the simple."*

"In comparison, let's look at James 1:17," Rachel said, "It says, *"Every good and perfect gift is from above, coming down from the Father of the heavenly lights, who does not change like the shifting shadows.'* You said the Word of the Lord never changes, right?"

"Right," Angel agreed.

"Who operates in the shadows?" the archangel asked.

"The other side. They even operate in people as Unnaturals."

"Right. Since we have looked at both sides, which one do *you* think is bad, and which do you think is good? I do not care what they said, or what we have said," the archangel said. "I care what *you* think...what you *know*. What does the Word of God say?"

"But when He, the Spirit of truth, comes, He will guide you into all the truth. He will not speak on His own; He will speak only what He hears, and He will tell you what is to come."

"John 16:13, good one, Angel!" Rachel smiled. "John 8:32 tell us, *'Then you will know the truth, and the truth will set you free.'* You *know* the truth, Angel. We have been taught since we were children to hide His Word in our hearts."

"I have hidden your word in my heart that I might not sin against you," Angel said, quoting Psalm 119:11. "I didn't sin

against Him. Allen did, though. He blasphemed the Spirit. He did the unforgiveable sin."

"And, for that, he will answer," the archangel said. "You did not, though. You hid His Word in your heart. You *know* the truth, and *the truth* is what set you free. You *know* you are a child of God. With that strength, you walked out of the caverns. You are free in Christ."

"Thank you," Angel said, as tears started to flow. "I *am* free. Thank you for showing me the truth."

"It hasn't been easy," Rachel admitted.

The archangel rested his hand on Angel's as he encouraged, "With time, you will heal."

"Psalm 147:3 reminds us that, *'He heals up the broken hearted, and binds up their wounds.'* You have a long journey ahead of you, Angel, but I think you've made the right steps." Rachel smiled. "You're not walking this alone. We're your family, and we're not leaving. Blood doesn't make a family…love makes a family. You have more than just your immediate family. You have team A.N.G.E.L., along with all of the angels, and the entire family of God behind you. You are a daughter of The King. You are bought with the priceless gift of the blood of Jesus. You have the saints before you, the A.N.G.E.L.s, and those in the family of God around you. And, you have The Spirit within you. You *will* be okay. I know this is only the start, and we will have a few more weeks of this, but I think I need to go take a break if you don't mind? I'll send Charlie and Jacob in, if that's okay?"

"What about Jesse?" Angel asked.

"I'd like to talk to Jesse for a bit."

"Okay. Are *you* staying?" she asked the archangel.

"I am not going anywhere until you want me to."

"Thank you both," Angel said, and nodded for Rachel to go.

Outside, Rachel closed the door behind her and leaned against the front of the house. "Thank you, Lord!" she whispered. "Without You, this could have gone sideways fast."

"Hey!" Charlie said, as he, Jacob, and Jesse got up from the table under the trees. Meeting in the middle, Charlie asked, "How's Angel?"

"I need to tag you blokes. I'm exhausted!"

"I'll bet! You've been going at it for like fifteen hours a day," Jacob pointed out.

"Jesse, I wanted to talk to you. Can just Jacob and Charlie go in?" Rachel asked.

"Sure!" He grinned, as his heart skipped a beat at spending more time alone with her.

While Charlie and Jacob went inside, Rachel and Jesse slowly made their way back to the table under the Boab trees. Sitting next to each other, they looked out over the brutally hot desert lands before them, dotted with the occasional flowered bush or tree, or an animal scurrying to find the precious shade.

Watching the heat radiate from the desert floor in waves for a few moments, Rachel finally broke the pensive silence. "We need to talk."

"I know. Our last conversation didn't go very well," Jesse admitted. "God and I have had many conversations since, and have worked things out. I'm not ready to talk to Angel about things yet, but when I get a chance, the archangel and I need to have a conversation."

"That's not what I meant, but that's good."

"What do you want to talk about then?"

"What I set out to talk to you about the first time."

"Which was what?"

Rachel took a deep breath, turned toward him, and blurted out, "Before something else happens, I want you to know that I am in love with you."

Wide-eyed, Jesse was stunned silent. He wanted to hear those words for so long from her, and now that she said them, he wasn't quite sure what to do with them.

When he didn't say anything, she spoke quickly, as she struggled to catch Jesse up in the conversations she had with God and others over the last several months. "I'm team lead, but that shouldn't make a difference when it comes to my heart. God wants us to live our lives to the fullest. Being an A.N.G.E.L., our lives tend to not last. In being in the field, and running into other A.N.G.E.L.s, I've learned that's not always true. Your mum and dad are a prime example. They, along with The Colonel, Danny, Ethan, Charlie, and Derek…they've all lived long lives. Some have been cut short, but they were lost in service to the Kingdom. If I'm going t' go," she said, her Australian accent getting thicker as she struggled to share her heart, "there's no way better to go than in His service…and in love." Looking up at him for his reaction, she saw his heart soften in his facial expression. "Please say something?"

He couldn't. She touched his heart deeply. Resting his hands on the sides of her face, he gently pulled her toward him in a kiss.

When they connected, Rachel couldn't hold the tears back anymore, and she started to cry.

"Why are you crying?"

"I haven't dated any guys before now. I've been afraid. Leah, Josh, Caleb, and I knew two of us would get the call, but we didn't know which ones. When Josh got it, Caleb was confident in pursuing a relationship with Willow. When I got the call, Leah knew it was okay to date Finn, her now fiancé. I was scared to say yes to you, because I have never had a boyfriend. I was also afraid that the others on the team would think I was favoring you."

"That still doesn't explain why you're crying?" he said, confused, as he wiped the tears off her face.

Smiling, shaking her head, she explained, "Because it was the most beautiful thing I ever experienced. I imagined what this would feel like, but it wasn't even close. To surrender to the call, meant that I trusted God with my heart and feelings. I know beyond a shadow of a doubt that He will take good care of them. To surrender to my feelings for you, meant that I trust *you* with those same feelings. That's terrifying for me."

"Believe it or not, it's terrifying for me too. But, I know you are a caring, kind, sweet, gentle woman of God. If things don't work, I know you will still do your best not to hurt me."

"And, I know the same about you."

"But…" Jesse shook his head.

"Tell me what you feel," she said, and kissed him again.

The tingling was instantaneous between them. Joining hands for a moment, Jesse released one to rest his hand on her cheek, as the love between them filled them from their inner core, and overflowed all around them.

Pulling a few inches away, Rachel asked, "What do you feel?"

"Joy. Unspeakable, unimaginable, indescribable joy."

"I have never felt that before." Resting her forehead on his, leaving their words between the two of them, she quietly said, "Thank you for not giving up on me."

"Thank *you* for trusting me. Rach, I don't want to date."

Sitting up in alarm, she asked. "What? What do you mean?"

Thinking for a moment on how to word it, he explained, "You mean more to me than a mere date. I want to have permission to court you."

"As in…?"

"As in, with the intention of one day marrying you. I know we were meant to be together as soon as I laid eyes on you. I know you feel the same."

"I do," she agreed.

"Then, may I have permission to ask your father for permission to court you? Obviously we have a long time until the marriage subject needs to be approached, but I don't want to look any further." Joining each of their hands together, Jesse rested his forehead on hers as he explained, "I know your heart. I know *you*. We've practically been with each other almost twenty-four/seven since we pulled up to your house on the station almost a year ago. I think we both know we are destined to eventually be together. Having said that, I would still like to take things slowly."

"I agree," she said, heart racing at how close his body was to hers. Looking into his eyes, she said, "Yes. You can talk to Dad about courting me. I would be honored."

A grin crossed his face that she hadn't seen in a long time. His dimples shown as his smile went from ear to ear. "Thank you."

"We need to talk with the team."

"No. I'm pretty sure they'll figure it out soon enough. Before we go back out to the field, we can sit our team down and talk to them. Things in the field won't change. I will still look out for you, as you will me…as we will the team. We are *still* a team. We are still A.N.G.E.L.s."

"We are still one of His, only now, we are one of His together."

"Exactly. And, together, we will continue to grow in Him, and as a team."

"Thank you for waiting." Rachel smiled.

"You are more than worth it."

"As are you."

Chapter 14
I Will Give Thanks To The Lord With All My Heart

On the night before graduation from their program, Mike, along with Ranger, and Jerrod, along with Chief, were in their room. "Hey, brother, I've been meaning to talk to you," Mike started.

"About what?" Jerrod asked, with Chief resting his head on Jerrod's chest, as they lay on their bed. Mike sat cross-legged on his, with Ranger beside him.

"I've been watching you through these last seven weeks."

Jerrod chuckled. "Is that supposed to be comforting?"

Grinning, Mike explained, "You've handled yourself very well. You and Chief are an example for the rest of us. Don't think me weird or anything –"

Jerrod smirked. "Ship sailed on that one a long time ago, brother."

Laughing, Mike said, "Funny, but seriously. You have a kind of light about you. It's hard to explain. I watched you defend yourself against Donny and Chase's continued grilling, and you didn't get angry at all. You calmly explained your perspective."

"Why would I get angry or upset with them? I don't appreciate the name calling, but it's ultimately their choice. It's my job to share. It's the Spirit's job to work on the heart. The choice, though, is theirs."

"See, that's what I mean," he said, leaning back on the wall next to his bed. "You have a way of saying things that makes one think."

"What do *you* think?"

"I *think* I'm talking to you for a reason."

"Which is?"

"To find out more about this Jesus, God, and Spirit you talk about. I've heard people talk about just God, or just Jesus, but in talking to you, there seems to be more of a connection. And then, there's the Spirit you talk about. I didn't know there were three of them."

"There is, but there isn't."

"Meaning?"

"Okay, let me see the best way to describe this?" he said, thinking, as he sat up. "Oh! I've heard Angel explain it this way…there are three parts to an egg, right? There's the shell, the yolk, and the egg whites."

"Right."

"But, they're all the egg."

"Right."

"There are three parts of God. There's God, the Father; God, the Son, Jesus; and, the Holy Spirit. They are all God, but They are three-in-one."

"Okay. Can you explain all three to me, so I know the difference?"

"Okay. God the Father is the creator. He spoke the world…the universe…into existence. He created the sun, moon, and stars. He created this beautiful planet we call earth, along with every plant, creature, and human on it. He created the vast universe around us – the planets, the Milky Way, black holes…everything. He even just spoke *us* into existence."

"You really believe that?"

"With every fiber of my being."

"How can you say that?"

"Genesis, chapters one to three for starters," he said, sitting up while opening his Bible that was on the nightstand. "We can go there in a bit. Let's go with the abbreviated version in John 1:1-3 instead. It says, *'In the beginning was the Word, and the Word was with God, and the Word was God. He was with God in the beginning. Through Him all things were made; without Him nothing was made that has been made.'* You see, They were there in the beginning – all three of Them. There's nothing here that God didn't create. There's nothing here by mistake…including you."

"Nothing like going for the target on the first shot," Mike said, tongue-in-cheek.

"We were military. That's what we were trained to do."

"Fair enough. Move on." Mike gestured for Jerrod to continue.

Flipping to another reference, Jerrod read, "Here's another one in Psalm 8:3-8. It says, *'When I consider Your heavens, the work of Your fingers, the moon and the stars, which You have set in place, what is mankind that You are mindful of them, human beings that you care for them?'* See, He created us, but He loves and cares for us. Here, there's more, *'You have made them a little lower than the angels and crowned them with glory and honor. You made them rulers over the works of Your hands; you put everything under their feet: all flocks and herds, and the animals of the wild, the birds in the sky, and the fish in the sea, all that swim the path of the seas.'* He created this world, and us, and then gave us dominion over it. He trusted us with the Earth and its contents."

"If we have so much power, why do we need Him?"

"Because we screwed up. He gave us one little rule, but we couldn't follow it," Jerrod said, and turned to Genesis 3:17-19. "It says here in Genesis, *'To Adam He said, "Because you listened to your wife and ate fruit from the tree about which I commanded you, 'You must not eat from it,' Cursed is the ground because of you; through painful toil you will eat food from it all the days of your life. It will produce thorns and thistles for you, and you will eat the plants of the field. By the sweat of your brow you will eat your food until you return to the ground, since from it you were taken; for dust you are and to dust you will return.'* He gave us everything, and we messed it up."

"Wait! Because of this guy's choice, we're all cursed?"

"Yes, and no. Look, you could have very well made the same choice. We *are* human. Regardless of who made the mistake, the human race was cursed to be separated from God from that point forward."

"Okay, again, then why do we need this God if He doesn't care about us?"

"Oh, I didn't say He doesn't care about us. On the contrary, this is the part where Jesus comes in."

"Okay," Mike leaned back, "Explain."

"You see, the Father doesn't *want* to be separated from us. Here, let me see if I can clear things up a bit. God loves each of us as His children. Some people see God, as they see their own Father. This causes issues at times, mainly if they didn't have a good dad."

"Yeah, mine wasn't the best."

"You'll have a more difficult time with understanding Him as the caring, loving, but fair-minded God that He is. You see, when Adam ate the fruit, he essentially cursed the entire human race to be separated from God forever. God already cast out an angel named Lucifer quite some time before. Lucifer is –"

"The Devil…I know," Mike cut him off. "Not a nice guy."

"Correct. He's actually the one who got Eve to eat the apple. He's going to spend eternity in a Lake of Fire, and wants to take as many of us as he can with him. He and his minions are working overtime, because they know they don't have forever."

"So, you're telling me that Hell is real?"

"Is Heaven real?"

"Well, yeah! I hope so!"

"Well, where you have light, you have dark. Where you have angels, you have demons. Where you have God, you have Satan. And, where you have Heaven, you have Hell. People don't mind looking at the good, but there's balance in the universe. Having said that, you have to remember that God is, was, and always will be stronger than the Devil. He created the entire universe, but still has time for each one of us individually. We are not worthy, but He still loves us. He is the King of Kings, and Lord of Lords, but those of us who are His, are taken care of and looked after."

"Sounds like a good guy. But, you said Satan wants us to go to the Lake of Fire with him. What if I don't want to? What if I just be as good as I can be?"

"You can't."

"Why not?" Mike asked, offended.

"You can never be good enough. Look, when sin entered the world, the only way to get forgiveness was through a sin offering. Have you ever heard about burnt offerings, or animal offerings on an alter before?"

"Yeah."

"There had to be blood shed in order to atone for sin. Not by just any animal either. It had to be the first, the best, and the most perfect one of the lot."

"Okay. I don't see or hear about any of those anymore, though. What changed?"

"Jesus made them null and void."

"I'm confused."

"Ephesians 2:8 and 9, says, *'For it is by grace you have been saved, through faith – and this in not from yourselves, it is the gift of God – not by works, so that no one can boast.'* There is *no way* you could *ever* be good enough. Let me put it this way. What if you came to my friend's house. I was already there. You knocked on the door, and asked to be let in."

"Why would they let me in? They don't know me."

"Exactly! Heaven is God's home. If He doesn't know you, why would He let you in?"

"Because I've been good."

"So, my friend should let you in because you are good?"

"No. Your friend should let me in because I know you, and you're there."

"My friend should just listen to you and expect that you're telling the truth?"

"Well, no." Mike rolled his eyes. "Of course he would ask you first, and then you'd vouch for me."

"You know I would, brother, but for the sake of the example, let's shift it back to Heaven. It's God's house…the castle. Jesus is the One inside who we know."

"Oh! I get it! So, I need to know Jesus to get in?"

Jerrod smiled. "Right!"

Furrowing his brow, Mike said, "We haven't gotten to Jesus yet."

"Nope."

"Okay, hurry this up. I want to get to the end of this story. You've got me more curious now," he said, impatiently.

"Okay, going to jump to John 3:16 and 17."

"I know John 3:16, but not 17."

"You have to put the two together to get the complete picture. They say, *'For God so loved the world, that He gave His only Son, that whoever believes in Him should not perish but have eternal life. For God did not send His Son into the world to condemn the world, but in order that the world might be saved through Him.'* You see –"

"Wait! You said that Jesus was in Heaven. But that verse says He's here. Which is it?"

"He *was* here."

"I heard something about that, but I don't believe it."

"Dude, your eternal security hinges on you believing it."

Wide-eyed, Mike said, "Explain! Immediately!"

"Okay, so, once sin entered the world, and throughout the next multiple thousands of years of history, God and humans wrestled with one another. For sake of cutting the story a bit, let's say that God was in Heaven, upset with the human race. Jesus came into the throne room to talk to Him about it. Being that He is the son of the King, He has full access to the Kingdom. After all, He is the King's one and only Son."

"True. I can see that."

"So, they have this conversation where God pours His heart out, and Jesus does the same. They get their minds together and figure out that there's only one way to save the human race."

"Which is?"

"For there to be the ultimate blood sacrifice. It had to be perfect, without sin."

"How is that possible, unless…?" Mike's voice faded as he realized where Jerrod was going with it. "The verse said, *God did not send His Son into the world to condemn the world, but in order that the world might be saved through Him.'* Are you saying *Jesus* was the sacrifice?"

"Yes. He came to Earth as a baby. Mary was a virgin when she conceived. Now, don't think that didn't freak her out, because it did! It totally threw Joseph, her fiancé for a loop too, but that's a story for another day. Point is, Jesus was born, and grew up here on Earth. He wanted each of us to understand that He knows our struggles. Satan even took a crack at Him when He was here too, but Jesus prevailed. He was without sin."

"This is the dying on the cross thing, isn't it?"

"Yep. Come over here," Jerrod said, patting the seat next to him. Chief went over and got on the bed beside Ranger, while Mike went over and sat beside Jerrod. Jerrod turned to John 15:9-17, and began to read, as Mike followed along, "Now, this is Jesus talking. He said, *'As the Father has loved Me, so have I loved you. Now remain in My love. If you keep my commandments, you will remain in My love, just as I have kept my Father's commands and remain in His love. I have told you this so that My joy may be in you and that your joy may be complete. My command is this: Love each other as I have loved you. Greater love has no one than this: to lay down one's life for one's friends. You are My friends –"*

"Did He really say that?" Mike asked, looking closer at the Bible.

"Yep!" Jerrod said with a smile, as his heart jumped in excitement. His friend was connecting the dots of the love of Jesus. Starting with verse fourteen, he continued, *"You are my friends if you do what I command. I no longer call you servants, because a servant does not know His master's business. Instead, I have called you friends, for everything that I learned from My Father, I have made known to you. You did not choose me, but I chose you and appointed you, so that you might go and bear fruit – fruit that will last – and so that whatever you ask in My name the Father will give you. This is my command: Love each other."* Quickly flipping to Romans 5:8, he said, "See, here, this is what happened. Pay attention, we're about to go fast here."

"Go ahead."

Reading Romans 5:8, he said, *" 'But God demonstrates His own love for us in this: While we were still sinners, Christ died for us.'* Now, in tying this in with John 3:16 and 17, what does that tell you?"

"That God and Jesus are love, and They would do anything for me."

"Yes. Now, this is where it gets good," Jerrod said, excitement unmistakable. "You see, when Jesus died, He went to Hell for three days. After those three days, He rose from the dead, victorious over Hell. Because of His sacrifice on the cross, we don't *have* to go to Hell when we die. All He asks is that we show His love to others, as He showed His love for us."

"By giving His life for us."

"Yes. Now, we put our lives on the line for our country. Wouldn't you like to give your life for an even higher purpose than freedom…freedom from the depths of Hell?"

Surprised, he asked, "I can do that?"

Turning to Romans 10:9, Jerrod read, *"If you declare with your mouth, "Jesus is Lord," and believe in your heart that God raised Him from the dead, you will be saved."* Turning to 2 Corinthians 5:17, he said, "Oh! And, check this out." Jerrod read, *"Therefore, if anyone is in Christ, he is a new creation. The old has passed away; behold, the new has come."* Looking up he explained, "You see, once you pray to Jesus, and confess with your mouth that He is Lord, He washes away all the sin that you've done before that point. You start with a clean slate. There may still be consequences here on earth that you will have to face, but in Heaven it's like it never happened. And, once you do, your name is written in the Lamb's Book of Life. So, when you go to the door after you die, and God asks you why He should let you into His Heaven, you can say that you are covered by the blood of Jesus! And, guess what?"

"What?"

"He already knows whose name is in the Book of Life, so He'll let you in, welcoming you as a child of God. You see, once Jesus made the sacrifice, He opened Heaven to all of those who choose to follow Him. I am a child of the King."

"I see."

"And the best part?"

"There's more?"

"Yeah. See," Jerrod said, turning to Romans 8:37-39. He read, *"No, in all these things we are more than conquerors through Him who loved us. For I am sure that neither death nor life, nor angels nor rulers, nor things present nor things to come, nor powers nor height nor depth, nor anything else in all creation, will be able to separate us from the love of God in Christ Jesus our Lord."* Then he turned to Jeremiah 29:11, and read, *"For I know the plans I have for you," declares the Lord, "plans to prosper you and not to harm you, plans to give you a hope and a future."* He's got the perfect plan for you, He's only waiting for you to come and talk to Him about it. He actually cares enough for each and every one of us to have a special plan just for us…for *you*."

Sitting back, Mike crossed his arms, deep in thought. After a heavy minute, he said, "So, what you're telling me is that light I see in you is Jesus?"

"Yes. The Spirit is the One who guides my thoughts and actions."

"We talked about God and Jesus, but not the Spirit."

"Right. Okay, before Jesus left back for Heaven, after He rose from the dead, He left the Spirit to help guide us here on Earth. It's that still small voice inside of us. If we listen to it, we will either have a blessing, or bless others through our actions. Here, this explains it better. The book of Acts was written by Luke, to Theophilus, so bear with me in the beginning. It'll become clear the more we read," Jerrod explained. Turning to Acts 1, he read verses 1-9, *"In my former book, Theophilus, I wrote about all that Jesus began to do and to teach until the day He was taken up to Heaven, after giving instructions through the Holy Spirit to the apostles He had chosen. After His suffering, He presented Himself to them and gave many convincing proofs that He was alive. He appeared to them over a period of forty days and spoke about the Kingdom of God. On one occasion, while He was eating with them, He gave them this command: "Do not leave Jerusalem, but wait for the gift My Father promised, which you have heard Me speak about. For John baptized with water, but in a few days you will be baptized with the Holy Spirit."*

"So God sent the Spirit as a gift? To help keep the communication between us and Him?"

"Yes. Once you are a child of God, you will be given a Spiritual gift from God. It will become stronger the more you use it. Some are prayer warriors, and are given times to pray, not always knowing why they are praying. Some will be given the gift of evangelism or preaching. Some will be given the gift of teaching. The list goes on, but you get the idea."

"Okay, I can roll with that. What else does it say?" Mike asked, looking down at the Bible.

Starting with verse six, Jerrod kept reading, *"Then they gathered around Him and asked Him, "Lord, are you at this time going to restore the kingdom to Israel?" He said to them: "It is not for you to know the times or dates the Father has set by His own authority. But you will receive power when the Holy Spirit comes on you; and you will be my witnesses in Jerusalem, and in all Judea and Samaria, and to the ends of the earth." After He said this, He was taken up before their very eyes, and a cloud hid Him from their sight."*

"I'll bet *that* was a wild day!" Mike laughed.

"I can't imagine. Now," Jerrod said, closing his Bible, "You have a choice, my friend. What are you going to do?"

"Honestly, I'd like to research this more," he said, going back to his bed. When he did, Chief jumped back on the bed with Jerrod. "Is there a way I can keep in communication with you? When I get home, I'm going to get in touch with some of my other friends who I know go to church. I want to know more."

"That's your choice, brother," Jerrod said, writing an email down on a piece of paper. "You can send an email. If I don't answer right away, don't worry. I'll get in touch with you as soon as I get back."

"Back from where?"

"From wherever God has sent me."

"What does *that* mean?"

"Well, I'll usually be here in the States, but there may be times where I'll be out of the country. I go where He sends me."

"Interesting," Mike said, tucking Jerrod's email into his wallet. "Do you have a phone number?"

"Nope. No social media either. That's the only way to get in touch with me. It may take me some time, but I *will* get back with you if you contact me. I'm here for you, brother."

"As am I for you," Mike said. Thinking for a moment, he asked, "What was that verse about giving one's life?"

"John 15:13. It says, *'Greater love has no one than this: to lay down one's life for one's friends.'* There *is* no greater sacrifice."

"And, Jesus did just that, huh?"

"Yep." Jerrod looked at him for a moment, and asked, "What are you thinking?"

"That I've got some serious thinking to do."

"While I'm not pushing by any means, I would be remiss if I didn't warn you not to wait until it's too late."

"What do you mean?"

"Once you die, it's too late to change your mind. I had a very good friend who was a Christian, but her friend was not. They were both killed in an accident. I'm pretty sure Terrik was not a Christian when he died. All of us around him were Christians, but he chose to wait until the situation at the time resolved before making a choice. I'm afraid it was more than likely too late for him."

"I see."

"Just think about it, brother," Jerrod said, lying back down.

"I will." Looking down at his wallet, containing Jerrod's email, he said, "I *will* be contacting you."

"I look forward to it."

*   *   *

After several weeks of chemo, Kit had enough! For the last few weeks, they would go into town the night before and rent a hotel room for three days. They found out just how rough the treatments were after the first one. Kit got so sick that Nico took her to the nearest hotel and checked them in. She threw up more than she thought she had in her. Lesson learned! Since the treatments would be scheduled for around nine in the morning, they would go into town the night before. After the treatments, which took about four to five hours, they would immediately go back to the hotel for the night. It would take Kit at least a day before she would be ready to travel back to the station, so they would stay through until the day after.

After the treatment that day, Nico rushed her to the hotel, barely getting their hotel room door open before she bolted for the bathroom to commence throwing up. "How are you able to keep anything down?"

"I –" Kit was cut off when she threw up again. When she finished, with tears in her eyes, she admitted, "I can't. I'm in so much pain, it's intense!"

"Where does it hurt the most?" he asked, crouching on the floor next to her. By this point, he didn't care that his bride was vomiting, he would be by her side through it all.

"All over," she groaned. "I don't know how people do this! I don't know how much more I can –" she was cut off again as she hurled into the toilet.

Just then, Nico's phone rang. "It's Mark," he explained.

"Take it. He may know information on Rachel."

Gently squeezing her shoulder, he left the bathroom to answer the phone. "Sullivan," he answered.

"Nico, this is Mark."

"G'day, Mark." Nico smiled. "How's it? You still in Australia?"

"Yes. Looks like we'll be able to go back to the States in a few more weeks. I can't wait. I miss my wife and kids."

"I'm sure she misses you too. I hear it's pretty chaotic over there."

"I'm sure. There are A.N.G.E.L.s crawling all over. I don't know how she's keeping it all organized. I was calling to check on Kit? Derek and I were prompted by the Spirit to pray for her, so we thought we'd call to see how she's doing? You're on speaker."

Hearing her vomiting again, he rubbed the back of his neck. Looking out the sliding glass doors that went out to a balcony from their room that overlooked the town, he admitted, "It's rough."

"How's she holding up?"

"She's not…really. She's struggling. She could use all the prayer she can get."

"How are *you* holding up?" Derek asked, sensing it in his voice.

"Honestly?" Nico asked.

"We wouldn't ask if we didn't want to know."

"I've seen a lot of ugly in my life, but t' be honest, this is the ugliest thing I've ever seen. Watching this stuff overtake your true love's body is horrendous! As I know you blokes are, I'm a fixer…and I can't fix this. She's in continuous pain, always throwing up, exhausted beyond measure, and often says she's not in control of her own body. She's just along for the ride. Honestly, this is a nightmare."

"I'm sure! I couldn't imagine what I would do if it were Casey," Mark said. "I *do* know that she's strong, though."

"Oh, she *is* a strong sheila. This isn't a matter of physical strength as much as it is mental. Yes, physical strength counts immensely, but the doctor warned us that the mental strength will be what ultimately pulls her through. Thing is…" he looked to make sure Kit couldn't hear him. Hearing her throwing up again, he walked out onto the balcony of the room, closing the sliding glass door behind him. Then he quietly explained, "With Leah's wedding coming, she wants to be there to help with the details, but she can't. Also, she's worried about ruining Leah's wedding. She knows she will look horrific in the photos and she doesn't want to be remembered like that. To hear her talk like that scares me. I pray she's not giving up."

"She can do this."

"Oh, *I* know she can do this. It's *her* I'm worried about."

"Look, I may not understand *exactly* what you're going through, but before Casey and I were married, we were taken captive and tortured. Having similar personalities, I know you understand the protective instinct we have in us."

"Yes!" Nico said, relieved someone understood his feelings. "Thank you!"

"Jackie tortured Casey, whipping her, lashing into her back to the point that the skin was broken down until the muscles were exposed. Then she poured warm salt water over her back.”

“Crikey! I knew it was bad, but I didn’t know it was *that* bad. I’m sorry, mate.”

“Oh, that was after she waterboarded her, drowning her over and over again. She went through it! The nightmares were horrible! The worse part, though, was that there was nothing I could do. I was chained to a wall in another room. I could hear her screaming, but there was absolutely nothing I could do to help her. Then, when we were rescued, I had to watch as other guys took care of her. Again, it was completely out of my control.”

“How did ya handle it?”

“Honestly? God, Derek, and The Colonel. Without them, I would have lost it.”

“Well, *you* have Derek –”

“Who is in desperate need to keep his friend here,” Derek put in. “You can’t have him *or* me right now.”

“I get it,” Nico chuckled. “I know you’re facing your own battles.”

“No joke!”

“When are *you* getting out?”

“In a few weeks.”

“Nico!” Kit yelled before she started throwing up again.

"I gotta go!" Nico said, and hung up, knowing he would be holding Kit's hair for the remainder of the night. And, he would gladly do so, only to have her wake up in his arms each morning. For that, he would give thanks to God with all his heart!

Chapter 15
Your Words Have I Hid In My Heart

"Girls, wake up!" Casey said, jostling Allie and Callie. "You guys need to wake up."

"Mo-o-o-om!" they whined in unison.

"Come on. Daddy's coming home! We need to go get him and Uncle Derek from the airport! Let's go!"

"Daddy!" Allie sat upright in her bed.

"Really?" Callie asked with a grin on her face.

"Yep! We need to get ready to go!"

After wrangling the wiggling, giggling twins into their clothes and through breakfast, Casey got everyone loaded into the van, with Josh driving. Josh had severe bruising from the explosion, but he was okay by that point. He still needed some recovery time when the others left to help find Angel, which is why he didn't go with them.

"Thank you for staying with us over the last several weeks," Casey said, as they waited at a table for Derek and Mark to come out of the terminal.

"My pleasure. I know you've had your hands full with Jon and Val's recovery, along with homeschooling, *and* the A.N.G.E.L.s coming in from all over. I can't imagine this has been all that easy."

"With you and Jon back up to full strength, and Val helping with homeschooling until his cast comes off, it's eased some of the stress. Cori and Kai help out in the kitchen and cleaning, and so do the other A.N.G.E.L.s when they can. Mark and Derek are coming home, and with the rest of the team coming in a few weeks for the memorial service, things may get a little more crazy, before they slow down, but we'll be together. Then a portion of you guys will head back to Australia for the wedding, and…" she sighed. "Okay, chaotic is a mild term for our life right now."

"What about Christmas?" Allie asked. "When are we going to celebrate Christmas?"

Casey groaned as she dropped her head on her hand. "Okay, maybe some things need to be adjusted."

"We'll sort it out. No worries," Josh encouraged. "Look, the only ones that *must* go to Australia are Rachel and I."

Casey laughed. "You don't seriously think my son will let your sister go anywhere without him, do you?"

"What do ya mean?"

"First of all, whether they want to fully admit it or not, Rachel and Jesse are in love. Secondly, they were separated for a few weeks on the opposite sides of the world, while you guys were getting yourselves blown up and shot at. I'm pretty sure if they're not together yet, it won't be too long before they *will* be together."

"Really?"

"You didn't see it? Do you not know your sister very well?"

"Well, I *do* know that they've talked about it, but do you really think they'll cross the line and go for it?"

"I'd put money on it. You didn't see her face when those bombs went off. Jesse's name was the one she whispered. She loves him. It's a matter of whether or not they're willing to take the risk."

"Time will tell," Josh acknowledged. "We haven't had any communication since Rachel went in. According to Caleb and Pete, the archangel basically took them off the map until they were ready. We'll have t' wait and –"

"Daddy!" the girls squealed in unison at seeing Mark and Derek.

They jumped up from the table, only to stop short. Both Mark and Derek were being pushed in wheelchairs, with Mark holding a crutch across his lap.

"What happened to Daddy and Uncle Derek?" Callie demanded, crossing her arms.

"Why are they in those chairs?" Allie asked.

"Remember, we told you guys about when Josh, Jon, and Val got hurt?" Casey asked them.

"Yes," Allie said, as Callie nodded.

"Well, Daddy and Uncle Derek got hurt too. That's why Uncle Derek hasn't been able to come home. Daddy was staying with him to help keep him company so he wouldn't be alone. Remember that? That's why we were able to see and talk to them on the computer."

Callie grinned. "Oh yeah!"

Casey smiled. "Yes, thank goodness for technology…and Cori and Kai."

"Let me get their luggage. Can you take the girls to the van and bring it around once you all say hello?" Josh asked, handing her the keys.

"Sounds like a plan." Casey smirked, as the girls ran over to Derek and Mark. While Casey and Josh walked, she said, "Too many little feet to trip over."

"Too true."

After greeting the guys, Casey took the girls to the van to bring it around, while Josh went with the guys, still being pushed by the wheelchair assistants to pick up the luggage.

After Josh loaded the luggage, he helped Derek and Mark into the van. Then after he loaded Derek's wheelchair into the van, he got into the driver's seat. "Good-ness! You blokes have turned into a lot of work!" he teased.

"Tell me about it," Mark said, slightly raising his crutch. "Can't wait until I can get rid of this."

"With a broken arm, you're lucky they aren't making you use a wheelchair until the cast comes off. When *does* it come off?" Casey asked.

"Well," Mark blushed, "the doctor said with my age, and it being a compound fracture, I'm stuck with this cast for about another six weeks, depending on how quickly it heals."

Covering the smile on his mouth, Josh kept his eyes on the road, as he commented, "With your age?"

"I'm getting older. I admit it. Trust me, I've already heard it from the archangel. Nico has too."

"Well then, I don't feel so bad about being put out to pasture." Derek grinned. "Looks like I'm in good company."

"Yes, and no. *You* still have a useful skill in doing papers and documents. *My* main skill is in the field."

"Not true," Casey disagreed.

"Really?"

"Really. You're more valuable with training others here at the Haven…also in being a daddy to those two, *and* you have two new ones."

"Katia and Liliya?" Mark asked.

"Yep. Liliya should be starting school when it starts back up in January. We've been working with her English, writing, as well as working through her recovery from her experience. She will still have a lot of extra work, but she says she's ready to start school."

"What grade will she be in?" Derek asked.

"Since her junior year was pretty much lost, she decided she would have enough trouble learning cultural differences, as well as basically a whole new language and history, so she will start in her sophomore year."

"Really?" Mark asked, surprised. "She *wants* to go backward?"

"She does," Casey confirmed. "She wants to get her feet wet. She said she would do better if she were adjusted. She didn't want to play catch up, along with learning everything else."

"Smart cookie!" Derek said, impressed.

"She is," Casey agreed. "She and Katia have also changed their names."

"So, they're English's as well?" Mark asked.

"Yes. They know it'll be an adjustment, but they both want to start fresh and new."

"They're keeping their first names, though?"

"Yep. Katia's is Katia Izabella English, and Liliya's is Liliya Mikhalia English. You can call her Lily for short."

"Nice. So, you're sure she's adjusting well?"

"Very much so. Between Kit, Rachel, Leah, and I, we've done a lot of work since she came into the house. She's much more stable. The first trip to the grocery store was a treat. She had never seen so many choices in her life. I let her put whatever she wanted in the cart."

"How'd that go?"

"Well, let's just say she likes her junk food," Casey laughed, as did Josh. He was there for that trip.

"I'm glad she's adjusting so well."

"How's my mum?" Josh asked. To be courteous, he let them get their own news out of the way before he asked, but he was chomping at the bit for information. His dad and brother usually had an audience with the station hands around, so he knew they weren't completely honest with him on the phone.

"She's not doing well," Mark admitted. "When I talked to your dad, they were both struggling. This is harder than either thought it would be."

"I'll have to get them to spill next time I get them on the phone over there," Josh said, irritated. "We also haven't heard any news from the Outback since Rachel went in."

"And, you won't until they're back to at least Alice Springs. There's no reception, and there's no way of knowing when their phones will come online," Derek pointed out.

"That's not for lack of trying on Kai and Cori's behalf," Casey explained. "They're down there every day trying to ping their cell phones. They can't even get that to go through. As soon as they do, I promise you they'll get a call through to them. They're incredible!"

"I'm sure!" Mark said, happy to know the new members were working out so well.

"It's driving them crazy not getting any news from them," Josh added.

"How's everyone else doing?" Mark asked.

"They're helping out," Casey said. "There are about fifty A.N.G.E.L.s here. We haven't seen the Mexican A.N.G.E.L.s yet. They called and said Rachel, Angel, and the rest will be coming home in a week or so, so they'll be coming in a few days."

Mark nodded. "That's good to know."

"Daddy?" Callie asked, as she was on one side, and Allie was on the other.

"Yes?" Mark asked.

"I think we need a vacation."

When everyone laughed, Allie added, "Mommy *definitely* needs a vacation!"

Laughing louder, the group was happy to be back together and heading home.

*   *   *

As the tiny group headed to the Haven, Jon headed back to the airport to pick up Jerrod. They tried to coincide the two flights, but there were too many variations in scheduling to make that possible, so Josh drove for one, and Jon did the other. Jon had the choice of which one to drive, so he chose to pick up Jerrod. Jerrod would still be another couple of hours, so Jon took his time, relishing in the silence that he was finally able to achieve. While he loved his family, sometimes the silence was priceless. He didn't even turn on the radio. He just wanted peace and quiet.

"Hello, Jon," an angel said, suddenly appearing in the passenger's seat.

Startled, Jon just about ran off the road. Thankfully, they were in a flat area, so when he went off the road, he didn't run

318

into a ditch or flip the van. Slamming on the brakes, Jon shouted, "*Don't do that*! Don't you people have some sort of early warning system? A bell around your neck or *something*?" he said, feeling his heart in his chest, as he struggled to catch his breath. "You just about got me in an accident!"

"You will not get into an accident with me in the vehicle," the angel said matter-of-factly. "Also, we are not people. We are angels."

Shaking his head, he reminded the angel, "My gift is sensing feelings, not knowing if you all are around. Seriously!" he said, with his hand on his chest. "*What* are you doing here?"

"I was sent with a message for you."

"Spill it!"

"Do not worry."

"*That* is your message?" he asked, his body still on edge. "After you give me a heart attack, *that* is your message?"

"No. I only wanted to calm you prior to giving you the message."

"What's the message?"

The angel gestured for Jon to move on. "You may continue driving."

"What's your name?"

"Raphael."

"Raphael, you just about gave me heart failure," Jon said, turning back onto the road, starting to calm his nerves.

"My apologies. I am thrilled to get face-to-face time with you."

"You know me?"

"The A.N.G.E.L.s are known throughout the Kingdom. You, however, are especially close to my heart. I have been your guardian angel for quite some time."

"*I'm meeting my guardian angel?*" Jon asked, wide-eyed, in shock. "Am I dying?"

"Oh," Raphael chuckled, "not right now."

"While this *is* wild, I gotta ask…*why* are you here?"

"I have a message from the archangel. He thought it would be…how did you put it? Oh yes, he thought it would be wild for you to meet me."

"Okay," Jon said, finally getting his heart rate and breathing under control, "What's the message?"

"Your family will need you, but the Lord will need you more."

"What does *that* mean?"

"Josh and Rachel will be going to Australia for the wedding of Finn and Leah."

"Yeah. I know that."

"You will need to stay and train the new team members while they are gone."

"Why not have Jesse train Rachel's team and I'll look after ours?"

"Because Jesse will be accompanying Rachel to the wedding."

"I see," Jon said, taken off guard once again.

"Their relationship will not interfere with the work your teams accomplish."

"Oh," Jon waved him off, "I wasn't worried about that."

"What is your concern?"

"Nothing. I was just thrown, is all. Jesse keeps his heart closed."

"Jesse is not the only one who does this," Raphael said knowingly.

"I don't know if I like talking to you or not. You know too much about me."

"I have been around you since the day you were born. I was in the field on that day."

"I see."

"I have been looking out for you since that day. Well, me and several others."

Jon burst out laughing. "I need more than one guardian angel?"

"Well," Raphael blushed, "you *are* rather active."

Still laughing, Jon said, "Well, at least I'm not boring. I keep you on your toes."

"That you do, young one."

"Young one? You look younger than me. How old are you?"

"That is a complicated question that I do not believe we have time to get into."

"I'm sure! So, how do I know you are from the archangel, and not from the other side? Both sides were in the field on that day."

"I follow the Jesus, the living Son of God. The Lord God Almighty is my King," he said, not batting an eye. "My job is to protect you. In this moment, it is to deliver a message. Does that sound like an angel or a fallen angel?"

"According to the Bible, that's an angel."

"Then?"

"Okay, Raphael, what do you know about my heart?"

"I know you do not give it lightly. I know there has only been one girl you have had feelings for, until…"

"Until *who*?" Jon demanded.

"Katia," Raphael said knowingly.

"No way. She doesn't like me in that way."

"She does more than you know. For someone who senses feelings, I am surprised you missed this one."

"Who knew angels could be sarcastic?"

"I learned from you, young one."

Chuckling, Jon said, "Ooo! I think I might actually like you."

Smiling, Raphael continued, "Jon, the Lord God wants you to live your life to the fullest, in *all* aspects. That is the other reason He sent me to you. You have shut your heart off since your relationship in college with Bianca."

Jon cringed. "Yeah, that didn't end well."

"It is not your fault she chose to pursue another man while she was still with you."

He cringed again. "No, but it still hurts."

"You connect with Katia in a way no one else can."

"That's because I can tell what she's feeling. She can't hide it from me."

"That scares her."

Jon shrugged. "I can't help that."

"I am aware."

"She's my sister now."

"Only in name."

"There's still a line there. Plus, I think Sasha likes her."

"Sasha has another interest," Raphael said knowingly.

"What about Val? Pretty sure he likes her."

"The choice will be hers, but I am to tell you to take the risk. She will respond."

"Really?" Jon chuckled. "How do you know all of this?"

"My job, besides being your guardian angel, is to help heal those hearts from their past, and to guide those to stay open to present and future love."

"So, you're an angel of love?"

"That is partially correct," Raphael chuckled. "I am one of the archangels. There is more than one archangel. As far as being your guardian angel, I have others who assist me in that capacity when it comes to you."

"An archangel needs help being my guardian angel?" Jon asked, wide-eyed.

When Raphael started laughing again, he mentioned, "You have a healthy sense of humor. It has amused me through the years."

"You're a mess!" Jon laughed.

"I enjoy humans. I find their passion intriguing, and their capacity for forgiveness, at times, is a relief in this dark world."

"I *do* think I like you after all." Jon smiled. "You're not as infuriating to talk to as the archangel." When Raphael laughed, Jon asked, "What?"

"You do not call him by name?"

"You know his name?" Jon asked, stunned.

Raphael raised an eyebrow. "You do not?"

"Okay," Jon grinned, "what's his name?"

"He is the archangel, Michael," Raphael simply said, as if it were no big deal.

"Oh!" Jon said, surprised. "Oh! This makes *so* much sense! Oh! I should have known! Oh wow! *Michael* is the archangel? How could I be so stupid that I didn't know that?"

"Why do you not know this?"

"I should have figured it out. We've just always known him as the archangel. Michael is the archangel of righteousness, mercy, justice, and protection. He's the most powerful of you guys, too, right? Man!" Jon said, smacking the steering wheel. "I seriously should have known!"

"Yes, he is. Does it make a difference now that you know his name?"

"Not really. It just makes *so* much sense!"

Chuckling, Raphael shook his head.

"Sorry, my mind is blown."

"No need to apologize to me. Why have you never inquired as to his identity?"

"Out of respect. He is *definitely* an archangel. We just weren't sure which one, so we just called him the archangel."

"This is amusing. He will find the humor in this situation."

"*Anyway,* back to why you're here. You're saying that I will need to lead and train both teams while the other three are gone?"

"Yes. What say you?"

"I have a choice? I thought I was more voluntold."

"What is this voluntold? I have never heard this colloquialism."

"It's where there is an appearance of volunteering, but you are in essence being told what you're going to do."

"I understand. No, you are not being voluntold, but you *are* the best person for the position. You always have the free will to say no."

"I may have the free will to do so, but I don't have the desire to tell the Lord God no."

"I informed Michael this would probably be your decision," Raphael said with a nod. "You must continue on to retrieve Jerrod and Chief."

"Chief? Is that puppy's name?"

"Yes."

"Kind of curious to see how Charm and Chief get along together?"

"They will get along famously."

"Perfect."

"I will leave you to your silence," Raphael said, and immediately disappeared without waiting for a response.

"Thanks for the warning," Jon said with a smirk. "Wow. I *love* working for God!" He grinned.

*   *   *

"Okay, we're all loaded up," Jesse told Charlie, as he slammed the back of the Jeep closed, deep in the Outback.

"No. We need to wait a moment," Charlie said knowingly, with his quirky grin. "They are bringing food – the good stuff."

"Oh, no need. We appreciate it, but we have taken enough of their food. We need to get out of here. There is a lot we have to do."

"The young are always in a hurry," Charlie said, shaking his head. His mom brought over a small bag, followed by several other women carrying food. Charlie explained that Jesse was grateful for their hospitality, but he didn't want to impose. After a few minutes arguing, Charlie took the special meal his mother made him, and sent the others away with thanks. "They are not happy, but are thankful for the food," Charlie explained. "I told them to have a feast in honor of the Lord."

"Sounds good. Thank you. Now, let's go. We have to get home," Jesse said. "We need to regroup. We also have to give Angel time to recover, and unfortunately, we also have a somber issue to take care of."

"Danny?" Charlie asked.

Jesse nodded. "Danny."

"Right-oh, let's go," Charlie said, and the group loaded up into the vehicles.

As the A.N.G.E.L.s drove away from the clan's tiny village, once they passed the border of the village, Jesse noticed that he couldn't see the village itself in the rearview mirror. It was like it wasn't there. When the angels and the archangel left the village in the form of streaks of light going toward Heaven, it was as if a veil was lifted, and the village appeared as if it was always there. "Wild," Jesse said, shaking his head. "I love my work!"

Chapter 16
Blessed Are The Pure In Heart

"Okay, love, we need to go. Caleb, Pete, and Leah are down at the truck," Nico said, leaning down, kissing Kit on the top of her head.

"I know you need to go. I'm just exhausted. Please pass on my condolences to the others."

"I will," Nico said, sitting on the side of the bed. "Willow, Kendra, and the kids will be staying here while we're gone. I know they're loud, but I really want you to have people here."

She smiled weakly. "Thank you. I appreciate that."

Nico ran his hand over her hair. When he did, he came back with a handful of it. "What in the world?"

"I've been losing it lately," she confessed.

"Oh, Kit," he said, shaking his head. "I can't leave you like this."

"You have to. You need closure. Please do it for me."

"I don't –"

"Please," she said, taking his hand. "For me?"

"Fine," he said in a sigh. "It's against my better judgment."

"Nico, you are my one and only. I need you to do this. I can't be there, but you can. The kids may need you. You need this too. He was your friend."

"Right-oh," he relented. "Please eat while we're gone?"

"I will do my best."

"Willow will go with you to your appointments. Go easy on her, eh?"

"I will," she smiled.

Leaning down, he kissed her lips. "I love you. Your name may be Kit, but you will always be my Katie."

"And, you will always be my Nick," Kit said with a wink.

When they said their former names, both has memories from their time in the United States go through their mind.

"I'll hold onto those memories until I see you again," Kit promised.

"As will I," Nico said, and left for Reno.

*   *   *

Bounding toward Alice Springs, the trio of Jeeps, fully loaded, did their best to get to Alice as quickly as possible. They wanted to get out of the Outback before anything else happened. While they wanted to get home as soon as possible, they also knew once they were home, they would once again be burying one of their own.

Jesse, who was driving in the last Jeep with Rachel, Angel, and Sasha, mentioned, "I'm actually going to miss being here."

"It's a beautiful place," Rachel said.

Hugging herself, Angel was beyond nervous. "Nothing personal, but I don't want to come back here for a long time."

"There are other places to go to in this big world," Sasha pointed out.

"I would be happy to go anywhere else," Angel said.

Suddenly, the back tire of their Jeep blew! Tightening his grip on the steering wheel, Jesse struggled for a few tense minutes to get the Jeep under control. Rachel gasped and grabbed the dash in front of her, while Angel screamed. Sasha wrapped both arms around Angel to keep her in place.

Once Jesse got the Jeep settled, they were instantly surrounded by those from the other Jeeps. "Are you okay? Are you guys hurt? What happened?" were some of the barrage of questions fired at Jesse, whose heart was still pounding out of control.

"Rach? Are you okay?" was the first thing Jesse asked.

Rachel nodded. "I…yeah. I'm okay."

"You two okay?" Jesse asked Angel and Sasha, who only nodded in response, as Sasha took a good look at Angel to see if she was all right.

"Is everyone all right?" Charlie asked the tiny group, who were shaken and pale. When they nodded, he said, "We can take two with us to get help, but not four. Two of you will have to wait here."

"I was the driver. I'll wait," Jesse immediately jumped to volunteer.

"I will too," Sasha said.

"No!" Both Rachel and Angel said at the same time.

"We can't be separated again," Rachel insisted, grabbing Jesse's hand.

"Right-oh, looks like you and Rachel will be staying," Charlie said, much to Angel's relief. Charlie looked at her, not sure what to think regarding her reactions. Shaking his head, he handed Rachel and Jesse some food and water. Feeling bad for leaving them, the food he left was the bag given to him by his mother, made special for just him. He decided if he was leaving them in the middle of the Outback, it was the least he could do. He also left them each three bottles of water. "It's going to get hot, so make sure to stay hydrated," Charlie warned. "We should be back here in about five or six hours. It may take us a bit to find someone to haul the Jeep out of here."

"We'll be fine." Jesse waved him off. "We have food and water. The main priority is to get Angel out of here."

"Consider it done."

"Get everyone settled into a hotel before you come back for us. Pretty sure Angel wants a long, hot shower," Jesse said, squeezing Angel's shoulder.

Angel nodded as she blushed. "It's been awhile. And, while the river worked, I would love to take a good shower."

"The sooner we go, the sooner we can return," Charlie reminded them, and they were off.

As they watched the Jeeps take off in a cloud of dust, Jesse and Rachel looked for somewhere to get in the shade. It was nearing the hottest point in the day, and they didn't want to take any chances in the scorching sunlight. Seeing a Boab tree in the distance, the pair headed directly toward it for relief.

*   *   *

"Hey! How was your trip?" Jon asked, hugging Jerrod in the airport near his terminal. Then he knelt in front of Chief, and asked, "How are you doing, buddy?"

"Chief, this is Jon. Shake," Jerrod said, and Chief put his paw out for Jon to shake.

"Cool!" Jon grinned. "I like him!"

"He's pretty cool. I have a feeling that he and Charm are going to get along."

"According to Raphael, they will," Jon said, standing. "Do you have any luggage?"

"I have one to pick up. Who's Raphael?" Jerrod asked, as they made their way to luggage pick up.

"He's one of the archangels. He's also my guardian angel."

"You have an archangel as your guardian angel?" Jerrod chuckled. "Is that good or bad?"

"Oh, it gets better," Jon said, laughing as he talked. "He has to have help. There are several *other* angels who help him with being my guardian angel."

"Are you serious?" Jerrod burst out in laughter. "And I thought mine had a tough time of it!"

"Yeah, we had a good laugh over it."

"So, that's the archangel's name? Raphael?"

"No, that's *one* of the archangel's names. Want to guess who *our* archangel is?"

"You know his name? I thought he was just 'the archangel'."

"I knew he had a name. I just never knew it."

"Who is it?"

"Guess."

"Well, there are two I can think of off the top of my head. Is it Gabrielle?"

"Nope. It's the other one in the Bible…Michael."

"Seriously?" Jerrod asked. Then he snapped his fingers and smacked his head. "Duh! Of course it is!"

"That's about the same reaction I had," Jon said, as they got to the luggage claim area.

"That makes so much sense."

"I know. Right?"

"He's going to get a good laugh over it too."

"I'm sure. So," Jon asked, as the luggage began its rotation around the carrousel, "Did they give you a hard time on the plane with Chief?"

"Nope. He was a good boy, too," he said, ruffling Chief's head. Chief stood beside Jerrod, keeping an eye in every direction.

"Good."

"There it is," Jerrod said, relieved they wouldn't have to wait for too long. Grabbing the suitcase, they headed for the van before heading home.

*   *   *

Still deep in the heart of the Outback, Jesse and Rachel sat under a Boab tree. "Not great shade, but it's better than nothing," Jesse mentioned, pulling out a bottle of water from his backpack.

"It'll work." Rachel shrugged. "It's not like we're camping out here," she said, opening her first bottle of water as well. "We should only be stuck out here for five or six hours. We just need to stay hydrated until they get back. We'll be fine."

"Sounds like a plan," Jesse said, taking a swig of his water. " I figure we'll wait a few hours before we crack open the baggies of food."

"Good idea."

"So," Jesse said, leaning against the tree with his legs stretched out in front of him, "Come here often?" he smirked.

"While I *do* like to come out here, honestly, in the summer it is not a good idea. December's weather is blasted hot," she said, in all seriousness.

"We didn't really have a choice. Well, that's not true. *You* had a choice. I was the driver, so there was no way I would not stay. That would be completely unfair."

"I understand, but you have to understand that there was no way I was going to be separated from you again. It was way too long for –"

"Rach?" Jesse said, suddenly sitting up, alert.

"What?"

"We need to leave this place," he said, rubbing his arms.

"We can't!" Rachel looked at him wide-eyed. "We could get lost out here in a heartbeat!"

"Stop drinking your water, and put it in your backpack," Jesse ordered, as he got off the ground.

"What's going on?"

"The other side is near, and coming closer. I think they know we're out here," he said, helping her up, his body on edge.

*   *   *

"Are they going to be okay out there?" Katia asked Charlie, while she, Charlie, Joe, and Delaney were in one Jeep, and Sasha, Angel, and Jacob were in the other.

"Rachel knows how to keep her head out there," Charlie said confidently.

"I'm glad they're together," Delaney said. "I couldn't imagine being out there alone."

"While we *could* have fit one more in, with all our luggage we couldn't squeeze in two…and I wasn't about to leave one person out there alone," Charlie said. "It's rough!"

"And hot!" Joe said, drinking his third bottle of water. "And, I thought Texas got hot!"

"While it's hot during the day, it gets cold at night."

"Like, how cold?" Joe asked Charlie.

"Well, let me rephrase that. It's not really cold," Charlie explained. "It's only about sixty or seventy at night, but you have to remember that the daytime temps are over one hundred degrees Fahrenheit," he used Fahrenheit, because Joe was the one who asked.

"That's quite a drastic difference!" Joe said, stunned.

"What is that in Celsius?" Katia asked. "While I know numbers, it will take me some time to adjust to the difference in how they feel."

"Sixty is about fifteen, and one hundred is about thirty-seven," Charlie explained.

"That *is* a big difference," Katia said in understanding.

"That's not even taking into account the wind that kicks up at night as well," Charlie pointed out.

"Uh, Charlie," Joe said, his heart racing, as he looked like he was looking in the distance.

Recognizing the look on his face, Delaney asked. "You had a vision, didn't you?"

"Yes."

"And?" Charlie asked.

"Rachel and Jesse could be in trouble."

"Why?"

"Some Unnaturals found the Jeep…and Jesse and Rachel aren't there anymore."

*   *   *

"So, who do we still have out?" Mark asked, as he, Derek, Casey, Jon, Val, Jerrod, Josh, Cori, and Kai were at the table after breakfast.

"Charlie, Joe, Delaney, Katia, Angel, Rachel, Jesse, Sasha, and Jacob," Kai said, checking his list. To keep track of everyone and where they were, and to make sure no one got left behind, Cori and Kai kept a list of the team members, and where they were at what time. It was a dry erase board in the kitchen. "Also, Nico, Leah, and Caleb are on their way in for the memorial service. The other group will be a while."

"Have we been able to ping their phones yet?" Derek asked.

"Not yet. I was going to try when we're done here," Cori said. "It's been awhile since we last tried."

"Mommy! Daddy!" Allie yelled, as she and Callie ran into the kitchen, pale.

"Something happened to Jesse and Rachel," Callie finished.

"What do you mean?" Casey asked, alarmed.

"The bad people found their car," Allie explained.

"And their car is messed up," Callie finished.

Stunned, Casey looked at Mark for help.

"Call them now," Val ordered. "If God sent the twins a vision, and they're not sleeping, they're in trouble."

"On it," Cori said, as she and Kai got up from the table, heading for the basement with Charm on their heels.

When they were gone, Jerrod asked, "The girls have visions?"

"Usually they're in the form of dreams," Casey explained.

"Casey," one of the Asian A.N.G.E.L.s, Akio Botan from Japan, came into the dining room, "I feel the need to go help those in the cyber cave. I get pushed by Spirit to assist."

"Sure. Go ahead, Akio," Casey said with a nod.

When he was out of earshot, Mark asked, "Who is that?"

"Pretty sure he's a new A.N.G.E.L., but I don't know for what team yet."

"Where's he from?" Mark asked, working on getting up from the table, balancing haphazardly.

"Why?" Jerrod asked. "Where are you going?"

"The list is in the safe," he said, maneuvering his way into the office, using his crutch with one arm, while the other arm was still in a cast. The group met him in there just as he pulled the list out of the safe. "What's his last name?" Mark asked, scanning the list until he got to the ones from Asia.

"Botan," Casey answered. "He said he was from Osaka, Japan."

"Yep. He's on the list. Are there more?"

"Hiroaki Jun Heng is a young one from China," Val offered.

"I have a Heng from Xia He?" Mark asked.

"Yes. That's where she's from," Val confirmed.

"Have you talked to the others who are younger?" Jerrod asked.

"Yes. I've talked to all of them at one point or another. Remember there are over fifty staying in Reno. That's quite a list of people to go through," Val explained. Looking at his watch, he added, "Those who aren't already here, should be here within an hour or so. They come in shifts so we don't get overwhelmed."

"Here, look at this and tell me if there are any more," Mark said, handing Val the list. Josh and Jon looked over his shoulder.

"This one is one of them," Josh said, pointing to a name. "Raphael Ecker is here already. He got here this morning about an hour ago. He's part of the team from Jordan."

"This one too." Jon pointed to another one. "Toby Harnick is also from Jordan."

"Oh! I know these two. They're both from Egypt," Val said pointing out two more. "Zahra Akins and Hanif Nassor got here about two weeks ago. They have some older A.N.G.E.L.s with them."

"Here's another one," Val said. "Isaac Braham is from Jordan as well. Wow," he said, looking up at the others, "they've been here for weeks, and we had no idea."

"I wonder if *they* do?" Jerrod asked.

"We could just ask them," Jon suggested.

"Simple, but effective," Mark said, accepting the list back from Val. "If we need to show them the list, we can. We'll meet with those who are already here, and we'll get with the others when they get here today. In the meantime, Josh and Jon, please check the cyber cave to see if Cori, Kai, and Akio have had any success yet."

"Yes, sir," they said, and disappeared.

When they were gone, Casey said, "God is good."

"All the time," Mark finished, with a smile.

* * *

"There!" Jesse said, pointing to some caves, as they were running.

"Let's go!" Rachel said, while Jesse pulled her by her hand.

Scurrying up the hillside, they ducked into a cave just as the four Unnaturals ran into view. Breathing heavy from running, Jesse glanced around the outside of the cave to see how far away they were from them. "If we can't see them, they can't see us."

"Right, but they can still sense us, just as you sense them," Rachel pointed out, as she tugged him deeper into the cave. "We need to get in here and find a good place to hide."

"While we *can* sense each other," Jesse said, as they tucked themselves into a hole, hidden between three boulders, "we can't tell *exactly* where the other side is."

"Good! We would *really* be in trouble if that were the case."

"Shhh! Here they come," Jesse said, wrapping his arm around Rachel, pulling her closer to him, into the darkness. While he was doing his best to keep calm, his body felt like there were thousands of tiny animals climbing all over him. Having this gift since he was sixteen, he learned to control how it affected him over time, but he knew he would never be immune to feeling them. The closer they got, the more his skin crawled.

"They are very close," an Unnatural male said, looking around.

"Right, but *where* are they?" another one asked.

"I cannot tell you that," the first one said.

"Why not?" the female asked.

"Basically, the closer they are, the worse I feel."

"I see."

Jesse covered Rachel's mouth as the first male got within two feet of them. Pulling her deeper into the shadows, the pair didn't make a sound. Rachel was in front of Jesse, smashed against him, close enough to feel each other's hearts pounding.

"So, do we stay around here?" the second Unnatural asked the one who had the sense.

"They *are* here," the first one confirmed.

"How long do we look?" the female asked.

"If we bring Cassius a few more A.N.G.E.L.s, we will be richly rewarded," the third one mentioned, as he checked behind a big rock.

"We cannot do this all day," the female said, impatiently, crossing her arms.

"We will do it as long as it takes," the second male insisted. "Agares said they were here."

"Do we know for sure that they are in *here*?" the female asked. "They could be in one of the other caves, but in this vicinity, right?"

"They could be," Agares confirmed. Rubbing his skin as if it broke out in hives, he reaffirmed, "They *are* here, though, and they *are very close*. She is right, though. I cannot tell if they are actually in here, or in another cave on either side."

"Then, we will check them all," the second one insisted.

As soon as the Unnaturals disappeared down another tunnel, thinking they checked the one they were in well enough, Rachel and Jesse snuck out of the cave. Knowing there was one among the group pursuing them who could sense them, they did not feel comfortable staying in those caves. Taking off in a full-sprint, they ran for a small section of trees and another set of caves.

"This way," Rachel said, now pulling him. Having to maneuver by bending in half to get back into the caves, Rachel's five foot nine frame made it a little easier for her than for Jesse's six foot two frame.

The darkness made it more of a challenge to finagle their way through the caves. Jesse hit his head a few times, and Rachel scraped her arms and legs, but they finally made their way to an opening that revealed several tunnels to choose from. As their eyes adjusted to the darkness, Rachel said, "This one."

"Whoa," Jesse pulled her hand to stop her from going down the tunnel, "How do we know it's the right one?"

She shrugged. "Because it's the one we're going down."

"How will we find our way back?"

Stopping, she looked at him, slightly alarmed. Grabbing a stone, she ran back and marked the tunnel that led to the outside by a line only a few inches from where the dirt met the granite wall. When she got back to Jesse, she said, "If we make a change, we'll mark the tunnel."

"Good idea."

After several minutes of walking, Rachel noted, "We have company in here."

"Who?"

"The bats," she said, referring to the bat-covered ceiling above them.

Looking up, to Jesse, the ceiling almost seemed to be alive. It looked like black waves as the bats shifted. "I hope they don't realize we're in here," he commented, keeping an eye on them as they went further into the caves. The idea of hundreds of bats above them sent a shiver down his spine. "I know a certain superhero who would love this cave, but I'm not one of them."

Chuckling, they snaked their way down a tunnel that had a small entryway. Doing their best to avoid hitting the rock, they hoped not to get cut any worse than they already were. Without light, they had to feel their way, hoping not to run into anything they couldn't handle.

"I hope I don't feel a spider," Rachel groaned, running her hand along the side of the cave as they went. It took them a good fifty yards before the cavern opened up again. Once it did, they felt their way up the rocks of the back of the pitch-black cavern. "Watch for the bats," Rachel warned again, as they ducked deeper behind a wall of boulders.

Feeling like the skin on his body was coated in bugs, Jesse said, "They're here."

*   *   *

"You are staying here," Charlie argued with Angel.

"No! Jesse came for me. I'm going for him!"

"Absolutely not!" Charlie put his foot down.

"Yes!" Angel's eyes flashed in defiance.

"Sit down…NOW!" Charlie shouted at her.

Knowing Charlie doesn't normally yell, Angel immediately sat down on a chair, resting her hands in front of her on her knees, glaring at Charlie.

"There is no reason to raise your voice," Sasha said to Charlie, as he sat on the bed near Angel.

Surprised by Sasha's assertiveness, Charlie quickly recovered and defended himself, "I do, because she's not listening."

Sasha stood and crossed his arms. "There is still no reason to shout at her."

"Are you kidding me?" Charlie snapped. "Do you really want to get into this now?"

Angel narrowed her eyes at Charlie. "What do you mean?"

Putting his hands on the arms of the chair, Charlie leaned down so he was eye-to-eye with her, and said in a low, but firm tone, "We will be having a memorial service for one of my best friends when we get back. A.N.G.E.L.s have been waiting for *weeks* to have his memorial, because we were waiting until *you* were stable enough to move. The reason he is dead, is because *you* chose to take matters into your own hands in Russia. You went against your team. Derek is permanently in a wheelchair, because of the choice *you* made to try to save Lily all by yourself. As much as I love you, your decision-making abilities are questionable right now. As far as my insistence for you to sit down and stop being stubborn, it is because your stubbornness got us into this mess in the first place." Standing, he turned to Sasha, and continued in the same tone, "While I understand you wanting to defend her, trust me, she does not need it at this moment."

Sasha backed down. "I understand."

"No, I don't think you do," Charlie continued. "Just ask Jesse and Jon how much they have had to clean up after her over the years. As A.N.G.E.L.s, we all talk to each other, despite being separated around the world. Now, as much as I love her, she needs to learn to listen before she can lead. She needs to *hear* her teammates. I am pulling rank right now, because I do not want to have to spend *another* six to eight weeks in the Outback trying to get her stabilized again, nor do I want to bury yet *another* A.N.G.E.L. anytime soon. I also don't want anyone else to land in the hospital."

"This is exactly my fear," Angel whimpered, tears overflowing her eyes onto her cheeks. "It *is* all my fault."

"While most of it *is* your fault, I do not want to tackle that at the moment. This is not all about you, Angel. Not everything in this world is about you," Charlie snapped again. When she looked at him, stunned, he took a deep breath to control his emotions before he continued, "Look, I am trying to get us all out of here alive. Joe has already told me Rachel and Jesse are in trouble. I can't leave you all here, yet I can't bring you all either."

Just then, there was a knock on the door. When Charlie looked through the peephole, he looked toward Heaven, and said, "Oh, thank you, Lord!"

"Who is it?" Jacob asked.

"It's Ethan and Kat," Charlie said, referring to his fellow team members, Ethan Carson and Kat Parker, as he opened the door.

"Hey, Kat." Charlie grinned as she walked in. "Hey, Ethan," he said to him, as Ethan walked in, giving him a 'bro hug.' "What brings you two here?"

"Is that a trick question?" Kat asked, leaning on the wall with her arms crossed, one foot on the wall behind her.

"What does that mean?" Katia asked, confused.

"It means that he knows *exactly* why we're here," Kat clarified. "Don't ya, mate?"

"Yes. I do," Charlie admitted. "We need more help."

"How are we going to find them in the Outback?" Jacob asked. "Joe said they're not where we left them."

"They're not," Ethan agreed. "They're on the run, because they're being tracked by Unnaturals."

"Then, how do we find them?" Katia asked.

Kat shrugged, and simply said, "We trust God, and the gifts He gave us."

"Are we to trust that He will lead us to them?" Katia asked.

"Dead or alive, we *will* find them," Kat assured them. "We will not leave without them."

"Who do you want to go?" Ethan asked Charlie.

"I'll take Sasha, Jacob, Ethan, and Katia," Charlie said. "That'll leave Kat, Joe, and Delaney to sit on Angel," he said, looking directly at Angel.

"Why can't Sasha stay?" Angel asked.

"Because he senses the other side. Any more questions?" Charlie asked, raising an eyebrow as he crossed his arms. He was irritated with her and he knew it. He knew he shouldn't be, but everything finally bubbled over. While he hoped she had learned her lesson, her actions since they got to town were telling him otherwise.

"No," she quickly said. "I'm good."

"Good. Let's go. We have two teammates to find."

Chapter 17
My Heart Will Not Fear

Hearing the four Unnaturals pursuing them, come down the tunnel toward the cavern where they were located, Rachel whispered close to Jesse's ear, "I can't see a thing. I wish we had the gift of spiritual sight."

"We were taught to see what we could not readily see. Trust God. Trust the training," Jesse whispered, holding a knife in his right hand, knowing Rachel did the same thing. Both were crouched in an attack position. Even though they couldn't see a thing, they trusted the Lord to help them…one way or another.

"Right. Psalm 27:3 says, *'Though an army besiege me, my heart will not fear; though war break out against me, even then will I be confident.'* God's got this," she whispered, reminding herself.

"Also, Isaiah 35:4 says, *'Say to those with fearful hearts, "Be strong, do not fear; your God will come with vengeance; with divine retribution He will come save you."* And, yes, that verse is for me too," he whispered with a smirk.

"Have I not commanded you? Be strong and courageous. Do not be afraid; do not be discouraged, for the Lord your God will be with you wherever you go, " Rachel whispered, quoting Joshua 1:9.

Giving Rachel's hand a gentle squeeze, Jesse whispered, "Shhh. Pray. They're here. I love you."

"I love you too," she whispered back. Closing her eyes, she took a deep cleansing breath. Imagining she was entering the throne room of the Lord, she felt the Spirit encompassing them, and began soaking in the Spirit in prayer as she imagined herself kneeling before the mighty throne of The Lord God.

*   *   *

"Okay, thank you. Keep us posted," Josh said into the computer microphone. Even though it was around midnight, there were still A.N.G.E.L.s at the Haven. Some had already returned to Reno for the night, but most were still there. When Joe called to catch them up, the thirty remaining A.N.G.E.L.s, along with those in the house, gathered in the cyber cave and on the steps. Cori and Kai had the speakers turned all the way up so the conversation could be heard throughout the basement, as well as on the stairs. When Joe called, the ruckus it made woke Allie and Callie, and they came down with Lily to listen.

"As soon as we know, you'll know," Joe assured him.

"You are all in our prayers," Josh said.

"That's the best place to be," Joe said, and he hung up on his end.

Turning to the group of A.N.G.E.L.s at the Haven, Josh instructed, "We need to pray in shifts. We all know the true power of prayer. We need to pray for the Lord to help Jesse and Rachel, and keep the rest of the team safe." With that, the group broke up into smaller groups throughout the ranch near

Reno, Nevada, to pray. Some were inside, broken up into groups of four or five, while others preferred to worship the Lord in prayer out in nature, and went outside in small groups.

"At least Angel's not mixed up in this one," Casey said, nibbling on her nails. "Unfortunately, Jesse and Rachel are in trouble now. I just wish they were all safe and at home for a breather."

"God has them," Mark said, giving her shoulders a gentle squeeze before he kissed her head.

"I know. I just wish *we* had them too."

"We do. We are praying them into the Lord's hands. C'mon," he said to Casey, Callie, Allie, and Lily, "let's go over to the corner and do our own praying for your brother and Rachel."

*   *   *

"I have a bad feeling Rachel's in trouble," Kit said, as she was resting on the couch in the main house at the station. She had another round of chemotherapy in a few days.

"Me too," Willow confirmed. Kit and Willow were taking a break right before calling the station hands in for dinner. They were about to call them when the phone rang in the kitchen. Kit and Willow were chatting while Pete ran to the kitchen to answer the phone.

"We need to pray," Pete said, returning to the living room from the kitchen. He rang the dinner bell before coming back in. "That was Josh. Rachel and Jesse are in trouble."

Kit gasped. "What happened?"

"Short version?"

"That would be appreciated," Willow said, exhausted from her daily activities. "Everyone will be here shortly."

"Jesse was driving, and the Jeep blew a tire. They couldn't fit all of them in, so Rach stayed with Jesse."

"Not surprised," Kit said. "Go on."

"Well, while the other group headed to Alice, and got themselves tucked safely into a hotel, Jesse and Rach were discovered by the other side," Pete continued. "Joe alerted them. Kat Parker and Ethan Carson have since joined them, and now Kat is with a few, and Ethan and Charlie took the rest back to try to find them."

Sitting up in her seat, alarmed, Willow asked, "How are they going to find them? If they're not where they left them, there's no telling *where* they are out there by now. They could all be running around in circles, barely missing each other for weeks on end! They could have heat stroke before they're found!"

"Charlie gave them each three water bottles and a bag of food before they left."

"*That's it?*" Kit asked, stunned. "He knows better."

"They were only supposed to be gone for a little bit. He felt bad, so he gave them the food his mum made him before they left," Pete explained. "You have no idea how much of a sacrifice that was for Charlie. That woman can cook! Besides, they were only supposed to be gone for four or five hours. How was Charlie supposed to know they would be found by the other side?"

"And, now they're lost," Kit said in a sigh.

"Right-oh, let's pray," Willow said, putting her hands out. Joining hands with the others, the group began to pray. Throughout the station, a cloud slowly covered the sun, creating a wave of darkness that slowly went over the station. Instead of running right to the main house to eat like they normally do, the station hands here and there felt led to pray, and did so. Dropping to their knees in the middle of the field or the barn around the station, the station hands from Serenity Wells, as well as the two stations around them, united together in prayer.

Other Christians throughout the world, feeling led by the Spirit, quickly joined the A.N.G.E.L.s and the Christians in prayer in Nevada and Australia, as they too felt the need to pray. Not sure as to why, whom, or what to pray for, those prayer warriors who did not know the situation, simply prayed with all of their might for the strong hand of the Lord to take over the situation, and for it to work out per His will.

"Father, I know You are a great and Mighty God," a fifty-year-old nurse in Ohio said, bowing her head in prayer in the break room at the hospital. Feeling the Spirit urge her to continue to pray, she went on, "There are many things in this world that I don't understand, but You're strength is one that I don't doubt. I have a bad feeling You are needed somewhere in this big world. I ask You to take the situation into Your hands. I ask…"

A small boy of eight got out of his bed in Ireland, and knelt next to it. Folding his tiny hands in front of him, he prayed, "Dear Jesus, I think I'm supposed to pray and ask for help, but I don't know who it's for. Please protect them, and bring them home to their family, yeah? Please keep them safe, and…"

In the middle of the night, a man in his sixties slowly dropped to his knees in his backyard in Oklahoma, hands raised toward the air in surrender, and prayed, "You are the King of Kings and the Lord of Lords. You are a great and mighty power. You are the Alpha and Omega. The Beginning and the End. Nothing is too much for You. The burden is strong right now to pray, and only You know why. You have carried me through many years of combat in the military. I fear there are more soldiers in trouble. These aren't soldiers for their country, but in *Your* Army. I ask that You carry those through this situation. I ask You to protect them, and get them home safely. I pray…"

In Jerusalem, four teenage girls were at the mall sitting down at a table to take a break from walking around, when one of them grabbed the hands of the girls on either side of her. The girl across from her also grabbed the hands of those on either side of her, creating a circle. When the two between them looked up at the other two confused, the first girl explained, "We need to pray."

"Yes," the girl across from her said, "there is a brother and sister in Christ in trouble."

"Do you know them?"

"No. I just feel led," she said, and bowed her head. Together, the group started in prayer, "Lord, we bring before you…"

In Wyoming, a sixteen-year-old girl with curly blond hair, and brown eyes got out of bed. Woken with a start around midnight, she instantly knew what she had to do. In order to not wake her sister in the bunk bed below her, she lay prostrate on her bed, hands folded in front of her. With her head on the bed, and eyes closed, she whispered, "Heavenly Father, You woke me up for a reason. Every other time You have done that, it's to pray for someone I know. You showed me the face of a man and woman, but I don't know them. You do. Your angels protect us down here, and I ask You to send them to this man and woman who are in trouble. I ask You to help them, and keep them safe. I ask You to make Your angels strong. I ask You to save them. I ask…"

In Texas, an older lady of about eighty-six, who had been a prayer warrior all of her life, sat in her chair with a Bible on her lap opened to her favorite passage. She couldn't sleep, so she opened her prayer journal, and rested it next to her Bible, opened to her prayer list. Heading into prayer time, the Spirit filled her, and instantly brought tears to her eyes. "I feel You, Lord," she whispered, closing her eyes. Soaking in the Spirit, she prayed, "I know You don't need us to do anything for You, but obviously someone does. I know they are not on this list either. While I may not know them, I know You do. I also know You don't put this on someone's heart lightly. I ask You to take over the situation. I ask You to send Your angels of protection to those in trouble," she prayed. "I ask them to surround those creating the problem, and to free those from possible harm. I ask that You strengthen Your angels with Your glory, giving them the strength to help those who need it."

Just as the four Unnaturals from the other side entered the cavern where Jesse and Rachel hid, several tremendously bright streaks of light immediately lit the cavern, temporarily blinding the small band.

"What is that?" Rachel asked, as she and Jesse immediately covered their eyes from the blinding light.

"It's either God, or a nuclear explosion and we're dead," Jesse said, shielding Rachel with his body. He wasn't sure what was going on near them, but he would do his best to put himself between Rachel and the danger.

"You will cease your pursuit!" the angel ordered the Unnaturals.

The four Unnaturals covered their eyes from the intense light and hissed. The head of the four shouted, "Never," and went to jump the angels.

Before the Unnaturals could move, the angels sliced them with swords glowing with God's glory. As soon as their swords came into contact with the Unnaturals, the four creatures instantly dissipated into ash, coating the floor where they stood only a split second before.

"Do not be afraid," one of the angels announced to Jesse and Rachel. "You are now safe."

As Jesse and Rachel came out from their hiding spot, the glowing went down to a minimal amount, allowing their eyes to adjust. "Where are they?" Jesse asked.

"They are no longer," the angel answered.

"Praise the Lord! Thank you," Jesse said, moving behind Rachel, holding her from behind, not wanting to let her go.

"The praying saints through the world have come together, hearts united in prayer for you. The Lord has answered swiftly and justly," the angel explained.

"Even though the Lord doesn't need any help, we are grateful, and thankful He sent you to assist. Thank the Lord for those who prayed, providing the extra help," Rachel acknowledged.

"Peace be with you," the angel said, and then the seven streaks disappeared toward Heaven, leaving the cavern once again pitch-black.

"Well, at least they let our eyes adjust first," Rachel said with a smirk.

"There aren't any more from the other side around. We need to go while we can," Jesse said, refocusing Rachel.

"How will the others find us?"

"Keep praying. He'll lead us to them." Grabbing her hand, Jesse tugged her back through the tunnel maze.

After navigating the underground cave system for over an hour, Jesse and Rachel felt a sense of relief when they exited into the vast openness of the Outback. Looking up at the sun setting in the distance, they got to see the brilliant orange and stark red of the sun as it said its last goodbye for the day. Rachel was grateful for so many things. As they walked hand-in-hand, she started by thanking the Lord for His mighty protection, and for the man He gave her to have in her life.

Chapter 18
Our Heart Is Open Wide

Pulling up behind the broken-down Jeep, Charlie shut the engine down, and sat there. Dumbfounded, Ethan pulled up behind him and shut his Jeep off. Watching no one in the other Jeep get out, Ethan said, "I don't know what they're waiting for. We're not going to find them sitting here. Let's go to the others and get moving," he said, getting out. When Sasha and Ethan walked up to the other Jeep, Ethan said, "Are you planning on waiting for them t' just walk out of the bush?"

Charlie laughed nervously, before he admitted, "I'm hoping."

Studying him for a moment, Ethan asked, "What's the plan, mate?"

"I don't know."

"What are you waiting for?"

"I *really* don't want to have to have another funeral. We watched Rachel grow up from a baby. We were there at Jesse's birth on the mountain in Mexico." Shaking his head, Charlie admitted, "If this ends in their death, I *do not* want to do this one. God may need to get someone else to do this mission."

"Don't get your knickers in a knot on a 'what if.' Let's go get them."

"*Are* we going to find them?"

"Yes," Ethan said firmly.

"Will they be alive?" Katia asked, getting out of the passenger's seat of the Jeep to let the others out.

"I believe they will be."

"Right-oh," Charlie said, giving up as he pulled himself out of the Jeep. "Let's go get them."

*   *   *

"I'm getting chilly," Rachel said, rubbing her arms. The sun went down a few hours before, bringing in the cold wind to replace the heat that released from the earth at sunset. They didn't have any jackets with them, because they were still in the Jeep…wherever that was.

"We could sit and make a fire, but that concerns me. If they see the fire, it could put a target on us."

"I understand. What if we just rest and eat?" Rachel asked.

"We can do that. Here," he said, gesturing toward a large, flat boulder. Rachel handed Jesse her backpack before she climbed up. Once she was safely up, Jesse knelt down, and got into his backpack where the food was held. "Uh-oh," he groaned.

"What?"

"Well, something happened to the food," he said, pulling them out. Opening one of the bags, he dumped one, only to have it plop onto the ground with a splat. "Seems they weren't sealed tightly, and in my rush to get away from the Unnaturals in the first place, I didn't get my water bottle closed all the way either. It leaked all over the food."

Jaw dropped, Rachel asked, "What are we going to eat?"

"Guess we'll see what the Lord'll provide. At least we have water. We can last a week without food, but only three days without water."

"We need to ration the water we have. We can combine our waters since you're now a bottle short. We're also in the summer," Rachel reminded him. "Water is scarce in the Outback during the summer."

"I was afraid you'd say that. Okay. I'm going to leave these here with you," he said, resting the backpacks next to her. "You'll be safe here. The other side is nowhere near us."

"Where are *you* going?" Rachel asked, stunned.

"I'm going to go find us something to eat. My stomach thinks it's been cut off from the rest of my body."

"Oh no you're not! You're not going anywhere without me!" she insisted, hopping off the boulder.

"Rachel, we need to conserve energy. The best way to do that is to trade off going and looking for resources. I'm better at finding things to eat at night."

"While this is true, I am more experienced in what is poisonous and what isn't out here. Remember, Australia's a stunning country, but the flora and fauna try to kill you."

"Fine," Jesse agreed. They took out the soggy food, and left it for some critter to indulge. Afterward, Jesse flipped his backpack onto his back before he put his hand out for hers.

"I told you I don't want to be separated from you again. Quit trying to separate us."

"You may regret saying that."

"Never," she said with a smile. After she slung her backpack onto her back, she took his hand, and they headed out into the Outback once again.

*   *   *

Back at the Haven, deep into the early morning hours, Mark, Josh, and Jon met with each person on the list from Mark's safe as they took a break from prayer. Keeping the continuous prayer vigil until they got word that Rachel and Jesse were found, they only took breaks to eat.

"That's the last one," Mark said, scanning the list as Akio headed back down to the cyber cave.

"So, they knew they were destined to join us," Josh said, curiously. "Why didn't they tell us?"

"I think they were waiting for Angel and Rachel," Jon suggested. "They are aware those two are in charge of the teams."

"Technically, you and I are in charge of one team, and Rachel's in charge of the other," Josh corrected.

"Only until the archangel deems she is ready to take over again," Jon reiterated.

"Which won't be any time soon," Mark said. "She was tortured. That's going to take some time for her to recover. She's going to be dealing with major post-traumatic stress."

"I think *I* may be able to help her with that," Casey said, walking up to the trio.

"What do you mean?" Jon asked.

"If you recall from the stories growing up, and the scars on my back, Jackie tortured me," Casey reminded him. When they nodded, she went on, "While mine wasn't anywhere near as long as Angel's, recovering from this is something I can sympathize with her on…and understand. Knowing Pete and Charlie's clan, I'm sure they've already laid the groundwork. I should be able to help her through the rest."

"This is true," Mark agreed.

"Besides, you are all men," Casey said. "Nothing personal, but women handle things differently."

"Then, when she gets here, she's all yours," Mark said.

"Nothing personal," Josh said, getting up from the table, "but better you than me. Have fun with that."

"Hold up!" Jon grabbed his arm. "Sit down and explain that."

Sitting back down, Josh organized his thoughts for a moment.

"Is this a meeting I can join, or is it private?" Derek asked, wheeling up to the table.

"You're always welcome," Mark said, and then turned back to Josh, waiting for him to explain his statement.

No one said a word until Josh explained, "Ever since we joined the A.N.G.E.L.s in Australia, Angel's had her eyes set on being a couple with me. That's not meant to sound like I'm bragging. On the contrary, I'm not. It's more irritating than anything. I mean, she's your daughter, so please don't take this personal."

"Oh no." Casey shook her head. "I get it. She can be stubborn."

"*Can* be stubborn?" Jon asked. "That girl is the epitome of stubborn! She couldn't be any more stubborn if she tried. That's the reason we got into this mess in the first place."

"Exactly," Josh continued. "We *thought* she sorted all this out with the archangel before we left, but obviously she didn't. When we lost Aden Knight, it threw her for a bigger loop than I think she even thought was possible. She fought us left and right to do the right thing, and to work as a team. Then, when I didn't think she could go any further off the tracks, she hits on the guy we were watching, in hopes that he would lead us to Liliya. Now," he put his hand up to stop Mark and Casey from jumping in, "under normal circumstances, I wouldn't have a problem with her hitting on whomever she wanted. However, she hit on him one minute, and then acted like we're an item the next. And for the record, I never agreed to be a couple with her. I was waiting to see if the changes would stick. She acted like I had no say, and I was hers. I never asked her out. I never even acted like I was interested. She approached it with me, and I told her we'd talk about it, but there was never a good time. She didn't seem to care what I had to say, though. I will admit I got sharp with her. I wasn't all that nice right before she snapped, but I was sick of it. She was going to get one of us hurt. In this case, it was Derek, Danny, *and* her."

"I can see your point," Mark said, mulling over Josh's thoughts.

Shaking his head, Jon said, "I give you a ton of credit, Mom. I couldn't do it. There's a lot inside me that I need to get sorted before I talk to her. I can't imagine it'll improve when I actually lay eyes on her. She's also furious at us because the archangel put us in charge until she could get herself straightened out."

"Seems there's a lot that she's not only going to have to work through, but the rest of us as well," Derek pointed out. "Anger, resentment, frustration, and mourning are just some of the emotions I can think of that people are going through."

"You've pretty much hit all of the ones flowing through those who are on our teams," Jon confirmed. "And to know that we're not even going to be able to work together as soon as they get back because of the wedding, is not exactly comforting. We're not supposed to be at odds with a brother or sister in Christ. We can't rectify any of this until we're all face-to-face for a decent amount of time."

"Agreed," Josh said. "And we also need to rectify it before we add people to the teams."

"Just remember to be open to the Lord's leading," Casey reminded Jon and Josh. "That will be of the utmost importance."

"Our hearts are open wide. Come on, Jon," Josh tugged on Jon's arm, "let's go get to know our new team members."

"They're going to be okay, right?" Casey asked Derek and Mark as they watched the pair leave.

"For that, we're going to have to trust the Lord," Mark said.

"I have faith in them," Derek said confidently. "The Lord wouldn't have passed the divine legacy to them if they weren't up to the task."

Chapter 19
Chained Hearts

"Jesse," Rachel said, as they had been walking around for over an hour and a half, "I don't know about you, but I'm tired and hungry."

"I am too. I'm looking. Keep on praying."

"I will," she assured him. Suddenly grabbing his arm, she pulled him back before whipping her three throwing knives out of their sheath, and into the ground in quick succession.

"What was that?" Jesse asked, stunned.

"*That* is the western brown snake. The Aboriginals lovingly call it *Gwardar*."

"Does that mean western brown snake?"

"Not hardly," Rachel chuckled as she watched to make sure it wasn't moving any more. When she was sure it was dead, she pulled her knife out of the head. One hit the head, the other two landed on either side. Slicing the head off the snake, Rachel explained, "Gwardar means 'go the long way around.' In other words, you need to give this big boy a wide berth. While it's normally a passive snake, if cornered, it'll kill you in a heartbeat. It's very fast, and highly venomous. That's why I threw the knives the way I did. It actually pulled back. I was aiming for around the middle of the buggar."

"Wow!" Jesse said, stunned. After she buried the head, he picked up the five and half foot long snake by the tail. "Dinner?"

"No way," she shook her head, chuckling. When she noticed Jesse wasn't laughing, her face dropped, and she asked, "Seriously?"

"Seriously. It's snake meat. You're going to tell me you've never had snake?"

"We grew up on a cattle and sheep farm. Why in the world would I purposely eat a snake?"

"It's dinner. Come on, I'll get a fire started. We'll cook it, and then move on so we're not by the fire very long. You can warm up a bit before we move on."

Sliding her knives back into their sheath, she grumbled, "You're going to make me go vegan."

*   *   *

"How are we going to find them?" Jacob asked, after a little over three hours of them walking around.

"How will we find the Jeeps again?" Sasha asked. "This is a big area, and we have been walking for a long time."

"The Lord will take care of both," Charlie said, searching the distance for some sign of the pair. "We just have to have faith."

"What if something has happened to them?" Katia asked. "The others will injure us if we do not find them."

"I think that saying is, '*the others will kill us if we don't find them.*'" Ethan corrected. "And, they won't. We're trying our best. I promise you that they're praying for us, waiting to hear from us."

Jacob stopped walking, and looked out toward the west. Cocking his head to the side, he asked, "What's that?"

"What's what?" Charlie looked at him, confused.

"There," Jacob pointed.

Shifting to get a better idea of what Jacob was looking at, Charlie said, "I don't see anything."

"There," Jacob pointed again. Taking Charlie's head, Jacob positioned it, lining it up with the orange glow in the distance. It was barely visible, but it was there.

Charlie took a moment to focus, before his eyes widened. "What *is* that?"

"What is what?" Ethan asked, when Charlie actually saw something.

Squinting to see better, Charlie asked, "Is that a fire?"

"I think so," Jacob agreed. "Is that them?"

"It's someone," Charlie said. "Follow me for a bit, and then let me sneak up on them. I'll be standing right behind them before they even know I'm there."

With that, as the group got closer, they could see the silhouette of man and woman who had their backs to the group, with the fire in front of them. Charlie made a fist with his hand, signaling the others to stop where they were. Then he slowly and stealthily made his way close to the pair. When he was within five feet of them, he said, "About bloody time!"

Rachel and Jesse jumped, knifes suddenly in their hands aimed at Charlie, who just stood there with a grin. His white teeth brightly shone in the fire light against his dark skin.

Dropping her knife on the ground, Rachel squealed in delight as she threw her arms around Charlie in a hug. "Praise God! Thank you for finding us! He was going to make me eat a snake!"

Hearing Charlie laugh, the rest of the group joined them. After Jesse doused the fire, and the group was on their way back to the Jeeps, Rachel and Jesse filled the group in on what happened.

"Seriously!" Rachel said at the end of the story, "to see you standing there while he was cooking the snake, I was never so relieved in my entire life. I was seriously freaking out! You have no idea! He almost single-handedly turned me into a vegetarian!"

"Oh yeah?" Charlie challenged. "Want to know how much snake I've eaten in my life?"

"No. It's just not right," Rachel said with a shudder.

Seeing her shudder, Jesse squeezed her hand while he chuckled.

"Here," Sasha said, taking off his coat, handing it to Rachel. When she appreciatively accepted it, he said, "You look cold. You have bumps on your arm."

"We call them goosebumps," Rachel said.

"The Russian term for them is *murashki po kozhe*," Sasha explained.

"Which means?" Jesse asked.

Katia smirked, as she simply responded, "Goosebumps."

"I cannot wait to get out of here," Rachel said. "How much farther is it to the Jeeps?"

"They're right over that hill," Ethan pointed out. "Baring anything else unforeseen, we'll have you in a hotel within a few hours."

"You have no idea how good that sounds."

"Nothing personal," Jesse said, "while I like Australia, I'll be happy to be home with the others. I feel like something keeps trying to suck us back here. I want to be free."

"We'll be home soon enough," Jacob said. "You can breathe as soon as we get back to Alice Springs. Once there, we'll be in civilization."

"I *know* Angel'll be happy to get out of here," Ethan said. "Ya know, it's kind of frustrating. Just when we think we've taken care of the other side, they pop back up. I'm not sure whether to wish they left Australia, or hope they stay here so we *know* where they are."

"Pretty sure they think the same thing about us," Charlie pointed out. "Having said that, I don't know that my clan will *let* them stay. They have just about had enough of them. My clan is a peaceful people, but seeing Angel in the shape she was in pushed them over the edge. And, knowing the other side has been kidnapping innocent Australians, threw them even further. One of the elders actually knew Allen."

"Wow! I'm so sorry," Jesse said, feeling bad for them. "And, knowing they're pretty much in their backyard can't be comforting."

"No. They'll wait to make their move after the wedding. There are many from my clan going to Leah and Finn's wedding. There are many clan members who work at Serenity Wells as soon as they come of age. The Sullivan family likes to hire from people they know," Charlie explained. "For example, Pete's dad, Bury, worked at the station for a long time before Pete came on. Pete and Victoria's two sons are now working on the station as well. Pete is training one of them to take over for him as the station doctor once he decides to move on."

"Wow! That's crazy!" Jesse exclaimed. "So, for generations, your clan and the Sullivan family have been connected?"

"Since they moved here from Ireland multiple generations ago and established their station," Charlie proudly declared.

"Their clan are good people," Rachel added. "They've taken care of us, just as much as we've taken care of them."

"It's mutually beneficial. When our men work for Serenity, it brings not only money into the clan, but the influence of the Sullivan family brings Christ to them as well," Charlie explained. "With Christ as our bond, it strengthens the bond we have that much more."

"Just as it does with the A.N.G.E.L.s," Jacob said in understanding. "We may not always get along, but we are family. I think Jesse once said, *blood doesn't make family, loyalty does*."

"And, I meant it," he said, momentarily letting go of Rachel in order to put Jacob in a headlock so he could ruffle his hair.

As soon as he went to go for Jacob, Jacob grabbed Jesse's wrist, and got it behind Jesse's back before he knew what was happening, and pulled up. Pulling up just enough to make his point, but not so much that he hurt Jesse. "Ha!" Jacob said proudly. "I *knew* I would get you one of these days."

"I give." Jesse put his other hand up in surrender. When Jacob let go, and Jesse stood back up, Jesse said, "You've learned a lot."

"Size matters a bit, but technique makes all the difference."

*　*　*

After spending the night in the hotel, the group got on a plane, bringing Ethan, Charlie, and Kat with them for Danny's memorial service. As they walked out of the terminal, Jon and Josh greeted everyone with a hug. As soon as both got to Angel, they gave her a light hug, but it was obvious by their reaction, they were less than thrilled to see her.

As they waited for their luggage, Angel asked Josh and Jon to talk off to the side. "Look guys," Angel started, "it doesn't take Jon's gift to know that you are both furious with me."

"We're not the only one," Jon mentioned, crossing his arms. "What you did caused major loss, serious, permanent damage, and a lot of people injuries and stress."

"Trust me. I know," Angel said, not fighting it. "God and I have wrestled about this for weeks. The archangel and I have gone rounds over the last few weeks about what went on. While I can't change the past, I *can* change the future. I'm sorry for causing so much damage and devastation. I know I have a *lot* of apologizing to do when we get to the Haven."

"You really have no idea." Josh shook his head. "While we would never leave you behind, you did that to us by taking off without us."

"The main emotions flying around are: anger, resentment, fury, frustration, depression, betrayal, anxiety, and worry," Jon said. "You have some major apologizing to do. This won't blow over anytime soon."

"This is a burden I must bear on my own. God and I are right. While I can't make things right with everyone, I *can* prove that I've changed."

"Well, you'll have to bear your soul before we even attempt to bridge that," Josh pointed out.

Angel asked, "What do you mean?"

"You *are* going to speak at Danny's funeral tomorrow. You will have to face all the A.N.G.E.L.s currently at the Haven as you do so. You will have your first chance to show remorse tomorrow morning at eleven," Josh explained, crossing his arms as well. "And, every person there had better feel it. Danny gave his life, and Derek is now in a wheelchair because of your actions." Getting in her face, he quietly, but sternly said, "You *will* understand just how much damage you have inflicted. Every time you look at Derek, I want you to remember that *you* caused that."

"Liliya could have been taken by Cassius without me jumping in!" Angel defended herself.

When she went to take a step back, she ran into Jon, who was standing directly behind her. "You will *not* run from *this* one."

"What do you mean I can't run from this?" Angel demanded.

"Growing up, you ran while Jesse and I cleaned up your messes," Jon pointed out. "You caused major damage to the new teams. The remaining team members have been at the Haven for weeks. They have not missed any of the stories floating around."

"What do you mean?" she asked, pale.

"They know," Josh simply said.

"Really?"

"Did you *honestly* think this would be kept quiet?" Josh shook his head, frustrated. "You basically caused an international incident – A.N.G.E.L. style."

"You're serious?"

"And, not just some small international incident either," Jon said, "it was a *major* one!"

"Your actions caused the loss of one of the A.N.G.E.L. legends…and, you caused another to never walk again," Josh reiterated. "That's not *even* including all the injuries, the resources, *and* the weeks spent bringing you back down to planet Earth."

Angel crossed her arms. "You're being cruel!"

"I'm being honest! You need to know what you're walking into," Josh explained. "What you did sent ripples through *all* of the A.N.G.E.L. teams."

"And," Jon continued, "just so you know, you'll have to face the Mexican A.N.G.E.L.s when we get home too. They came yesterday."

Pale again, Angel gulped in response. "How many A.N.G.E.L.s are there?"

"Everyone who is alive," Josh said. "This one's going to go down in the A.N.G.E.L. archives. This was a doozy!"

"Yikes," Angel whispered.

"Just trying to prepare you. No one is going easy on you."

Putting her hands up in surrender, Angel gave up. "Okay. I'll own it. I will do what I need to in order for all of you to trust me again."

"That will take a *major* life change," Josh said, matter-of-factly. "What you've done is inexcusable. What you've done has caused serious, and in some cases, permanent damage."

"I can prove to you that I've changed and am sorry."

"Angel," Josh said calmly, "if you were to drop a plate onto the floor, what would happen to it?"

"It would shatter."

"That's what you've done to the trust level in our team." When Josh said that, Angel's bottom lip trembled, but she fought the tears at the realization of just how big of a mess this created. "Now, let's say you were able to pick up all the pieces and glued it all back together again. Do you think that plate will ever be the same?"

Taking a moment to really think about it, she attempted to justify it, before she shook her head. Holding her arms, almost hugging herself, the tears flowed freely.

Placing his hands on her shoulders, Josh explained, "No matter how much you try to fix this, it's not going to happen. You will make your apologies, but it will take a *lot* of time for the team to trust you again. And, even then, they will keep an eye on you. You cannot take over the team again until we have confidence in your leadership abilities. We will be adding new team members, and you can start fresh with them, but you and Val need to have a deep conversation. He may even want to change teams. That will be up to him, Rachel, and God. You will not have a say in the matter."

"But he's on my team!" Angel objected.

"That is *exactly* the wrong mindset. It's *not your* team. It's God's first, and *ours* next. You are supposed to be a guiding force, not a dictator," Josh said. "Once you understand the difference, and what that looks like, only then will you be able to attempt to recover what you've lost. Having said that, you will *never* be able to fix what you've done…ever."

"I understand," Angel said, wiping the tears.

"Crying won't help this either," Jon pointed out. "Hearts are angry. Hearts felt betrayed, frustrated, and even depressed. You have a lot of work to do in order to bring this team together for the Lord. You need to remember that it's *not-all-about-you.*"

"That's the second time I've heard that!" Angel snapped, fire in her eyes. "You make me feel like I'm selfish."

"First of all," Jon jumped in, "no one can make you feel anything. That's *you* doing that. Secondly, what you did in Russia *was* selfish. You were trying to promote yourself. It *was* all about you. It wasn't about Lily. You wanted to prove yourself. That's selfish."

"I wanted to rescue Liliya."

"If you truly wanted to rescue her, you would have done it *with* us, instead of trying to prove that you could do it yourself. Tell me I'm wrong," Jon challenged. "Tell me you didn't do it to prove to the team and the archangel that you deserved to be team lead."

"I…" Angel's voice faded. Then she admitted, "I can't."

"Finally! You're being real to yourself!" Jon threw his hands in the air in exasperation.

"*That's* what everyone needs to see," Josh said. "If you continue to be real with yourself and others, then you may actually recover from this."

"Lord willing," Angel said under her breath.

*   *   *

Once everyone reunited at the Haven for the evening, they had dinner. Things between the younger A.N.G.E.L.s were tense at best regarding their feelings toward Angel. Mark knew it would be a while before the teams would forgive her on this one. He prayed for grace on behalf of the A.N.G.E.L.s, and for strength on Angel's behalf. He knew both sides would need it if they were to become hearts united once again in the Lord.

*   *   *

Around eleven the next morning, the group of A.N.G.E.L.s who had been there, along with those who finally joined them the night before, stood together around the boulder with the names of A.N.G.E.L.s who passed before. There were ropes out about two feet, surrounding the boulder in order to give a guideline on where to place the roses around it. A table containing an Australian flag draped over Danny's urn, sat just inside the ropes. There was also a framed photo of Danny right next to the table on an easel.

Charlie got up first. Placing a rose inside the roped-off area, Charlie then stood and said, "Thank you all for coming here today. Thank you for being here for all of us in prayer as well until we could all return home. Without the Lord, and the power behind your united prayers, I do not believe we would all be here today." Resting his hand on the table for a moment, he then turned back to the group, and said, "Not all of us made it back from this mission. John 15:13 reminds us that, *'Greater love hath no man than this, that a man lay down his life for his friends.'* Danny did more than that. He laid down his life for strangers. He didn't know any of the four who were rescued that day, but he knew they needed to get away." Taking a deep breath, allowing him a moment to refocus, Charlie then continued, "Danny Hawk was my best friend. I remember when I first met him. I was young and stupid." He grinned as he added, "And, as he would say, now I'm old and stupid." Everyone chuckled. Giving people a moment to settle, he organized his thoughts. "When I was of age, I went on a walkabout. Here I was, in the middle of nowhere, when I hear this ear-piercing scream. It was one of those that sent a shiver down my spine, and I had to go and investigate. It was Casey. They had just rescued her and Mark from the other side. Through the time of her healing, I was able to help teach them some of our techniques, while they taught me some of theirs. The most valuable thing I learned during those weeks in the Outback so long ago, though, was who Jesus is. I learned about Jesus Christ and what He did for me. I learned who the Lord God Almighty is, and just how much He loves me. I learned about the Holy Spirit, and how to listen to His guidance. Out in the middle of nowhere, I finally learned the truth. And for that, I cannot thank Danny enough. He not only saved my soul, but he also gave me a purpose."

Looking up toward the sky, Charlie blinked away the tears before he continued. "I watched as they took off in a helicopter on that day. I promised myself, in that moment, that I would find the A.N.G.E.L.s, and I would be a part of them. Their mission was important. And, I did just that. I walked all the way to Perth, and found them. From that day on, Danny took me under his wing. He was not only a mentor, but also a brother. Through the years, we became close. He became my best friend."

Crossing his arms, he did his best to keep control of his emotions. "I cannot thank Jon enough for pulling him out of that cave on that day." Looking directly at Jon and Jesse, he said, "There is no telling what they would have done to his body. By you pulling him out, Jon, and by Jesse carrying him back to the Jeep, you guys gave me the time in the end for me to comfort my friend, and to say goodbye. There is nothing I can say or do to thank you for those few precious moments."

They nodded in appreciation. "That's what an A.N.G.E.L. does, though. We look out for not only those who are Christ's, but for each other as well. We may not know each other's names. We may not even speak the same language. We *do* have an unbreakable bond in the Lord, though. It's one that unites us together in heart and soul. It's one that allows us to face each day with faith, strength, and courage. Thank you, Danny," Charlie said, resting his hand on top of the urn, "for taking the chance on a scrawny young kid. Thank you for allowing me to be a part of this amazing group of people. Thank you most of all for being my friend. Rest in Jesus now. I'm sure you were welcomed with open arms to the greeting we all wish to hear from our Lord, 'Well done thy good and faithful servant.'" He finished, and stood between Jesse and Jon, who each put an arm over his shoulder in comfort.

Nico got up next. Placing a rose at the end of Charlie's to start a circle, Nico then stood next to the urn, "Danny was a good mate. He was quirky, fun, brilliant, and a strong man of God. He not only taught my children the ways of the A.N.G.E.L.s, but he also taught me some lessons in faith. He seemed to pop up just when we needed him the most. At first, it was here or there, but when he realized two out of four of our children were destined to be A.N.G.E.L.s, we saw him at least weekly, if not more. We became great mates. You will be missed, Danny. Your strength, your smile, your encouragement, and your wisdom are irreplaceable. You have more than earned your time of rest and peace with the Lord. You stayed focused on missions before you. You stayed focused on keeping your own team safe, while looking out for others. I wish I could say more, but I'm trying not to cry here, so I'll say, until we see you in the Kingdom…rest well, my friend."

Mark got up next. After continuing the circle around the boulder with his rose, he stood and looked out among the many faces of the A.N.G.E.L.s there. "Danny has touched each and every life here either directly or indirectly. To have this many lives changed by one person would be an incredible honor. Those who have run into us as A.N.G.E.L.s over the years only see a couple of us. What they don't know is that we are many. We are members of the Lord's army, bound by our faith and trust in the Lord and His leading." Looking down at the urn for a moment, several memories flashed through his mind. "There are many stories I could tell you from over the years. Charlie touched on one. What he didn't see, though, was Danny's face on that day. He didn't see Danny's heart break when he found out that Shawn and Victoria's lives were lost in trying to get Casey and I out. That was the first lost to his immediate team. The devastation was written all over his body, but he stayed focused on the mission – which was to get Casey, Derek, The Colonel, and I out of the Outback, and safely on a plane to Mexico." Rubbing his neck, he looked toward the sky to blink away his tears for a moment. Taking a deep, cleansing breath, he then said, "I cannot thank that man enough for what he did for us during that time. He played a critical role in helping us get away. He paid a heavy price with the loss of two of his team members. When we lose one of us, we all feel it. When we lose an immediate team member, it's as if you've been gutted. We all felt it when The Colonel *and* when Danny left this earth for Heaven. That speaks volumes to who they were. They were handpicked by the archangel to find the lost A.N.G.E.L.s, and begin the legacy once again after the World Wars. They helped to reignite a flame that was doused by those wars."

Taking a deep breath, Mark did his best to keep himself collected as he continued, "I know I seem like I'm all over the place. I knew this was coming, but nothing prepares you for seeing that flag once again draped over the remains of your friend. He was a friend to all; a mentor to many; and a faithful servant to the Lord. Danny, you have been, and will be missed until we can get to Heaven and give you a hug. We know you and The Colonel are up there together, looking down on us, cheering us on. Thank you," he said, and went next to Casey and the kids.

Angel didn't want to, but she knew she was next, so she made her way through the crowd, and placed her rose near her father's. Rubbing her arms, she nervously cleared her throat before she began, "Um, wow. There is so much to say *about* Danny. I want to say something *to* him, though. You see, while I was being held captive, Danny was among those who came in to rescue me. They tried to get me free, but I knew Cassius and his followers wouldn't kill me. They needed me. So, I made them leave me. But, this isn't about me. The reason I shared that story is because Danny could have ran on that day with the others, but he chose to stay and block, so the others could get away. That was his heart. It was always for others." Tears overflowed onto her cheeks in a steady stream as she did her best to wipe them away. "You all know the story, but you didn't see his face. You didn't see the bravery I saw just feet away, as he stood between the demons and those trying to get away. You didn't see Jon's face when he saw the demon slash into Danny. Jon wasn't going to leave him there."

Her body shaking from emotion and adrenaline, she did her best to focus. "Danny," she said, resting her hand on the table, "I want to say thank you for being the man who helped my mother. You have been helping us since before I was even thought of. Because of you, my brothers and I are here. Because of you, there are many here today, who wouldn't otherwise be here. Because of you, I now have two new sisters in Katia and Lily. Because of you, and your sacrifice, there are many who found the Lord. You have been a good and faithful servant of God. Please rest in that knowledge. Please don't stop looking after us. I hope from this point forward to be a good witness for the Lord; a good leader to my team; and as good of a person as you were. Thank you," she said, and returned to her mother's arms in the group, sobbing quietly.

Rachel then made her way to the front of the group and placed her rose at the base of the boulder. Tears already flowing, she shook her head for a moment as she wiped her eyes. Looking toward Heaven, she whispered, "Help me, Lord."

Jesse couldn't take seeing her struggle anymore, and walked up and held her for a moment, letting her cry. "It's okay. You don't have to if you don't want to."

"No." Rachel shook her head. "I need to." Turning back to the group, she cleared her throat. Jesse turned to go back to his spot, but she grabbed his hand, not wanting him to go. When Jesse resumed his position slightly behind her, with his hand resting on the small of her back, she said, "Danny was an amazing man. He was around for as long as I can remember. Growing up, for the longest time, I just assumed he was an uncle," she said, and those from Australia chuckled. "He instructed me in techniques and weapons, as much as he did in the Lord. He encouraged me when I got discouraged, and made sure to discipline me when I royally screwed up," she said, and the group chuckled again. "He and The Colonel have a legacy they left behind that can never be touched. Having said that, they didn't do it for the notoriety. They did it for the Lord. They did it for the sake of humanity. They answered the call when it was placed before them, just as much as we did when it was placed before us. Their lives were for others and for the Lord. Their hearts were in the right place…with God. While one might hope to be strong like them, I hope to be strong like Jesus. They didn't hope to be like each other, their hope was to be more like Jesus. Their goal was to follow Jesus, and for the Lord to be proud of them. They didn't care what the world thought of them. Their concern was doing the right thing in the eyes of the Lord. *That* needs to be our goal as an A.N.G.E.L. of the Lord. Our goal is to reach those who are lost and to find those of His who need us. Our main goal is to do the missions put before us to the best of our ability. The battle is the Lord's. We are His hands and feet here on the ground."

There were nods from many of those in attendance. Taking a deep breath, she then placed her hand on the flag, and said, "You will be missed more than you know, but we know you are with Jesus right now. We know you are not resting, but encouraging each of us to continue to focus on the Lord. We know you are still being you in Heaven, just waiting for us to get there. And when we do, I know beyond a shadow of a doubt that you and The Colonel will be there waiting for us, standing there with Jesus. So, until that day, my friend, well done, thy good and faithful servant."

One-by-one, other lives that were touched by Danny came up, placed a rose around the boulder, and said a few words. They each had a different story. While some needed translators, the sentiment was the same. "Well done, thy good and faithful servant."

As a couple older A.N.G.E.L.s from Ireland and Scotland played *Amazing Grace* on the bagpipes, Josh stood next to the table, and Ethan, Kat, Charlie, Nico, Caleb, and Leah walked over and picked up the flag. As they properly folded it, and the song continued, the rest of the A.N.G.E.L.s stood at attention and saluted. Once they finished folding the flag, the six folding stood at attention as well, with Charlie holding the flag until the last note was played.

Once finished, the group stood at ease. Charlie then went to hand the flag to Josh, but he shook his head 'no.' When Charlie insisted, with both of them holding it, Josh explained, "He was your best friend. This flag is meant for you. You were with him when he went home. You held him in your arms as he passed from this world to be with the Lord. The honor of keeping this flag goes to you. We all agree that you will hold it in the same honor and high regard that you held Danny. It would be *our* honor if you would accept this flag on behalf of all of the A.N.G.E.L.s." Letting the flag go, leaving it in Charlie's arms, Josh's heart broke at seeing Charlie openly weeping as he hugged the flag to his chest. Hugging Charlie, through his own tears, Josh said, "He was a good, Godly man, and a brother. A man we were all proud to know."

"Thank you," Charlie whispered, before returning to the others, who had already rejoined the group once the song completed.

Josh wiped the tears before he spoke, addressing the crowd. He started by quoting Revelation 21:4, "'*And God shall wipe away all tears from their eyes, and there shall be no more death, neither sorrow, nor crying, neither shall there be any more pain: for the former things are passed away.*' While Danny Hawk was a legend among the A.N.G.E.L.s, he was my friend, my mentor, and like a member of the family to us. Along with the other Australian A.N.G.E.L.s, he trained my siblings and I since we were little. We also recently lost The Colonel. Now, the pair are watching us, cheering us on together until we can see them again in Heaven. They have joined the other Saints to encourage us daily. What else is there to say about Danny Hawk that hasn't already been said? He cared about people. He cared about their hearts and souls. As the leader of the Australian A.N.G.E.L.s, this brought about a deeper responsibility to not only to those on the missions he was on, but on those under him as well. He led with courage and wisdom. He and The Colonel were given many assignments over the years, but none was so important as the one to find the A.N.G.E.L.s of this world, and get the teams started again. They did this with discernment, clear thinking, and by being continuously focused on God. They had the foresight to not only get the teams going in their generation, but to begin to train the next generation as well. This was their time, and they used it to the best of their ability for the Lord. It's now our time, and our opportunity to carry on the legacy granted to us by these beloved men. Danny never let an opportunity pass to share some sort of insight or pearl of wisdom as he trained us. Some of his lessons were painful," Josh said, rubbing his chin as he remembered his first challenger/aggressor game. "Some of his lessons saved me from future pain and misery. *All* of his lessons, though, were practical and sound. What I'm trying to say," Josh said, hoping they understood his heart, "is despite the moments in time where we don't get along, we are all united with God as the center. He is our main focus, and Danny, as well as The Colonel, believed that. I believe that, as do all of you here. Whether we're connected personally, or in the Spirit, it's the Lord that binds us. As an A.N.G.E.L., and a brother and sister in Christ, we are never alone in this world. When the older generation passed the legacy on to us, I'm sure they were terrified," he said, and some of the older A.N.G.E.L.s snickered. "Trusting such an important mission to rookies must have been their worst nightmare. But, they trusted in the Lord's timing. While they didn't pass it onto us lightly, they *did* do it with confidence in the faith we have in the Lord our God and each other. We are all joined together with one purpose. Let's prove to them, and to God, that they made the right decision. Let's join together, hearts united, to continue the divine legacy that was passed down to us."

Epilogue
Chains Broken

The final book in the Divine Legacy Series, **Chains Broken**, follows the A.N.G.E.L.s as they continue on their journey. There will be wedding, Christmas, and New Year's celebrations, which should bring about a fresh start…but will it?

Kit's battle is coming to a head. Can she overcome what is trying to lay hold, or will she succumb like her mother? Have the issues of anger been worked out within the team? Who will win the battle for the Outback? What about the other box? Do the A.N.G.E.L.s have a lead on it?

These questions and more will be answered as this exciting series wraps up. Chains will be loosened, and hearts and lives will be connected in ***Chains Broken***. (Book 4 of the ***Divine Legacy Series***.)

1 Peter 5:8 *"Be alert and of sober mind. Your enemy the devil prowls around like a roaring lion looking for someone to devour."*

John 8:32 *"Then you will know the truth, and the truth will set you free."*

The books in the Divine Legacy Series –

Connect with CJ – *CJPetersonWrites.com*

Meet the previous generation of A.N.G.E.L.s -

Grace Restored Series

Book 1

Book 2

Book 3

Book 4

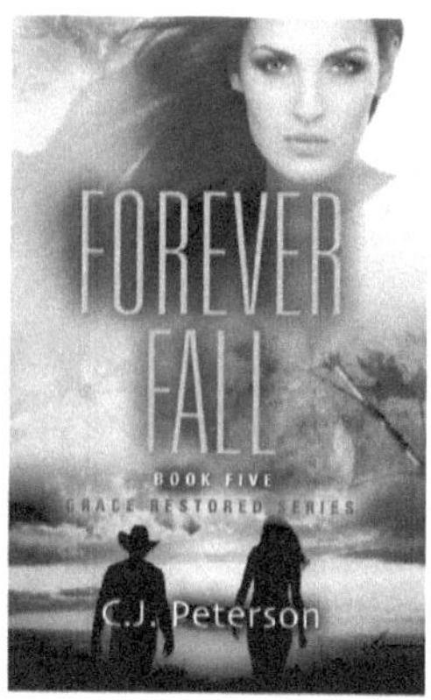

Book 5

Katie MacKenna experienced one storm after another in her life. When Leukemia stole her mother from her and her father, Katie was only seven-years-old, and her father didn't know how to cope after such a catastrophic loss. His response was to shut down and become abusive. The overwhelming devastation which surrounded Katie throughout her journey in life forced her to shut down just to survive as well.

Trust is a difficult thing for many people, but for Katie it's virtually impossible. Every life has Seasons of Change. Will those seasons open Katie to new opportunities or will they forever isolate her in survival mode? Will she be able to overcome the storms that have surrounded her to answer a call for help?

Meet the previous generation of A.N.G.E.L.s -

The Holy Flame Trilogy.

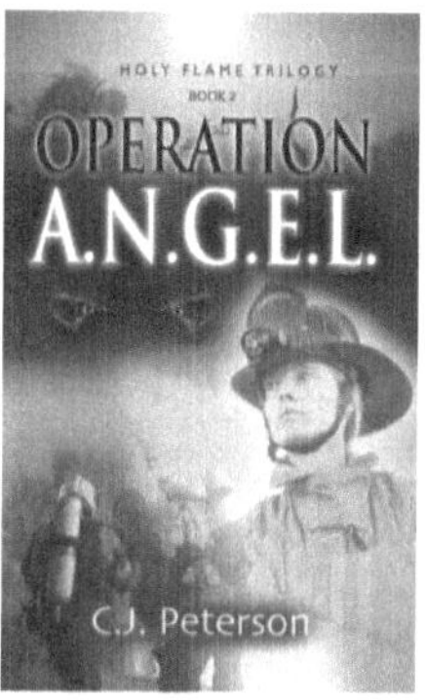

| Book 1 | Book 2 | Book 3 |

Summary

Courageous. Brave. Fearless. Valiant. These synonyms are often used to describe firefighters/paramedics, police officers, and military personnel. They face danger and lay their lives on the line when they leave for work. What are their struggles? Could that hinder their job proficiency? Who is taking care of those who are taking care of the citizens of this country?

Casey Carter is a 'newbie' to the firefighting family of Engine Company 15. Not only does she have to prove herself as a probationary firefighter, but she also has to battle misconceptions of females within her newly chosen profession. As situations begin to arise, can she count on the firefighter brotherhood to have her back? Will she be able to pass the tests placed before her, or are there aspects that she was not even aware existed?

Often in life there are two realms in play. There is the physical realm - what is right before you; the other is the spiritual realm - what is unseen. Each can directly affect you, whether you believe they exist or not. Can Casey keep them in balance when she is not exactly sure what she is fighting? Can a group of men help her see what cannot be readily seen, hear what cannot be readily heard, and be able to overcome what she never knew existed? Will they be able to show Casey her true Call To Duty?